The Florist

C. L. Pattison spent twenty years as an
entertainment journalist in London, before moving
to the country and joining Hampshire Constabulary
as a PCSO. Her previous psychological thrillers,
The Housemate and *The Guest Book*,
were both eBook bestsellers.

Also by C. L. Pattison

The Housemate

The Guest Book

C. L. PATTISON

THE FLORIST

HEADLINE

First published in 2023 by
HEADLINE PUBLISHING GROUP

1

Cataloguing in Publication Data is available from the British Library

Paperback ISBN 978 1 0354 0476 6

Typeset in Sabon LT Pro by EM&EN
Printed and bound in Great Britain by Clays Ltd, Elcograf S.p.A.

Headline's policy is to use papers that are natural, renewable and recyclable
products and made from wood grown in well-managed forests and other
controlled sources. The logging and manufacturing processes are expected
to conform to the environmental regulations of the country of origin.

HEADLINE PUBLISHING GROUP
An Hachette UK Company
Carmelite House
50 Victoria Embankment
London EC4Y 0DZ

www.headline.co.uk
www.hachette.co.uk

THE FLORIST

Now

'If you could just tell us in your own words what happened at The Sanctuary.'

I place two fingers on the tender spot between my eyebrows. 'It's all a bit of a blur, to be honest,' I say, the words feeling sticky in my mouth. 'I think I'm still in shock.'

Detective Inspector Kate Kilner's face fills with sympathy as she leans forward, resting an elbow on the starched white sheet of my hospital bed. 'You've just had a very traumatic experience, it's perfectly natural to feel a little confused.'

I lie back on the pillows and take a few long, slow breaths. It's barely twenty-four hours since I regained consciousness and my brain feels sore. There's a long silence. It stretches out, thinning until it becomes awkward.

'What if we rewind . . . go right back to the beginning?' says DI Kilner's colleague, whose name has momentarily escaped me. He's a big man; his corpulent bulk fills the room in a way that feels slightly intrusive. 'How did you first come to meet the Elliott family?'

If only they knew the truth: that this all began way before I ever laid eyes on the Elliotts. Before I even knew they existed.

'Through work,' I tell him. 'Darling Buds has been doing the flowers for James Elliott's office premises for several years. He's one of our best customers.'

'And his wife, Eleanor?'

'Also a client. We supplied the floral arrangements for a couple of social events at her home.'

DI Kilner steps in. 'So were you at the Elliotts' home in a professional capacity on the morning of the twenty-second of September?'

A wave of exhaustion washes over me. The kind of tiredness that creeps up behind you and climbs on your back, its clammy tentacles slithering round your throat. I don't think I can do this now. I need more time to get the facts straight in my head; iron out any creases.

'I'm sorry, I know you're only doing your job, but I don't think I'm in any fit state to answer questions right now. Perhaps you could come back tomorrow.'

DS Pearce, whose name has just popped into my head, smiles stiffly. 'Your doctor's given us clearance to speak to you. It really would be better to get this out of the way now, while events are still fresh in your mind. One person is dead and another is in a critical condition. You're the only one who can tell us what happened.'

'Actually, that's not strictly true,' Kilner corrects him. 'We do have another witness.'

A flicker of surprise in the centre of my spine. What does she mean? It was just the three of us in that room.

She pulls out her mobile phone. 'Here, let me show

you.' She presses a button to adjust the volume, then places the phone on the bed where I can see it.

As I look down at the screen, Kilner's eyes are on me, alert to the smallest tell. I manage to maintain a neutral expression, but it takes every ounce of energy I can muster.

When the video has finished playing, I shut my eyes. I can feel the throb of a headache starting in my temples. My thoughts are like rats in a burning building, running along one wall after another, desperately looking for the escape route. I'm inclined to take DS Pearce's advice. Tell them everything.

In light of the surprising new information DI Kilner has just presented me with, what other choice do I have?

Three Months Earlier

1

The man on the end of the phone has a guilty conscience. His tone is slightly sheepish and he's speaking a little more loudly than he needs to, trying to convince himself that this is just another boring business transaction in his oh-so-busy day. One he wishes he could hand off to his PA, except he's not sure he can trust her to get it right – not when there's so much at stake.

'I'm looking for something really special,' he says. 'It's for my wife.'

'OK, what sort of thing did you have in mind?'

'I don't know; I was hoping you could point me in the right direction.'

'That's fine. How much did you want to spend?'

'There's no upper limit.'

Okaaay. Sounds like this guy's really in the doghouse.

'Is it a special occasion?'

'Not as such.' He hesitates. 'It's more a case that I've been taking my wife for granted. I need to show her how much she means to me.'

In other words he cheated and was careless enough to get caught. Pulling on my bottom lip, I run through a few options in my mind. Freesias won't be enough to get him out of jail, or even a lavish bouquet of floribundas. Nope, I'll need to bring out the big guns for this one.

'What's your wife's favourite colour?'

'I haven't got a clue.'

Seriously?

'No problem. Let me ask you this then: how would you describe your wife's personality?'

He heaves a sigh. 'Is this necessary? I just want some beautiful flowers for my wife; it's quite simple.'

Except it isn't; it's actually very complex, but I wouldn't expect a man like him – a man who doesn't even know what his wife's favourite colour is – to understand that.

'Just run with it, all right? If your wife isn't delighted with the end result, I'll give you your money back, I promise.'

Another sigh. 'She's quiet and sensitive; definitely more introvert than extrovert.' He gives a little snort. 'Mind you, her inhibitions go out the window when she's had a few gin and tonics.'

I ignore the barb. 'Does she prefer the city or the countryside?'

'The countryside, definitely. She's been saying we should move out of London for ages.'

I scribble some notes on the pad in front of me; that's narrowed down the field considerably.

'What about her taste in interior decor? Traditional? Minimalist? Contemporary?'

'Erm . . . how about *rustic*? Will that do?'

'Rustic will do nicely.'

We proceed in a similar fashion for another minute or two until finally I'm ready to present my recommendation. 'Based on the information you've given me, I suggest one of our handwoven willow baskets, filled with pink and white ranunculus, pastel Himalayan Musk roses – trust me when I say their scent is out of this world – purple delphiniums and pure white baby orchids.' He won't get much change out of a hundred and fifty quid for that lot – but hey, forgiveness doesn't come cheap. 'How does that sound?'

'Good,' he says briskly. 'When can you deliver?'

I glance at the clock above the door. 'It'll be tomorrow morning now.'

'Oh.' He sounds disappointed. 'Is there no way you can get them to her today?'

Poor bastard, he's scared that by morning his wife could be gone.

'Just hold the line a second for me, please.'

Pressing the handset to my chest, I turn to my assistant, Claire. The muscles of her jaw are tight as she strips the leaves from dozens of gerbera stems (not one of my favourite flowers, I must admit, but they're such a crowd-pleaser we'd be stupid not to stock them). Our regular delivery guy's already clocked off, but the van's parked up outside and Claire's job description is pretty loose.

'How do you fancy a quick run over to Clapham in about half an hour?' I ask her.

'Whatever you need, Amy,' she says, glancing up. 'Just let me know when the order's ready.'

I put the phone back to my ear. 'Yes, Mr Prout, we can deliver this afternoon, but there will be a fifteen-pound surcharge.'

His relief is palpable. 'That's great, thank you for being so accommodating.'

I pick up my biro. 'And what message would you like on the card?'

'All my love, Antony,' he says. 'Without an H.'

My eyebrows knit in a frown. This guy really isn't doing himself any favours. 'I don't mean to be presumptuous, but I wonder if your wife might appreciate a few more words, something a little more . . . *meaningful*.'

There's such a long silence I actually think he's hung up.

'I'm sorry,' he says at last and I hear the catch in his voice. 'You can put that on the card. *I'm sorry and I promise faithfully it will never happen again. All my love, Antony.*'

Weddings, birthdays, anniversaries, make-up flowers, break-up flowers, flowers to celebrate new life, comfort the sick and honour the dead: my couture creations mark every milestone and human drama you can think of. Behind each and every order lies a story and if you want to get it right, then a grasp of basic psychology is vital. You see, floristry isn't just about colour combinations and knowing what's in season; it's about being able to evoke an emotion and change someone's mood in an instant. As I often say to people, I don't just sell flowers; I sell *feelings*.

When I was younger, I was convinced my future lay in graphic design, but by the end of my first year at art college, I was already having serious doubts. During the summer break I answered an ad for a part-time job in a florist's shop. And that was it – the beginning of my love affair with flowers. I never went back to art college.

Within six months, I was managing the shop and studying for a floristry qualification in my spare time. Within a year, I'd landed a much better paid job at a self-styled 'artisan' florist's in Shoreditch. I worked there until five years ago, when I spotted a derelict shop on Forest Hill high street, not far from my flat. That was where Darling Buds was born.

Running your own business is hard work, and there were times I wondered whether I'd made the right decision. I plodded along for a couple of years, honing my craft and developing my marketing skills, but the truth was I was barely earning enough to pay the bills.

The turning point came when a boutique hotel in West London commissioned me to create a large and daring floral installation (think Amazon rainforest meets English country garden) for the launch of their new spa. I knew the hotel's PR through a friend of a friend and agreed to do the job for a fraction of what anyone else would've charged, just for the experience.

The installation was a big hit – more popular even

than the free hand massages, and I landed several lucrative commissions on the back of the publicity. Things just snowballed from there.

Of course, my bread and butter is still the gifting market, but every now and then I get the chance to do a large-scale project – an extravagant doorway arch for a restaurant opening, or a lavish flower wall for a high-end wedding. That's when my creativity runs riot and I get the chance to show what I'm really capable of. Which reminds me – as soon as I've finished Antony-without-an-H's order, I must update my Instagram. I post as often as I can. I have to, I can't risk dropping off the radar, even momentarily, not when so many other florists – younger, hungrier, with perpetually churning Insta feeds and chirpy instructive vlogs – are competing for a limited amount of work.

An hour and a half later, I'm sitting in the studio, sipping a cup of peppermint tea and staring at my laptop screen. Social media has done wonders for Darling Buds. All those likes and shares are worth more than any ad campaign, and best of all, I get to be a whole other Amy Mackenzie – an Amy who's flamboyant and fun-loving and completely at home in any social milieu. My fifteen-point-seven thousand Instagram followers would probably be horribly disappointed if they ever met me in person. Sometimes I feel as if I have lots of different versions of myself tucked up inside me – a whole cast of understudies, some more likeable than others, all waiting in the wings for their turn on stage.

Today's photo is a delicate wedding corsage – a frothy confection of roses, snapdragons, sweet peas, pelargonium, phlox and eucalyptus. The bride was a total bitch, a pedantic control freak, who wanted to dictate the minutiae of the flowers a year in advance. I tried to explain to her that thanks to climate change, it was impossible to predict what would be available next spring and that she wouldn't be able to have peonies for love or money if they finished flowering a month early. Of course, I'm not going to put any of that in my post. This isn't reality after all; it's a carefully curated, fragrant fantasy.

On the day of the wedding, I delivered the flowers to the venue – a historic pile in the arse end of nowhere (no pun intended). As I pulled up in the van, I spotted a vintage Norton motorbike, parked in the dappled shade of a cherry tree. I didn't know who it belonged to and frankly, I didn't care; I know a photo opportunity when I see one. Moments later, I was laying the posy carefully on the motorcycle's worn leather saddle, praying that its owner wasn't about to appear and ask me what the hell I was doing.

Navigating to the photos folder on my laptop, I open the half dozen or so pictures I took. They're even better than I remember. The bike, with its sinuous curves and gleaming chrome, provides a pleasing contrast to the delicate flowers, while the early morning sunshine lends the scene a soft, almost ethereal glow.

After selecting one of the images, I spend several minutes editing it to perfection. All it needs then is a snappy caption. I think for a few moments and then my fingers return to the keyboard.

Put the petal to the metal! Thank you, Kayla, for being the loveliest bride to work with and for entrusting Darling Buds to inject some floral va-va-voom into your big day.

Perfect, I think to myself as I click *Share*. If only real life were this straightforward. Everything polished, filtered and posted in a neat little square.

2

I hoist the Venetian blinds and throw open the sash window overlooking the garden. The sun is glinting in the sky and I can hear the fluting song of a blackbird. I love the fact I have a private outdoor space; it's part of the reason I wanted a ground-floor flat. When I bought the property last year, the garden was a complete mess, a sun-scorched patch of grass, surrounded by thuggish clumps of weeds and the odd diseased hosta. But slowly, painstakingly, I brought it back to life and filled it with my favourite flowers – azaleas, hollyhocks, pinks and hypericum. And roses, of course. Lots of them, in just about every shade of pink you can imagine, from the palest blush all the way through to deep raspberry. It's such a beautiful, tranquil space. There's something about the colours, the pleasing lack of symmetry that loosens the dark knots inside of me.

Shoving my feet into ballerina slippers, I make my way through to the kitchen. It's the room where I spend most of my time – not because I do much cooking, but because of its pleasing proportions and the natural light that floods in through the lantern roof. As I move around the room, assembling my breakfast things, I think how nice it is having no one else to look after but myself. I've been single for a while now. I was with my last boyfriend, Rob, for six years. There was no big drama surrounding our break-up;

it was more of a gradual withdrawal of love. However many times I go over the minutiae of our life together, there was never any satisfactory explanation as to how we had unravelled so spectacularly.

It took me a long while to even realise anything was amiss. After all, the fabric of our relationship was still there – the joint tenancy, the shared record collection, our Maine Coon, Delilah (I didn't fight Rob for custody – she always preferred him to me). But slowly, drip drip slowly, the sparkle went and everything got just a little bit darker. At first, I pretended not to notice, but eventually it got to the point where I couldn't ignore the warning signs any longer. Rob, sitting in the living room, a music magazine in his hands, not reading it, just gazing over the top into space. When I'd catch his eye, he'd give me a quick, over-bright smile before returning hastily to the gig guide. There were subtle changes in his appearance too: he lost half a stone and splashed out on some expensive linen shirts for work (this from a man who'd previously been perfectly happy to defile himself with a polyester blend). And then one day, he told me that he'd met someone at work; some-one he'd rather be with than me. Some tears were shed, but no insults were hurled, no last-minute plea to stay was made. A civilised ending to a civilised relationship. I wish now I'd put up more of a fight.

After breakfast, I shower and dress, taking a little more care with my outfit than usual. Then I get in the car for the short drive to work.

When I arrive at the shop, Claire's standing outside, helping a customer choose from the colourful selection in our pavement display. I'm very proud of our frontage. There are no ugly plastic buckets in sight, just an eclectic array of 'props' that include a milk churn, some old packing crates, a pair of ornate jardinieres and my personal favourite – a vintage pram. I give Claire a nod of acknowledgement before making my way down the narrow alley at the side of the shop, which leads to my studio. It used to be the storeroom for the greengrocer's that once occupied the premises, but now it's where we make up our custom orders. It's not luxurious, but it has natural light from several large windows and there's room for a long workbench, big enough for two of us to work side-by-side, as well as a compact kitchen area with a table and chairs.

Inside, I find Ewan tucking into a McDonald's. Ewan's our part-time courier. He's only been with us a couple of months. He's a nice guy. Late thirties. Fit-looking. Split up with his long-term partner last year and is living with a friend while he looks for a place of his own. He's certainly a vast improvement on his predecessor – a surly man with a deathly pallor who would furtively sniff-check his armpits when he thought no one was looking.

The minute Ewan sees me, he puts down his food and starts rising to his feet. 'Sorry, Amy, I was just grabbing a bit of breakfast before I hit the road, but if I'm in your way . . .'

'It's fine, Ewan, there's no rush.'

He sits back down. 'Busy day ahead?'

'I've got a funeral later.' I take off my denim jacket and hang it on one of the wall hooks. 'For a young lady called Iris.'

'When you say *young* . . .'

'Twenty-two.'

'Shit,' he says, looking at me aghast. 'Was she sick?'

I shake my head. 'Car accident. Her best friend was driving. She took a corner too fast and the car hit a tree head-on.'

'And the friend?'

'Survived with barely a scratch.'

Ewan takes a gulp from his cardboard cup, then dabs the corners of his mouth with surprising delicacy. 'Don't you find those sorts of jobs a bit depressing?'

I give a one-shouldered shrug. 'I actually like doing funeral flowers. It feels good knowing I've done something – albeit a very small something – to help people who've lost a loved one. It's amazing how flowers can help turn a really ugly occasion into something quite beautiful.'

'That's a nice way of looking at it.'

I take down an apron and slip it over my head, looping the strings twice around my waist and tying them in a double knot at the front. 'Of course, back in the day flowers at funerals weren't there to make the place look pretty – they served a much more practical purpose.'

'Oh yeah, what's that?'

'To mask the stench emanating from the coffin.'

He makes a gagging noise. 'That's gross.'

'Sorry, am I putting you off your McMuffin?'

He pats his stomach. 'Don't worry, it's already down the hatch.' He stands up and carries the packaging from his meal over to the swing bin. 'I'd love to stick around and hear more of your grisly anecdotes, but it's time for me to hit the road.'

'Do you have the delivery schedule?'

'Yep, Claire printed it off for me. I asked her to give me a few business cards as well, just in case any customers ask for one.'

I smile at him appreciatively. I like an employee with initiative.

As I watch him go I find myself wondering – and not for the first time – why someone like Ewan would want to do a monotonous, low-paid job like this one. It was actually one of my interview questions, although I didn't put it quite so bluntly. He said he'd found his previous job in sales very stressful and wanted to do something less demanding. I got the feeling there was a bit more to it than that. I wondered if perhaps he'd had some sort of breakdown, but that's not the sort of question one can ask in an interview these days without finding oneself in front of a tribunal. In any case, it's none of my business. I liked Ewan, his references checked out and he had a clean driving licence which, at the end of the day, is all that really matters.

Brushing the thought aside, I refocus my mind and set to work. First port of call is the metal storage unit that was custom-built to my exacting specifications. Filling an entire wall, it's loaded with water-filled buckets of blooms in every size, shape and colour. I make my selections quickly, confidently, going back and forth between shelf unit and workbench until I have everything I need. Next, I go to a rack on the wall and remove a handful of tools: knife, stem strippers, spool wire, twine.

I start by preparing my raw materials, carefully stripping excess foliage, removing any damaged petals and trimming the stems to the required length. It's only then the fun part begins: the construction. My aim is not just to create something beautiful, but to bring out the inner qualities of the flowers, the same way a sculptor brings life to a lump of clay. Although each one of my creations is highly individual, I do have a certain aesthetic and it's important that everyone who sees the flowers feels welcomed, rather than overwhelmed, by them.

This is the first funeral I've done in months. We don't get as many requests as we used to; a lot of people ask for charity donations in lieu of flowers. That's their prerogative, of course, but I do think it's a shame. In my experience, flowers can bring a great deal of comfort to people in times of sorrow or distress.

In my first floristry job, the owner of the shop had put together a ring binder of laminated pages that he would present to the bereaved with a flourish, as if it were a first edition. A dozen or so wreaths, distinguished only by serial numbers – ghastly, formulaic offerings that practically screamed 'funeral' and made you depressed just looking at them. No custom alternative was offered; it was that or nothing. Just thinking about it now makes my blood come to a rolling boil. In my opinion, flowers for the dead should be just as unique as flowers for the living. That's why I always try to meet the bereaved in person, rather than making do with a snatched phone chat or a few lines in an instant message. I've found that it's the best way to gather the information I need to create a fitting floral tribute, one that accurately reflects the deceased's personality and passions. At the same time, I don't want my designs to appear trite, or predictable – it's the reason irises won't be featuring in today's funeral.

Unusually, Iris's parents have given me complete carte blanche. 'Just make the flowers really special,' her mother said when she came into the shop. 'Exactly like my daughter.' To be honest, I think she was glad to offload the responsibility of choosing the flowers on to someone else. I don't blame her. A funeral director I work with a lot once told me that the average funeral requires around two thousand decisions. So at a time when your brain and heart feel like they're being fed through a shredder, you're expected to organise one of the most important events of your life – and worst of all, you only have a couple of weeks to do it. It's a huge burden and something a lot of people struggle with. If I can take off some of the pressure, even just a little bit, then I feel as if I've done something truly worthwhile.

By the time I've completed the order, it's coming up to eleven, which leaves me with an hour or so to dress the church before the first mourners arrive. While Ewan does the residential deliveries and most of our corporate clients (offices, hotels, restaurants and the like), I take care of our 'event' business, where a personal touch is so important. If, like now, Darling Buds' liveried van isn't available, then I make use of my spacious SUV.

The church is only a short drive away, and today God must be smiling on me because I manage to bag a parking spot right outside. I know the building's interior well and it doesn't take me long to position the arrangements. But every time I step back, I feel the need to make a small adjustment. Shorten the ribbon on a pew end; move a jug by a couple of centimetres; pinch off a disobedient piece of foliage. It's funny how something can look completely 'wrong' and yet the tiniest tweak can render it absolutely perfect, even if one can't articulate precisely why. Once I'm happy with the close-up views, I start walking backwards down the centre aisle so I can get the full effect. I'm concentrating so hard that I manage to walk straight into someone, who lets out a loud gasp as I catch them with my elbow. Spinning round, I discover to my embarrassment that it's Iris's mum, Jill.

'I'm so sorry, Jill, I didn't see you there,' I say, wincing. 'I didn't hurt you, did I?'

She smiles weakly. 'No, I'm fine, honestly.' Her shoulders are high and tense and dark shadows bloom beneath her eyes. Despite her smart navy dress and matching heels, she looks so defeated, so pitiful, I have to resist the temptation to hold out my arms and give her a hug. 'I just came to see how you were getting on.'

I move to the side, so she has an unobstructed view of the nave. 'I'm pretty much there. What do you think?'

She walks forward a few paces, her hand drawn up against her stomach in a protective gesture. She studies the nosegays that hang from the end of every pew – vivid yellow sunflowers jostle for position alongside spiky blue globe thistles, delicate orange nasturtiums and bright pink dahlias – a cacophony of clashing colours and contrasting shapes. As she brushes her hand lightly over the petals, she sighs softly but doesn't say anything. Her attention moves to the stained-glass windows and the deep stone sills beneath them, now lined with a cornucopia of mismatching milk jugs and teacups, each one exploding with miniature blooms – lobelia, forget-me-nots, fluffy clouds of gypsophila.

When she still doesn't offer an opinion I start to feel anxious, worried I might've overcooked it. Perhaps if I explained my thought process . . .

'You told me Iris was a free spirit, a true one-off,' I say. 'I've tried to represent all those wonderful qualities in the flowers – her zest for life, her quirky sense of humour, her eclectic fashion sense. You may not know this, but Iris was the Greek goddess of the rainbow. That's why I've used every single colour imaginable, from the violet of the lavender to the red of the amaryllis.'

Jill looks at me and the tense lines of her face melt as if she's been caught in a sudden shaft of soft, warm light. 'Oh, Amy,' she murmurs as a single fat tear rolls down her cheek. 'They're absolutely perfect.'

I give a relieved smile. 'That's good to hear. The last thing I wanted to do was to let you – or Iris – down.' I point to the small wooden table next to the font. On it lies a visitor's book, and next to it a cream cardboard box. 'There's something else I want to show you.'

She follows me over to the table and watches as I ease the lid from the box. Nestling in its tissue paper folds are dozens of fragrant herb sprigs, simply tied with raffia.

'It's rosemary, for remembrance,' I explain. 'There's one for every guest. They can wear it as a buttonhole, or take it away as a keepsake. It's something I do for every funeral I have the privilege of working on; there's no additional charge.'

Before she can reply, a man appears in the vestibule. He's tall and bearded and he wears his tailored black suit like a punishment.

'Amy, I'd like you to meet my husband, Liam,' Jill says as he comes over to join us.

He shakes my hand – a single dry pump. Not knowing what else to say, I ask him what he thinks of the flowers.

He casts around the nave, his eyebrows shooting up when he notices the teacups.

'It's not quite what I was expecting. Isn't it a bit . . . I don't know . . . *frivolous?*'

Jill throws her shoulders back, straightening like a thirsty plant freshly watered. 'Today isn't for us, darling, it's for Iris,' she reminds him gently. 'And I know, without a shadow of a doubt, that she would've *adored* Amy's flowers.'

He takes a deep breath that flutters several of the coarse hairs on his moustache. 'Of course, my love, you're absolutely right – as usual.' He turns to me. 'I'm sorry, Amy, I didn't mean to sound unappreciative; I can see you've put a great deal of effort into this. I just wish Iris were here to see it for herself.' His mouth twists into a grimace. 'But she isn't; she's been stolen away from us by that . . . that *person* who had the nerve to call herself my daughter's best friend.'

His words stir something in me and my stomach twists with a sensation I can't quite identify. Feeling uncomfortable, I start moving towards the pew where I dumped all the packaging from the flowers. 'I'll just tidy up and then I'll get going,' I say, figuring the couple could probably use a few moments alone before their daughter's nearest and dearest start to arrive.

Before I return to the shop, I have one more delivery to make. Cole & Elliott is a prestigious firm of architects and their office is just a few minutes' drive from the church. I've been doing the flowers for their reception area for years; they were actually Darling Buds' first ever corporate client. I could easily add their weekly order to Ewan's roster, but for various reasons I prefer to make the delivery in person.

Today, my least favourite of the two job-share receptionists is on duty – a young woman with too much eye make-up and an irritating drawl. When I enter the building, she barely registers my presence; she's too busy texting on her mobile phone, her fuchsia shellacs hitting the screen with a flinty click. As I lay the flowers on the horseshoe-shaped desk, she glares at me reproachfully.

'Thanks,' she says, sounding as far away from grateful as it's possible to be.

'I'll send the invoice by email as usual,' I tell her.

'Great,' she says with a yawn.

I glance around, reluctant to go just yet. The glass-walled meeting room to my left is occupied by two men engaged in the kind of gesticulation-heavy discussion that characterises serious business. I recognise one of them as Adam Cole. He's one of the partners and the guy who took a punt on me when I was just starting out. I'll always be grateful to him for that – and for the glowing testimonial he provided for Darling Buds' website.

'Was there anything else?' the receptionist asks.

'Er no,' I reply. 'I guess I'll see you next week then.'

Glancing down, I notice that the lace on one of my shoes is about to come undone. Bending down, I start to re-tie it. And then, in a stroke of sublime good fortune, my delaying tactics are rewarded.

'Is that my favourite florist?' comes a familiar booming voice.

I stand up quickly as James Elliott comes striding down the hall towards me. James is the other half of the business and, in the interests of full disclosure, I do have the teensiest crush on him. He has strong, even features and bright blue eyes that are the colour of cornflowers. Beneath his fitted white shirt, a ripple of muscle is just visible. Not gym-obsessive muscle, but the understated strength of a man who could, if required, be relied upon to wrestle an unyielding lid from a jar of chutney, or push a broken-down car into the nearest layby.

'Hi James,' I say. 'How are you today?'

'Looking forward to Friday; it's been a hell of a week.'

His gaze snags on my shift dress. I've had it for years, but it's one of my favourites; the bold geometric print conveniently distracts the eye from my non-existent bust.

'I like your outfit,' he says. 'I don't think I've seen you in a dress before, have I?'

Heat creeps up my neck. 'Thanks, I was doing the flowers for a funeral earlier, so I made an effort to look smart.'

He notices the flowers lying on the desk. 'So what surprises have you got for us this week?'

I peel back the edge of the paper cone that's shrouding them. 'Birds of paradise, heliconia, protea and tiger lilies,' I say, pointing out each one in turn. 'I've tied the stems together, so you just need to pop them in the vase and they'll pretty much arrange themselves.' I cut my eyes towards the square glass vessel that bears last week's offerings. Gratifyingly, they're barely wilting, although the water is a rather unedifying shade of grey.

'Would you like me to swap those out for you, while I'm here?'

'That's kind of you to offer, but I'm sure Olivia won't mind doing it, will you, Olivia?'

'Of course not, Mr Elliott.' Despite the receptionist's apparent willingness, her tone has a strained, martyr-like inflection.

James turns back to me. 'Before you rush off, Amy, I wonder if you have five minutes to spare; there's something I'd like to discuss with you.'

'Sure,' I say, not needing to think about it. James is a highly valued customer – on a personal, as well as a corporate level. He comes into the shop fairly regularly to buy flowers for his wife. Unlike a lot of men, he doesn't just pick up the first thing he sees; he chooses carefully, thoughtfully – putting as much effort into the choice of wrapping as the flowers themselves. We'll chat easily as he makes his selections – not just about the flowers, but all sorts of things. I'm sure James isn't just being polite either; he seems genuinely interested in what's going on in my life. He can be talking to me about something quite mundane – the weather, the price of petrol, the new vinyl lettering on the shop window – but the way he looks at me when he does it makes me feel as if the rest of the world is spinning and he's the only fixed point. I don't have that sort of connection with most people. With *anyone*, in fact. It's part of the reason I look forward to seeing him so much.

'We'll go in my office; that way we won't have any interruptions.' James looks at Olivia. 'Can you bring us some coffee, please – unless Amy would prefer tea?'

'Coffee would be great, thanks.'

Olivia hauls her pert backside up off the chair. As she sets off down the hallway in her four-inch heels, I find myself uncharitably wishing she would trip and break her ankle.

I've never been in James's office before. There's a large pale wood desk and behind it a designer chair that looks comfy enough to sleep in. But the dominant feature of the room is the table at its centre, on which a scale model of a house is displayed. It's not the sort of home *I'd* like to live in, all sharp angles and vast floor-to-ceiling windows, but it's very impressive all the same.

'Did you make this yourself?' I ask him.

'God, no – even if I had the requisite skills, I wouldn't have the patience. All our models are made by a specialist company. They use a laser-cutting technique that provides exceptional accuracy.'

I cringe inwardly, embarrassed that I even asked. Did I really think a man like James sat up late into the night, fashioning tiny cornices out of balsa wood?

'It's my latest project,' he goes on. 'All eight thousand square feet of it. The location's spectacular; the house sits on the edge of a private lake.'

He comes to stand next to me and I catch a faint scent of citrus from his aftershave. I have a sudden urge to step closer in order to get a deeper breath.

He points to a narrow structure on stilts that leads to a little circle of blue Perspex. 'The house has a raised walkway from the front deck all the way down to the water.'

'It's stunning,' I say, my voice tinged with envy. I can't even begin to imagine what it must be like to be so rich, so *privileged*. 'I bet a house like that doesn't come cheap.'

He chuckles. 'You're not wrong there. Fortunately, my client is a highly successful hedge fund manager with very deep pockets.'

Our conversation is interrupted by the appearance of Olivia. She's carrying a tray with a cafetière and a plate of biscuits. Not the sort of biscuits we have in the kitchen at Darling Buds – Jaffa Cakes or chocolate digestives – but thick shortbread fingers, studded with chocolate and chunks of stem ginger. She sets the tray down on the desk and goes to pour the coffee. I'm pleased when James waves her away. 'It's fine, thanks, we can help ourselves.'

He goes over to the desk and invites me to sit in one of the retro-looking chairs positioned in front of it. 'Help yourself to a biscuit,' he says as he starts to pour the coffee.

I hesitate, not wanting to appear greedy. 'Are you going to have one?'

'You bet I am; the only time I get to eat them is when I'm in the office.' He pulls a mock-angry face as he hands me my coffee. 'Biscuits are banned at home. My wife has a terrible sweet tooth; she says that if we have them in the house, she won't be able to stop until she's eaten the whole packet.'

'I'm the same.' I pick up a shortbread finger, careful to keep my elbows pinned to my sides, lest James spot the dark flowers of perspiration blossoming at the armholes of my dress. It's a warm day and being in such close proximity to him is making me nervous.

Resisting the urge to push the shortbread into my mouth like a log into a sawmill, I take a dainty nibble. I notice a photo in a silver frame on James's desk. It shows an attractive blonde woman, holding a toddler in her arms. 'Is that Eleanor?' I say, dredging his wife's name from the depths of my memory.

'Yeah.' He gives a rumpled smile. 'And that's our son, Toby; he's two and a half.

'Awww, he looks adorable.' He doesn't especially; I'm just being polite.

'He is . . . *sometimes*,' says James. 'And sometimes he's a little horror. But I can't complain, I was exactly the same at his age. It's only now I'm a father myself that I realise what my poor parents had to put up with.'

He leans back in his chair, one hand cupped to the back of his neck, his fingers kneading the tendons there. 'Do you have kids?'

'No.' Feeling the need to justify my childlessness, I add, 'But it's down to personal choice rather any biological malfunction – or my inability to find a suitable co-parent.'

He laughs, a deep throaty laugh that sends vibrations up my spine. 'Good to know. What about a significant other?'

I shake my head. 'Single and very happy, thank you.'

'Best way to be,' he says with a wink. 'There are times I wish I was still single – not because I don't love my wife and son, but because being a husband and father can be very hard work at times.'

Our eyes meet and in that moment it seems like something passes between us, although it's probably just wishful thinking on my part.

'Actually, it's my wife I wanted to talk to you about – or rather Eleanor's sister, Isabel.' He reaches for his mug and takes a slug of coffee. 'Izzy's had a rough time of it lately. She went through a rather nasty divorce at the beginning of the year and then she got made redundant.'

'Poor thing,' I murmur sympathetically, wishing he'd cut to the chase as the suspense is killing me.

'Her fortieth birthday's coming up and Eleanor and I are throwing a party for her on the August bank holiday. We're pushing the boat out – marquee, caterers, live band . . . the works.' He reaches for another piece of shortbread. 'We'd love it if you could do the flowers, but seeing as it's a bank holiday, I fully understand if you have other commitments.'

I don't. The truth is I haven't had much of a social life since Rob and I split up. It's not unusual for me to go an entire weekend without speaking to anyone except the postman. I know I should do something about it – join a community choir or enrol in an evening class – but for some reason I can't quite fathom, I keep putting it off.

'No, no,' I say quickly. 'I'd love to do the flowers for your sister-in-law's party, and thank you very much for thinking of me. What sort of arrangements did you have in mind?'

'I'm afraid it's no good asking me, I'm totally clueless on the subject. It's probably best if you and Eleanor talk through some ideas together. Nothing's set in stone at this stage and I'm sure she'd be interested to hear any suggestions you might have.'

'Great, I'll give her a call, shall I?'

'I think she'd rather meet you in person, if that's OK. I've got her calendar on my phone; we can get a date in the diary now if you like. Maybe some time next week, if you're free?'

'Sounds good.'

He picks his phone up off the desk. 'We're in West Dulwich. Do you normally visit people at home, or would you prefer it if Eleanor came to the shop?'

I hesitate. It would be more convenient if she came to me, but I'm very curious to see where James lives. 'I'd be happy to pop in and see your wife at home if that's easier for her.'

He consults the calendar on his phone. 'How about Thursday – can we say two p.m?'

My eyes crimp into a smile. 'It's a date.'

As I leave the offices of Cole & Elliott, I can't help feeling excited. This could be an amazing opportunity for Darling Buds. It's clear the Elliotts are wealthy people. It's woven into the crispness of James's shirt, the carelessness of his posture, the heavy gold links of the watch band on his wrist. I've been thinking for a while now that in order to move the business on, I need access to bigger fish – bankers, lawyers, people with money and taste – the sort of circles that James and Eleanor doubtless move in. It's all very well flogging mid-priced 'occasion' bouquets to commuters and doing the odd smart wedding and corporate installation, but if I want to take Darling Buds to the next level, I need different customers – better connected ones, with more disposable income. The sort of people for whom fresh flowers are a necessity, rather than a luxury. If I do a good job, this party could be a stepping stone to higher-end clients, more lucrative commissions. All I have to do is make sure I don't screw it up.

3

The Elliotts' home is an estate agent's wet dream: a jaw-dropping church conversion – pure Gothic Revival with arches, corbels, gargoyles, finials and a host of other architectural features I don't know the names of. A beautiful rose window dominates the right side of the building, its individual stained-glass panes divided into segments by delicate stonework tracery. Even more impressive is the squat bell tower at the opposite end, with its pretty mullioned windows. The steeple, if there ever was one, is long gone and in its place is a contemporary glass box that cantilevers from the side of the tower. This juxtaposition of old and new ought to jar, and yet the overall effect is wholly pleasing. I'm still staring up at it, quite awestruck, when the front door opens.

Eleanor Elliott and I are both in our thirties, but that's where the similarities end. When I wear linen, I look like an unmade bed, but on her it's effortlessly chic. Her wide-legged trousers and flowing top are perfectly accessorised with a statement necklace and diamond stud earrings that snatch greedily at the light. Her honey-coloured hair is wound into a loose knot and her face has the subtle sheen of expensive skincare. Standing on her doorstep in my pollen-stained blouse and faded capri pants, I feel like a dandelion next to a calla lily.

After greeting me, Eleanor leads the way through an imposing entrance hall and into a vast open-plan living space with a vaulted wooden ceiling. I've visited some lovely homes in the course of my career, but none quite as impressive as this. At one end lies the dazzling rose window; at the other a pair of modern French doors look out on to the garden, acting as a neat counterpoint to the ancient-looking stone jambs that bear their weight.

Everywhere I look I see elements of the building's ecclesiastical architecture, nestling comfortably alongside minimal modern interventions. Bare walls are warmed by wooden floors; shadowy corners are lit by stainless steel sconces. Carvings have been left intact, arches unfilled. Past and present in perfect harmony.

My hostess pauses for a moment in front of a feature wall, framed against the Colefax and Fowler foliate wallpaper like an exotic bird.

'Would you like something to drink, Amy – tea, perhaps?'

'I don't want to put you to any trouble,' I say, even though I could murder a cuppa.

'It's no trouble; I have an au pair.'

Of course you do, I think to myself.

She urges me to sit down, before she disappears through a stone archway. After checking my trousers for plant detritus, I lower myself into one of a pair of wittily mismatched armchairs and stare down at the grubby half-moons of my fingernails until she reappears.

'You have a beautiful home,' I tell her. 'I've never seen anything quite like it.'

'Thank you,' she says, sinking gracefully on to a mid-century rocker. 'I can't claim too much credit for it though. I chose the furnishings, but everything else is down to James.'

'He did the conversion himself?' I say, my eyes widening.

She nods. 'When he first showed me the listing in the auction catalogue, I couldn't see how it could ever be a practical family home, but James convinced me he could make it work for us. He was absolutely right, too. He's created such a peaceful haven here; that's why we decided to call our home "The Sanctuary".'

'I think that's a great choice of name,' I say. 'And what a super showcase for James's talents.'

'It is, isn't it? It was featured in a series the *Evening Standard* did on London's best church conversions – James got several new commissions as a result. Not that the project was plain sailing; far from it. Originally we wanted six bedrooms, but that would've meant building a ground-floor extension and we couldn't get it past planning.' She throws a hand in the air. 'And yet they were happy for us to stick a glass box on top of the bell tower to house the master suite. Where's the logic in that, huh?'

I smile. 'I bet the views up there are amazing.'

'They are, you can see all the way to the Houses of Parliament on a clear day; definitely worth climbing up three flights of stairs for.'

Jealousy brews inside me. What I wouldn't do to live in a house like this – *and* be married to someone as wonderful as James.

'Let's talk flowers, shall we?' Eleanor kicks off her thong sandals and curls her legs up beneath her, a manoeuvre few people could manage with such elegance on a rocking chair. 'I googled you this morning.'

Her innocuous comment triggers an instant physiological reaction. My pulse quickens and my heartbeat seems to echo around the room, every surface reflecting a different timbre: glass, wood, granite, exposed brickwork.

'I found your Instagram,' she goes on. 'I love your style – and your attention to detail is incredible.'

Instantly my shoulders relax. I don't know why I assumed the worst; force of habit, I guess.

'I was particularly impressed by your Crystal Palace Park installation – you know, the one to commemorate the Queen.'

The piece she's referring to is a huge, tiara-shaped floral sculpture, inspired by the planting at Balmoral. Commissioned by the local council as part of a 'best-dressed park' competition organised by the London Mayor, it earned me some useful publicity, as well as the runner-up prize.

'Thanks. It's certainly one of the most challenging projects I've worked on.'

'How long did it take?'

'Nearly three days.'

'Gosh,' she says admiringly. 'Your fingers must've been bleeding by the end of it.'

I laugh. 'Not quite, but I did have a few blisters from the secateurs.'

She gives a tinkling laugh. 'I do hope this birthday party for my sister won't cause you any pain.'

'Have you had any ideas about colours or themes?'

'Yes, but I keep changing my mind. I was hoping you could offer some guidance.'

'Of course, that's what I'm here for.' Reaching into the tote at my feet, I remove a small notebook. 'How many guests are you expecting?'

'Sixty or thereabouts. We've only just sent out the invites, so I don't have an exact number just yet. The party's going to be in the garden, weather permitting. Drinks first and then a buffet meal. All pretty informal.'

'Would you like flowers for the dining tables?'

'Yes, just a small centrepiece – nine to ten in total, depending on the final numbers.'

I jot down a few words in my notebook. 'Do you want the centrepieces to be the same or different?'

'Oh,' she says, her brow crinkling. 'I hadn't thought about that. Different ones would be nice. What do you think?'

'I agree. Different, but all sharing the same colour palette. How does that sound?'

Eleanor beams. I notice the faint asymmetry of her teeth and how white they are. 'Perfect.'

'I can show you some photos of the table arrangements I've done in the past. If you point out the ones you like, it will give me a good idea of your style – but of course the final design will be utterly unique to you. Did you want flowers for the house as well?'

'Yes. I was thinking of something quite dramatic; something that will really make a statement.' She points to a low, glass-topped table in the centre of the room. 'I thought we could display it over there.'

I tap my biro against my chin. 'It's not an ideal location, to be honest. That'll be a heavy traffic area on the day of the party, especially if you've got caterers shuttling between the kitchen and the garden. There's a risk the vase might get knocked over.'

I look around for a few moments, my gaze finally settling on a row of stone niches set deep into the wall, each one crowned with a delightful Gothic arch.

'Those niches would look lovely filled with flowers.'

'Really?' she says doubtfully. 'They're not very big.'

'You'd be surprised – lots of smaller arrangements can have more of a visual impact than a single large display.' I delve into my bag and pull out my laptop. 'Let me show you.'

A few moments later, we're staring at a close-up image of six identical vases, each one filled with a tightly bound posy of white hydrangeas. 'This was for a luxury hotel in Islington.' It wasn't really; it was a baby shower in Hackney, but what does it matter? 'The hotel owner has *very* exacting standards,' I add, warming to the theme. 'I guess you have to when you count celebrities and European royalty among your clientele.'

She touches the screen to enlarge the photo. 'I see what you mean,' she says thoughtfully. 'And you think something as simple as that would work well in here?'

'Absolutely. People tend to think a show-stopping arrangement is all about cramming as many different varieties into a vase as possible, but sometimes less is more. Of course, we don't have to go with hydrangeas, but they do have the advantage of being in season during August, which is always a bonus.'

Judging by the look on her face, she's won over. 'I think hydrangeas would be lovely. Perhaps we could go with blue ones though, it's Izzy's favourite colour.'

'Blue it is,' I say, making an entry in my notebook. 'I forgot to ask – what's your budget? A ballpark figure will do at this stage.'

She names an amount that most people spend on their wedding flowers. It's way more than she needs to shell out for an event of this size. Still, if the Elliotts have got it, I'm more than happy to help them spend it. 'Does your sister want to have some input into the flowers, or is she happy to leave it up to you?'

'Oh, didn't James tell you? It's a surprise party. Izzy thinks she's coming over here for a simple birthday lunch, *en famille*. I can't wait to see her face when I take her into the garden and she sees all our friends and family there.' She squeezes her shoulders close to her ears, as if I were sharing her excited feeling. I'm not, but I squeeze my shoulders back anyway.

'How exciting, I'm sure your sister's going to be thrilled when she finds out. I hear she's been through a tough time just lately.'

Eleanor turns her face to the side, staring off into the middle distance. Her profile is that of a ballerina in repose: perfectly straight nose, chin tilted upwards and a poise that suggests a woman used to being looked at. 'God, yes . . . that ghastly divorce. Hugh, Izzy's ex, made the process so much more difficult than it needed to be. It got so bad they were only communicating through their solicitors in the end. You'd think he'd have been a bit more accommodating, especially as he was the one who initiated the split. Izzy was devastated; she had no idea Hugh was even unhappy. He insisted there was no one else involved, but he was clearly lying through his teeth.' She pauses, checks herself. 'Sorry, you don't even know Izzy – why would you care about her marriage break-up?'

'Oh, but I do care,' I say with emphasis. 'Whenever I'm doing the flowers for a family occasion, I always try and find out as much about the client as possible. For me, it isn't just about making the place look pretty, you see; it's about creating a mood. For someone like your sister, for example – someone who sounds like she could do with a bit of a lift – I'd focus on what I call "happy flowers". Tulips, lily of the valley, calendula and roses; flowers that raise the spirits and make people feel good about themselves.'

'I like your holistic approach,' Eleanor says, nodding slowly. 'I'm beginning to see why James thinks so highly of you.'

I feel a thrust of pleasure. It's always nice to have one's efforts recognised, and James's opinion means more to me than most. I cast my eyes towards the French doors. The sunlight that filled them when I arrived is gone and clouds are scudding across the darkening sky. 'I was wondering . . . would it be possible to have a quick look at the garden?'

Eleanor swings her feet back to the floor. 'Yes, of course, but we'd better be quick. It looks as if the heavens are about to open.'

The garden is pretty and very generous by London standards. I do a slow three-sixty, taking it all in: the gently undulating box hedge, the lovely old cherry tree, the eye-catching copper water feature with its soothing gurgle. Roughly two-thirds of the space is laid to lawn and at the far end stands an imposing gazebo.

'Originally, we were going to hire a marquee, but then I had second thoughts,' Eleanor tells me. 'We'll have the meal in the gazebo instead. It'll be so much nicer than sweltering inside a stuffy tent, don't you think?'

She touches my bare arm with her long, delicate fingers and it sets off a kind of shiver in my bones.

'For sure – and the flowers will look so much better outdoors, in their natural habitat.'

'Let me talk you through the table placement,' she says, setting off down the garden.

Close up, the gazebo is even more impressive. A handsome wooden structure with a hipped roof, perfect for alfresco dining. Definitely not the sort of thing you'd get off the peg at a DIY warehouse. The ground underneath is laid with honey-coloured flagstones and there's some attractive planting in the surrounding flowerbeds. My client starts moving around, indicating the location of the tables. 'The catering company's providing the furniture. I can give you the dimensions if that would be helpful.'

'Yes, please.'

'I don't suppose you know of any reliable employment agencies, do you – ones that supply waiting staff? My au pair did say she had some friends who'd be willing to help out, but I think we'd be better off with professionals.'

'I can certainly give you one or two recommendations. A lot of the events I work at use agency staff. I'll text you some numbers when I get back to the shop.'

'That would be great, thank you.' She places her hands on her slender hips. 'I was thinking about a floral arch at the entrance to the gazebo, but I was worried it might look too wedding-y.'

'Oh no, I think an arch would be awesome – a real focal point.' Hell, I've got to find some way of spending their money. 'And if we steer clear of pastel colours it won't look like a bridal arch at all.' I chew on my bottom lip, as if I'm weighing up the options. 'A Carmen Miranda theme might work – something bold and exotic, with lots of vibrant colours.'

Eleanor's glossed pink lips twitch with approval. 'You must be a mind reader, Amy. My sister's travelled all over South America, it's her favourite part of the world. A Carmen Miranda theme would be spot on.'

Not a mind reader. Just observant. One wall of the living room was covered in family photos. They included several of a woman who looked just like Eleanor, but her fair hair had an auburn tinge and her nose was slightly more upturned. In one of them, she was sitting in a canoe on a wide river, surrounded by rainforest, a backpack at her feet. In another, she was posing with a fellow traveller at a colourful street festival. Judging by the costumes, I'd hazard a guess at Brazil or Colombia.

'Great, I'll speak to my supplier in Holland and see what's available. I prefer to build larger installations in situ, so I'd need to come here the day before the party to start work on it.'

'That would no problem at—' Before she can finish her sentence, a loud rumble of thunder echoes above our heads. We both look up in surprise. Seconds later the rain begins to fall, heavy drops the size of pennies that soak through our clothes in an instant.

'Quick, let's get back inside,' Eleanor shrieks. I'm hot on her heels as she starts running towards the house.

We stumble through the French doors and stand for a few minutes on the coir matting, catching our breath. We both look pretty bedraggled and Eleanor's thin shirt has practically turned see-through. She calls out a name and seconds later a young woman appears; she doesn't look much older than twenty and on her hip is a young child, who I assume is James's progeny.

'Bring us some towels from the airing cupboard, will you, Katya?' says Eleanor. 'I don't want Amy here catching her death.' She waggles her fingers at the little boy, who's staring at me with unabashed interest. 'Silly Mummy and her friend got caught in the rain,' she tells him. 'We forgot to put our coats and wellington boots on.'

'Silly Mummy,' he repeats, giggling with glee as Katya carries him towards the staircase in the corner of the room.

Spotting the tray of tea things that Katya must have laid out for us, Eleanor beckons me over. 'Come and sit down,' she says, stepping out of her sandals and padding barefoot to the seating area.

I'm reluctant to remove my own footwear (it's been a while since I had a pedicure), but I do because I don't want to track shoe prints across what looks like a very expensive rug.

'Milk and sugar?' Eleanor asks as she gives the contents of the teapot a stir.

'Yes – and two spoons, please.'

I sit down on the edge of an armchair, not wanting to ruin the upholstery with my damp clothing.

'Has Katya been with you long?'

'Nearly a year. She's the second au pair we've had. The first girl was absolutely brilliant, but she had to go back to Poland for family reasons. She was the one who put us in touch with Katya; I think they were at school together.' She lowers her voice. 'She's not the hardest worker, but Toby adores her.'

She begins pouring the tea into two slender mugs. 'James works incredibly long hours and doesn't have much time for childcare,' she confides. 'There's simply no way I could manage Toby on my own, not with everything else going on in my life.'

'What do you do?' I ask, assuming she must have a very demanding career.

'I used to be in HR, but that was a long time ago.'

I wait for her to offer some explanation as to why a person who doesn't work needs an au pair to take care of their child, but none is forthcoming.

Soon, Katya reappears with the towels but minus her young charge. 'I've put Toby down for his nap,' she announces.

'Good,' says Eleanor. 'We don't want him tired and grizzly for his playdate with Hebe this afternoon.' She gives me a quick conspiratorial look, as if dealing with an overwrought child is a scenario I can readily identify with.

Katya hands me a towel. Like everything else in this house, it's immaculate – thick and soft and fragrant.

I spend the next half an hour showing Eleanor more photos from my portfolio and helping her make the final selections for the flowers for the party. Then it's time for me to make a move. I need to get back to the shop to see how Claire's getting on with the buttonholes for tomorrow's wedding. It's not a complicated task and left to her own devices she'll do a decent job – but decent isn't good enough for Darling Buds and nothing leaves the shop until I've given it my personal seal of approval.

My bladder is fit to burst after the two-and-a-half cups of tea I've drunk, so I ask Eleanor if I can use her loo before I go. She directs me to a room in the entrance hall that she says was created from the former vestry. It's twice as big as my bathroom at home, with wood-panelled walls and the sort of accessories you'd see in a high-end hotel.

After I've finished drying my hands I open the doors of the little cupboard under the sink, just out of curiosity. I don't know what I'm hoping to find – a ratty old cleaning sponge, perhaps, or a tube of anti-fungal ointment; something to make me feel less inadequate. But all it contains is a beautifully wrapped bar of luxury soap and a bottle of Jo Malone room spray that smells so gorgeous I'm tempted to spritz it on my wrists.

On exiting, I'm greeted by the sound of an angry voice. I hover by the door that leads to the living area, thinking Eleanor must be admonishing the au pair. But then, realising I can only hear one half of the conversation, I surmise that she's talking to someone on the phone.

'You can't keep doing this, Izzy,' I hear her say.

Ah. It's her sister. I lean forward slightly, holding my ear to the gap in the door.

'What are you talking about?' Eleanor snaps. 'James and I have bent over backwards to help you these past few months.'

A thirty-second silence ensues.

'Well, I'm sorry if you feel suffocated.' There's a sarcastic emphasis on the final word. 'But you're my big sister and I can't help worrying about you.'

A shorter silence.

'Have you been drinking, Iz?'

A rapid pull of breath.

'Yes, you have, I can always tell.'

A momentary pause.

'I don't *care* if it's only one drink. For God's sake, Izzy, it's three o'clock in the afternoon. Wouldn't you be better off scouring the job sites or polishing your interview technique, instead of kicking back with a double vodka?'

Whatever Izzy says next clearly hits Eleanor where it hurts because her voice breaks like a fine crack running through a piece of porcelain.

'How can you say that, after everything I've done for you? . . . Izzy? . . . *Izzy? Are* you still there?'

A huff of breath.

The conversation has apparently been terminated.

When I walk back into the room, Eleanor is standing there, staring down at her phone. Her cheeks are rather flushed.

'Is everything all right?'

'Yes.' She sighs. 'No, not really. I've just had a row with my sister. She actually hung up on me, would you believe?'

I bend down to pick up my bag. 'I shouldn't worry about it. We always fight with the people we care about the most.' I read that on a fridge magnet once; I have no idea if it's actually true.

She forces a smile. 'Do you get on with your siblings?'

'I'm an only child, but I always wanted a sister.'

'Believe me, you wouldn't want a sister like mine.' She puts her phone down on the table. 'I love Izzy to bits, but she can be terribly self-centred – especially since her divorce. It seems like we can barely have a conversation these days without falling out.'

'What were you arguing about this time?' I ask, my nosiness getting the better of me.

'Izzy was angling for a supper invite this weekend. When I told her James and I had other plans, she accused me of not caring that she's going to be spending the entire weekend by herself. I know she hates being on her own, she always has done – but divorce or not, she's got to understand that the whole world doesn't revolve around her. James and I have busy lives, we simply can't be there for her twenty-four-seven.' Eleanor pulls in a long breath of air and suddenly it seems as if she's on the edge of tears. 'What makes it even harder is that Izzy's a completely different person whenever James is around . . . charming, witty, relaxed. I find it rather hurtful that she makes so much of an effort with him, but not with her own sister.'

She folds her arms across her chest, gripping her tiny, childlike shoulders. 'I'm not sure she deserves this birthday party,' she says, the jagged edge in her voice hardening. 'I've half a mind to cancel the whole damn thing,'

My stomach constricts. She can't cancel. I want this job. More than that, I *need* it.

'But you've already sent out the invites,' I say. 'In any case, isn't the party the perfect way to show Izzy just how much you *do* care about her?'

'You're probably right,' she concedes. 'I just hope she's suitably grateful.' She looks at me from under her eyelashes. 'You must think I'm a terrible person, bitching about my sister to someone I hardly know.'

'Not at all. Family relationships often trigger powerful feelings; it's nothing to be embarrassed about,' I say, thinking of the slow, involuntary petrification of my emotions that always occurs when I'm in the presence of my own family.

As Eleanor walks me to the front door, she thanks me for my expertise – and for my understanding. Then, almost as an afterthought, she adds, 'I'd be grateful if you didn't mention my little outburst to James. He already reckons I'm too sensitive as far as Izzy is concerned; I don't want him thinking I'm completely neurotic.'

I smile reassuringly, thrilled to be taken into Eleanor's confidence. 'I wouldn't dream of it.'

4

I feel the familiar heaviness descend the second I pull up outside Mum and Dad's uninspiring seventies bungalow. It's not that we don't get on; it's just that whenever I see them it feels as if I'm returning to a soap opera after not watching it for several years and I'm still trying to piece together the plot.

My parents live on an island off the Essex coast that's cut off from the mainland by a high tide twice a day. It's either a delightful quirk of the place or a massive inconvenience, depending on your point of view. We see each other every few months. Sometimes they visit me in London, but usually I go to Essex; that way, I can leave when I've had enough, tide permitting.

As soon as he opens the door, my father draws me in for a hug. When I pull away I see that my foundation has applied itself to the fabric of his navy polo shirt: a little pale impression of my cheek and nose.

Mum's waiting for me in the sitting room-cum-diner, pale-faced and erect. Her lips are slightly pursed and she's strumming the rope of turquoise beads at her throat.

'Your mother had a bad night,' says Dad by way of explanation.

Mum and I sit down on the sofa while Dad goes to the kitchen to check on the roast chicken. The ceiling above me shows cracks running through the plasterwork from one side of the room to the other, snaking right through to the cornicing. I feel a bit like this house sometimes. In need of some support. A bit of careful underpinning.

'How have you been?' I ask her.

I listen as Mum catalogues her latest ailments. Some are real, but the vast majority are imagined. My mother – and there's no way of putting this kindly – is a card-carrying hypochondriac. A mild headache is instantly upgraded to migraine status, a new freckle becomes a suspected tumour, a slight fatigue incontrovertible evidence of long Covid. She's like one of those people with haunted eyes you see on the evening news who's just been winched from the roof of a flooded building, trying to convey to everyone watching from the safety and comfort of their own homes what it feels like to be so close to death. I shouldn't really judge; she's had a lot to contend with in her life. We all have.

I do my best to look interested, but I've never been one of life's natural empaths. It's another reason I don't look forward to these familial get-togethers – they wipe out every emotional resource I have for at least twenty-four hours. When Mum's finished telling me about the rash on her arm that she's convinced is an allergic reaction to a new furniture polish, she enquires after my own well-being.

'I'm good, thanks,' I reply as I cast an anxious glance upwards. There's a heavy brass chandelier right above our heads that I can never look at without thinking, *now what if that accursed thing should fall down?*

'How's work – still busy at the shop?'

'Yes, rushed off my feet.'

'You need to get yourself some help.'

'I did – at the end of last year. I told you all about her.'

'I don't think so.'

'I did, Mum. I distinctly remember telling you Claire was head and shoulders above all the other interview candidates.'

She frowns. 'Strange . . . I have no recollection of that conversation at all.'

We sit in silence for several minutes, the sunshine outside bleeding weakly through the Venetian blinds that, inexplicably, my parents always keep at half-mast. Then Mum jumps on another one of her hobby horses.

'Have you met any nice men lately?'

'Yes, actually,' I reply. 'I had a date with a theatre director last night. We went to see a new exhibition at the National Portrait Gallery and then he treated me to a very expensive dinner.'

Mum's face, as she processes this information, is like watching time-lapse photography on one of those nature documentaries, her face turning from winter to summer all in the space of a few seconds.

'How lovely,' she says breathily. I experience a stab of irritation at her guilelessness and then immediately feel guilty.

Mum turns her head towards the serving hatch which was amusingly highlighted on the selling agent's details as an 'appealing original feature', as I recall.

'Did you hear that, Neil? Amy had a date with a theatre director last night.'

Dad's head appears through the hatch. 'That's fantastic news, love. I always said you could do better than that Bob character you were so stuck on.'

'Rob,' I say wearily. 'His name was Rob.'

'You want to keep your options open though,' says Mum. 'That's the beauty of online dating . . . so many fish in the sea.'

'That's good advice your mother's giving you,' says Dad. 'No point settling for second best. If this fella phones and asks you for a second date, don't say yes straight away, make him w—'

'Actually, he already has – and we're meeting for lunch on Friday.' I know Dad means well, but I can't bear to hear more pearls of wisdom from a man who has only ever slept with one woman in his entire life (I don't know this for a fact, but I'd stake my business on it).

Just then, my mobile gives a bright ping. I take it out of my cardigan pocket and look down at the screen. It's the surgery, reminding me for the third time that my cervical smear is overdue. 'That's him now,' I say. 'He wants to know if I'd like a private backstage tour of the Old Vic before our lunch.'

'Oooh,' Mum squeals. 'This one's definitely a keeper.'

I should point out at this juncture that the theatre director doesn't exist. I was so sick of Mum asking me when I was going to find a husband and settle down that I told her I was using a dating app, when really I've done no such thing. Everyone knows those apps promise more than they can possibly deliver: the facade of intelligence, wit and instant chemistry conjured through the phone screen belies heavily Photoshopped images, crashing bores and unrequested dick pics. Besides which, I can't keep up with the ever-evolving jargon. *Benching, bread-crumbing, submarining* . . . whatever happened to just being a shit?

'I'll go and lay the table for you, shall I, Dad?' I call out, keen to change the subject.

'That would be a big help – thanks, love.'

I go over to the sideboard. Sitting on top of it is a photo of me with some school friends. It was taken on the beach when I was in Year 9. I look at that photo now and I am struck by the irony of the figure I cut: a happy teenager without a care in the world. No hint of the bad weather to come.

I open the top drawer and start removing cutlery. 'Where are the table mats, Dad?'

'Bottom drawer,' he replies, shouting to be heard over the whir of the extractor.

I take the mats and cutlery over to the dining table, which is dominated by a gratuitous arrangement of exotic flowers I wouldn't have thought was available in this part of Essex. I lean in to smell them. They're fake. Good fake – but still.

Half an hour later we're all sitting round the table. As Dad sets heavily laden plates of food in front of us, Mum looks down at hers like a death-row prisoner who's just been delivered the wrong last meal. 'I thought were having *roast* parsnips,' she says.

'I decided to do mashed in the end; I thought it would be nicer.'

'Nicer for who?' Mum says, half under her breath.

Dad smiles benignly. He's been living with Mum too long to take offence. He and I both know she's one of those people who's doomed to live in a state of mild dissatisfaction. People, places, things – they never seem to quite live up to her expectations. It's like sleeping with a mosquito in the room; hearing the low hum and knowing the inevitable bite is on its way, fixing you in a state of constant awareness.

'I loved that photo you sent on WhatsApp,' Dad says as he joins us at the table.

I reach for the gravy boat. 'Which one?'

'The Mexican restaurant opening.'

'Oh, the cactus arrangements. They were fun, weren't they?'

Dad chuckles. 'I bet you were removing the prickles for weeks afterwards.'

I chuckle back.

'Have you done any other interesting jobs lately?'

'Not really, just the usual weddings and funerals.' I pour gravy over my roast potatoes. 'One of my corporate clients has asked me to do a birthday party for his sister-in-law. I met his wife the other day to go through some ideas. Their house was amazing; it's a converted church. There was a whole article about it in the *Evening Standard*.'

I offer the gravy boat to Mum, but she shakes her head. 'If I play it right, it could be a really good advertisement for my work.'

'Good, good,' says Dad, but he seems a little distracted.

He unscrews the lid from a bottle of Pinot and pours a small amount into my wine glass. Something about the way he does this and the set of his jaw forewarns me of some serious conversation coming up.

'You know it's the anniversary soon, don't you?' he remarks. He doesn't need to supply further details; I know exactly what he's referring to.

'Twenty years,' says Mum. 'I can hardly believe it. The time's gone by in a flash.'

Not for me it hasn't. It's crawled by with agonising lethargy – a bit like a life sentence, but without any likelihood of parole.

'The family's holding a candlelit vigil to mark the occasion. Your mother just happened to see something about it online.'

I throw Mum a sharp look. *Just happened to see?* I don't think so.

'You've been looking at their social media, haven't you?' I can't keep the accusing tone out of my voice. 'If you remember, my solicitor said we weren't to have any contact with them.'

'I haven't had contact, I just looked at a couple of things on the internet,' Mum says.

'But *why*?' I say. 'What can you possibly get out of it?'

She gives an awkward shrug – her sharp shoulders hitching themselves too high and then staying there too long, as if she hasn't quite perfected the technique. 'I just like to know they're all right – after what you did to them.'

Her comment stings. It's like stepping on a wasp, a sharp attack into soft flesh.

Dad clears his throat. 'Obviously, our family wouldn't be welcome at the vigil, but perhaps we could mark the anniversary in some other way. It doesn't seem right to just ignore it.' He takes a sip of wine. 'Perhaps we could have our own candlelit vigil in the garden; you could even stay the night if you wanted to.'

An ache starts to pulsate at the corners of my temples, and I instinctively reach a hand to my forehead, pushing the pads of my fingers into the pressure points. 'I'm not sure,' I say.

Mum begins cutting her chicken breast into tiny uniform pieces, arranges them in rows, then begins ferrying each one to her mouth on the back of her fork in a complicated manoeuvre that seems to absorb her entirely.

'Just think about it, OK, love?' says Dad. 'And if you don't want to do a vigil, then that's absolutely fine with us.'

We limp through the rest of the meal and then I offer to do the washing-up, insisting I can manage on my own; anything for a few minutes to myself. Afterwards, Dad takes me on a tour of the garden. He doesn't bring up the anniversary again, for which I am grateful. Instead, he talks about the latest additions to his vegetable patch and the unseasonably bad weather we've been having.

Back at the house, we have coffee and Elizabeth Shaw mints and then I make my excuses, pretending I'm concerned about the incoming tide, even though we all know there's a good two hours before the road becomes impassable. As I kiss them both goodbye, I think that perhaps I'll leave it a bit longer than the usual three or four months before I see them again. I'm not being selfish; it will be easier for all of us.

The drive back to London is a nightmare. There's an accident on the motorway and I'm stuck in stationary traffic for what seems like forever. I feel on the verge of tears, but it's not down to my frustration with the hold-up; my parents' words have burrowed deeper than I care to admit. I have to say I'm surprised they brought the subject up, anniversary or not. As a family, we've become adept at ignoring this unpleasant chapter in our shared history. But secrets never go away completely. Like moths in a wardrobe, they nibble away unseen, until one day you hold your favourite angora jumper up to the light and the whole thing falls apart in your hands.

Now

5

WITNESS STATEMENT

This statement is true to the best of my knowledge and belief and I make it knowing that, if it is tendered in evidence, I shall be liable to prosecution if I have wilfully stated in it anything which I know to be false, or do not believe to be true.

Signature: *Andrea Jennings*

My name is Andrea Jennings and I am employed by Eleanor Elliott as a domestic cleaner at The Sanctuary in Oakwood Road, West Dulwich.

My usual hours are midday to 5pm every Thursday. However on 22nd September I'd arranged to come in first thing, as I had to take my elderly father to a doctor's appointment in the afternoon.

I arrived at eight forty-five and rang the doorbell first, just like I always do. When no one answered, I let myself in with the key Mrs Elliott had given me. I didn't have any cause for concern at that stage because it wasn't unusual for the house to be empty when I arrived.

After I'd hung up my coat and bag, I went into the kitchen. I always start in the kitchen because it's usually the untidiest place in the house and I like to get it out of the way first. When I got the cleaning things out from under the sink I noticed that the limescale remover was missing. I knew Mrs Elliott kept a second bottle of limescale remover in the first-floor bathroom, so I decided to go upstairs and get it.

When I got to the landing, I noticed that the door to Toby Elliott's bedroom was slightly ajar. I didn't think anything of it and continued on to the bathroom. It was only when I was coming back out with the limescale remover that I realised there was someone lying on the floor in Toby's room. All I could see through the gap in the door was an arm and a hand – but it looked like the person was unconscious because they weren't moving.

I was so shocked, I dropped the limescale remover and ran straight over to the door. I'm quite a large person and the gap wasn't big enough for me to fit through it. I tried to push the door open, but it wouldn't budge because the person was lying right behind it and I didn't want to use too much force in case I hurt them. I could see that the hand belonged to a woman, so I said Mrs Elliott's name out loud, although I had no idea if it was her or not. When there was no reply, I put my arm through the gap in the door and touched the hand. The person didn't react, but their skin felt warm, so I assumed they were still alive. That's when I decided to go downstairs and use the house phone to call for an ambulance.

Two Months Earlier

6

'I'm going to head off now, if that's all right.'

I jump at the sound of Claire's voice and my knee catches the rough underside of the workbench. Turning to look over my shoulder, I see her standing in the studio's open door.

'Sorry, Amy, did I startle you?' she asks.

'Just a bit.' I glance at my laptop screen: twenty to six. I was so absorbed in my task I'd totally lost track of the time.

'Have you locked up?'

'Yep – and before you ask I've also mopped the floor, drawn the blinds and stuck the cash in the safe.'

I flash her a grateful smile. 'Thanks, Claire, you're an angel.'

I mean it as well. I deliberately didn't set the bar too high when I was recruiting for the role. How could I, when the salary I was offering was barely above minimum wage? A glorified shop assistant was all I was hoping for, someone to deal with walk-ins and help me with the more tedious aspects of flower prep. In the event, Claire exceeded all my expectations. She might not have an extensive knowledge of plants, or a natural talent for flower arranging, but she's enthusiastic and hard-working, which counts for a lot in my book. The customers like her too. She has one of those faces, all straight lines and agreeable angles that people instinctively trust. Whether it's helping a shy teenager choose flowers for his first girlfriend, or dealing with someone recently bereaved, she handles every person with sensitivity and patience – and those aren't skills you can teach.

'I'm happy to stick around a bit longer if there's anything else you need me to do,' she says. 'Kyle's just texted to say he's stuck in Deptford, dealing with a blocked sewer, so there's nobody waiting for me at home.'

Kyle is Claire's partner. He's a plumber and often works unsocial hours. We've never met, but I feel as if I know him because Claire talks about him all the time.

'No, it's fine, you get off. What are you guys up to this weekend – anything exciting?' It's only Thursday, but as Claire works a four-day week, her weekend effectively starts now.

'Yeah, actually, we are.' She comes over and rests a buttock on the edge of the workbench. 'We're going to a surf festival in Newquay; I'm really looking forward to it.'

'I didn't know you guys surfed.'

'We don't, but one of Kyle's friends is competing.'

'Are you taking the camper van?'

'Yeah, we packed all our gear up last night. The plan is to hit the road as soon as Kyle gets home from work. It's a pretty long drive, but with any luck we'll be at the campsite by midnight.'

I feel a childish pang of envy. Claire's a few years older than me, but she doesn't have kids and leads the kind of gloriously uncomplicated life that most people have in their teens and twenties. She and Kyle are always doing fun stuff – festivals, mountain bike rides, canoeing trips, weekend breaks with friends. It was one of the reasons Claire took the job at Darling Buds – because it gives her plenty of free time to plan, and execute, her next adventure. It must be wonderful to have so few responsibilities, to be so utterly carefree.

'I bet you'll have an amazing time,' I say.

She picks up a stray dahlia petal from the workbench and rolls it between her thumb and index finger. 'How about you? What have you got planned for the weekend?'

I made the decision early on to keep the shop closed on a Saturday and Sunday as I knew it would limit my availability for weddings but, unusually for this time of year, I don't have any booked in for this weekend.

'Oh, just meeting up with a couple of friends,' I say vaguely. 'I'm not sure what we're doing yet.' I'm too ashamed to admit the truth: that my own weekend stretches ahead of me, flat and featureless, the only excitement on the horizon a trip to the supermarket and, if I can summon the energy, a spin class at the gym.

Claire points to my laptop. 'Is that one of your friends?'

My eyes cut to the profile that fills the screen. Staring back at me is the tanned face of an attractive woman dressed in hiking gear. She's standing in a dense pine forest, one foot up on a fallen tree trunk, as she poses for a selfie like a pro.

'Mmm, she's an old pal from college.' I close the lid of the laptop and rest my forearms on top of it. 'We haven't hooked up in a while; I was just checking to see what she's been up to. I really must find the time to give her a call.'

Claire's face takes on a wistful look. 'I wish I'd made more of an effort to stay in touch with my friends from college,' she says. 'Trouble is, I keep making new ones and now I've got so many, it's a full-time job just keeping up with them all.' She cocks her head to one side. 'That's the great thing about London – it's ridiculously easy to meet new people.'

'Yeah, I know what you mean; I might have to have a cull of my Christmas card list pretty soon.' I'm talking utter bollocks. I can't remember the last time I made a new friend – a proper friend, I mean. Work colleagues like Claire don't count, nor does Janet, the middle-aged woman who lives in the flat above mine. We'll stop to chat if we happen to run into each other, but we don't socialise together as such, which I've always thought was a bit of a shame. I extended a few casual invitations when she first moved in, but she never seemed terribly interested.

There was a woman at the gym recently who I thought had friend potential. We chatted a few times on the treadmills and made each other laugh, but when I suggested exchanging phone numbers, she made an excuse – something about having a new phone and not being able to remember the number. I knew she was fibbing because I could see the rectangular bulge in the pocket of her leggings. It would've been the easiest thing in the world to get her phone out and punch in my number – if she actually wanted to progress our friendship, that is. Maybe she thought I was hitting on her. I guess I'll never know.

'Amy?'

I zone back in to the conversation. 'Sorry, Claire, what was that?'

'I was just saying that the keys to the van are in the safe. You'll need to get them out for Ewan when you come in tomorrow morning.'

'Great, thanks for reminding me.'

She slides off the workbench. 'Well, if there's nothing else, I'll get off home. See you next week.'

'Yep, see you then.'

She starts walking towards the door, but then she stops and half turns. 'I nearly forgot, James Elliott came by when you were out at the printer's.'

Instantly my heart beats a little faster. An automatic reaction, like an animal reacting to its mate's pheromones. Stupid really, when (a) he's married, and (b) even if he were single, he wouldn't look twice at the likes of me.

'To buy flowers?'

'No, to see you. Sorry, Amy, I should've said something sooner. He asked me to pass on a message.'

My pulse rate ratchets up another couple of notches.

'He says thank you for meeting with his wife the other day. He really appreciates you going over to the house and he knows you're going to do an amazing job.'

I stick out my lower lip, slightly disbelieving. 'He came into the shop just to say that?'

'He said he happened to be passing. I think he has a client in the area.' She flips her shiny dark hair over her shoulders. 'It's nice when people make the effort to show their appreciation, isn't it?'

My lips twitch upwards into a smile. 'It certainly is.'

Once I have the studio to myself again, I open the lid of my laptop. I hope Claire didn't look too closely at the Facebook profile on my screen. She caught me by surprise and the untruth just slipped out. I ought to be more careful. I know from experience that lies are spindly, unwieldy things. Delicate filaments that are easy to twist and hard to control.

This is the first time I've looked at Facebook in ages. I do have a profile, but I don't pay much attention to the vapid updates of my several dozen so-called 'Friends', most of whom are business contacts or people I met through Rob and am no longer in touch with. Whenever I read their smug little posts, the photos of their families and pets and foreign holidays, I have the disturbing feeling I often get when I reflect on my own life and come up against the fuzzy grey blanket that shrouds significant chunks of it. I know that something dark lies beneath it, but I can't quite bring myself to lift it up and take a look.

I was surprised how easy it was to track Izzy down. As I don't know her surname, I searched for Eleanor's social media instead. I found her Instagram and scrolled through the comments until I found a gushing affirmation from @isabelharkness, posted in response to a pic of Toby, wearing one of those kids' bath towels that have a hood and animal ears. That led me in turn to Izzy's own Insta account, which was rather dull and consisted almost entirely of pictures that looked as if they'd been lifted from National Geographic. I didn't hold out much hope for Facebook. If she was on there, I assumed her profile would be locked down; that there would be nothing to see but a thumbnail-sized photo and, if I was lucky, the name of a former school or employer. But, by some massive stroke of luck, it was wide open. I'd only just found it when Claire interrupted me and now that I'm alone, I can gorge myself on the wealth of information there. I don't usually do so much research into the lives of the people I work for, but for some reason I'm intrigued by this seemingly capricious and self-absorbed creature that the Elliotts are lavishing so much time and money on.

I start by checking out Izzy's photos. She's not as sleek as Eleanor, but she has a robust, farm-girl beauty with strong limbs and eyes that are a deep ficus green. Whatever shortcomings she may have as a sister, she clearly has a wide circle of friends. As I observe her drinking cocktails in a fashionable Chelsea bar, it almost feels as if I'm there with her. I can taste the salt from the Margarita on my lips, hear the chink of glass as we toast each other. Three months later and we're spending Christmas in a Verbier ski lodge with a tight group of university mates, all of us in garish jumpers, posing in front of a lavishly decorated tree. Fast forward to summer and we're sunbathing on the beach, unfurling our towels on the warm sand, massaging sun lotion into each other's shoulders. Izzy's life burns so brightly on my screen, it practically leaves scorch marks on my eyeballs.

Next, I scroll through her recent posts. She's gushing about a climate change documentary she saw on Prime, sharing a video clip of someone bottle-feeding a baby gorilla, asking if anyone knows where she can donate her unwanted towels; all pretty mundane stuff. But then something catches my eye. A friend called Maria, posting three days ago, with a one-line query:

'Are you up for this?'

Seeing that Izzy has liked the comment, I click on the link Maria has provided. It redirects me to the Facebook page of a South London-based hiking group called Your Pace or Mine, a name that immediately endears me to them. The pinned post advertises their next event: a ten-mile hike along the South Downs Way on Sunday. Twenty-four people have already said they're going, but since I'm not friends with any of them on Facebook I can't see their names.

Discover hidden churches, beautiful chalk streams and ancient drove ways in this stunning circular walk, says the blurb. *There are a few climbs and descents, but nothing too strenuous. Please bring sufficient food and drink for the duration as there will be no opportunities to purchase any along the way. New members welcome, but please contact the event organiser in advance to book your place. A £5 contribution is payable on the day.* Driving directions are helpfully provided, as well as the train times from Waterloo.

It sounds like fun – except for the walking part. Personally, I've never seen the point of hiking in a country where the ground is soggy and the sky is grey for at least seventy percent of the year. Still, the weather forecast for this weekend does look favourable.

I only looked Izzy up out of idle curiosity, but all of a sudden this feels like one of those wonderful treats that life doles out when you're not looking.

It seems I do have plans for this weekend after all.

7

The next two days seem to drag by. Business is unusually slow on Friday – so slow that I end up shutting the shop early and heading to the gym. On Saturday morning I go to the supermarket and then to one of those vast sporting goods warehouses. Walking boots and socks are purchased, along with a pair of racer sunglasses that almost make me look cool.

Back at home, I put away my shopping. Then I rummage in the hall cupboard until I find my old rucksack. The seams are coming apart in several places, but in the absence of anything better it will have to be deemed fit for purpose. Afterwards, I clean the house from top to bottom, which takes me up to lunchtime. I eat a bowl of soup and then, unable to conjure up a more scintillating diversion, I decide to reorganise the contents of my chest of drawers.

Folding each one of my T-shirts into a neat oblong and stacking it vertically in colour order proves surprisingly therapeutic. It's only when I open my knicker drawer that my enthusiasm starts to wane. I own a handful of items that could reasonably be described as 'lingerie', bought when Rob and I were in our honeymoon phase. The rest is a collection of mismatched items, many of which are ready to be relegated to the duster division. I suppose I ought to replace them, but I'm reluctant to spend money on anything that requires hand washing and that nobody but me is ever going to see.

Determined to see my task through to the end, I spend twenty minutes folding each pair of pants into a perfect square, before lining them up in an old shoebox. If only I could give myself a similar makeover, I think as I slide the shoebox into the drawer – dress myself in delicate neutrals, trim my frayed edges and smooth away my ugly creases.

Finally Sunday rolls around – the day of my Big Adventure. The initial signs are inauspicious. For starters, it's overcast, which means I won't be able to wear my new sunglasses. Then, when I go to assemble my packed lunch, I discover that the ham I was planning to use in my sandwiches is out of date. The only other option is egg mayonnaise – not the most socially acceptable of fillings, but a double wrapping of clingfilm manages to contain the worst of the stink.

Having donned a pair of combats (the closest thing I own to walking trousers), a cotton top, lightweight fleece and my new socks and boots, I set off for the bus stop in what should be plenty of time to catch the recommended 09:06 from Waterloo. Frustratingly, my bus gets stuck in roadworks, meaning I miss the aforementioned train. Luckily, there's only a twenty-minute gap before the next one, even if it does call at every godforsaken market town and rural outpost en route.

Once safely on board, Costa coffee cup in hand, I walk from carriage to carriage. I'm hoping to spot some of my fellow walkers, but the only person with appropriate footwear is drinking from a can of lager. I feel I can rule him out with a reasonable degree of confidence.

It's a sixty-five-minute journey to the East Sussex village where the walk begins. Three minutes after the train leaves the platform, the first doubts start to creep in. I'm not exactly sure what I'm hoping to achieve with this merry jaunt. I'm not even certain that Izzy will be there. And if she is there, there's no guarantee I'll have an opportunity to speak to her. And if I do have an opportunity, what am I going to say?

It strikes me that my behaviour is slightly . . . I swallow down the first word that comes to mind, replacing it with something more palatable: *eccentric*.

I consider getting off at the next stop and returning to Waterloo. But then what – go back home to my empty flat and reorganise a few more drawers? No, I tell myself resolutely. I shan't give up; I shall press on. So what if Izzy's a no-show? The hike will be a break from my usual routine; a chance to meet new people and get some fresh air. And best of all, I'll have something to tell Claire about on Monday.

I arrive at my destination four minutes before the walk is due to start and make my way to the appointed meeting place outside the village church, where a large group is assembled, the majority youngish and fashionably clad in breathable synthetics. Identifying the walk leader from the clipboard in his hand, I go over and introduce myself. He thrusts out a hand, leaning in as we shake, his elbow jutting at a vigorous angle, before taking my five pounds and ticking me off his list. It appears I'm the last to arrive because we set off almost immediately, making our way in a snaking formation along a field edge and through a patch of woodland, before emerging on to a well-marked trail.

In the first bit of good fortune I've had all day, the sun suddenly emerges from behind a scalloped row of clouds. I slide my sunglasses down from my head on to my face and shake my hair free of its ponytail. It's nice to get away from London with its concrete and its fumes, and the scenery here really is quite lovely. There's a red kite wheeling overhead and at knee level a profusion of flowers, pink, white and blue, embroiders the long grass by the rutted track. I list their names in my head, repeating them over and over like a mantra.

It isn't long before I fall into step with another walker, an older woman with hooded eyes and the skittish gait of a creature emerging from an unscheduled hibernation. After the obligatory chit chat about where we both live in London, she embarks on a passionate monologue about wild swimming and the spiritual awakening she had at the ladies' pond in Hampstead Heath. I'm faintly relieved when she stops to re-tie her bootlace.

The group is now spread out over some distance. Conscious that I still haven't spotted Izzy, I pick up my pace, overtaking other walkers whenever I get the chance. It's only when I'm almost at the head of the group, slightly sweaty after my exertions, that I see someone who fits the bill. She has the right hair and build and she's dressed in a pleasing soft-fruits palette – raspberry leggings, knee-high apricot socks and a blueberry gilet. I can't see the whole of her face, just her profile as she turns her head to talk to her female companion, but the tip-tilted nose and softly rounded chin look awfully familiar.

For the next half a mile or so, I stay a couple of metres behind the pair of them, wondering if the woman in my sights can feel the hungry tug of my stare. I love how she walks, so stable and assured, limbs flexing, arms pumping, hair rippling in the breeze. If it is Izzy, then presumably the dark-haired woman she's talking to so animatedly is the same one who messaged her on Facebook. Every now and then tantalising snatches of their conversation drift over to me and it isn't long before I hear the name of Izzy's ex-husband, confirming my suspicions.

'I'm pretty sure Hugh's been bad-mouthing me every chance he gets,' the woman I'm now convinced is Izzy tells her friend, an unmistakable note of bitterness saturating her words. 'Half our mutual friends have stopped responding to my texts; two of them have even had the cheek to unfriend me on Facebook.'

'I don't know why people always think they have to take sides after a marriage break-up,' the friend remarks. 'I wouldn't let it get you down; you can always make some new friends.'

'I suppose so, but that takes time and energy – and in the meantime, I'm stuck at home on a Friday night, while everyone else is out enjoying themselves. Speaking of which, are you free at all next weekend? I thought we could go out for dinner – my treat.'

'I'd love to, Iz, but the kids have got their cousins coming to stay.'

'Can't that adorable husband of yours hold the fort? It'll only be for a few hours.'

'You're joking, aren't you? He can barely keep control when I leave him on his own with our two, and his brother's kids are practically feral.'

I don't catch Izzy's reply because just then a tall man with a hairline in rapid retreat sidles up to me. 'Are you enjoying the walk?' he enquires pleasantly.

Annoyed that my eavesdropping has been interrupted, I hesitate for a moment, searching for some loophole in the laws of etiquette that might spare me from having to engage with him. Finding none, I answer in the affirmative. After that, I'm stuck with him for another four miles although, to be fair, he's perfectly nice and incredibly knowledgeable about woodland fauna.

At twelve-thirty, we stop for lunch atop a grassy hill that offers panoramic views. It comes not a moment too soon as I have a sore heel that urgently needs attending to. But before I do anything else, I must eat; the combination of fresh air and exercise has given me quite an appetite. To minimise any sulphurous wafts, I wolf my sandwiches as quickly as possible, washing them down with several swigs from my water bottle. Then I pick up my rucksack and go over to a nearby tree stump, where I sit down before gingerly removing my left boot and sock. When I see the inflamed skin on the back of my heel, I congratulate myself for having the foresight to bring an assortment of plasters. After selecting one in an appropriate size, I bend over double and begin to tear off the wrapping.

'Little bastard,' someone says.

As the plaster slips through my fingers, I look up to find the person addressing me is none other than Izzy.

'I'm sorry,' I say, confused.

She points to my bare foot. 'Blisters,' she says. 'The bane of every walker's life.'

My facial muscles relax. 'It's probably these new boots; it's the first time I've worn them.'

'Yeah, they generally take a bit of time to break in.' She picks the plaster up off the ground and hands it back to me. 'I don't want to sound like a know-it-all – and please feel free to tell me to butt out – but it would help a lot if you laced your boots the right way.'

I smile to show that her advice is not unwelcome; quite the contrary. 'I didn't realise there was a *wrong* way.'

'You'd be surprised – and I speak from experience.' A starburst of fine lines spread congenially from the corners of her eyes. 'I can show you if you like.'

'Yes, please, that would be most helpful.'

She waits for me to apply the plaster and pull on my sock.

'The problem is your feet are moving about inside your boots,' she explains. 'It's the constant friction that causes blisters.' She kneels down in front of me and begins pulling the lace out of my right boot. I notice that her fingernails aren't manicured like Eleanor's but cut short and gently shaped.

'For someone like you, with high arches, it's better not to use criss-cross lacing,' she says as she begins rethreading my boot. 'If you lace straight across you won't feel so much pressure on the top of your foot.'

She glances up at me. 'Stand up, will you? We need to see how your foot sits when it's bearing your weight.'

Obediently, I rise to my feet.

'Now, flex your toes up and push your heel down. We want your foot sitting nice and snugly in the heel cap before we tighten the laces.'

I do as instructed, whereupon she starts pulling out the slack in the lace, one row at a time, starting at the toe and working her way backwards. It feels strange, and actually rather nice to have someone lavish so much attention on me.

Once Izzy is satisfied that the tension is correct, she takes one end of the lace and doubles it back on itself, creating a bunny ear. She wraps the other lace around it, using her thumb to create a loop underneath. After that, her hands are moving so quickly that I lose track of what she's doing.

'How does that feel?' she says when she's tied off the knot.

I lift my left foot up off the ground. 'Comfortable – and also very secure.'

'Try walking.'

I take a few steps forward, my mouth dropping open when I feel the contrast with my right boot. 'Wow, the difference is amazing! My foot isn't moving about inside the boot at all.'

'That's what we want to hear.' She leans back on her haunches. 'If you sit down again I'll sort out your other boot so you'll have a matching pair.'

'Are you sure? I don't want to take you away from your lunch.'

'Don't worry, I'd eaten most of it before we even sat down. I have zero willpower, that's why I'm carrying a few extra pounds.'

From where I'm standing, Izzy has the perfect figure (and there really is nowhere to hide in those leggings) – but I don't want to sound like a sycophant, so I resist the temptation to say as much.

'I'm Amy, by the way,' I say, retaking my seat on the tree stump.

'Izzy,' she replies. 'Nice to meet you.'

'It really is very kind of you to help me like this; I'm a total novice when it comes to walking.' I give an exaggerated simper. 'When I say walking, I don't mean putting one foot in front of the other.'

She grins. 'It's OK, I know what you meant – and big respect for throwing yourself in at the deep end with a ten-miler.' She holds out her hand for my right boot. 'How did you hear about the group?'

'On Facebook. A friend of mine knew I was looking to join a walking club and sent me a link,' I say, the lie sliding easily off my tongue. 'How long have you been a member?'

She gives a one-shouldered shrug. 'A year or so. We're a pretty friendly crowd; I hope everyone's making you feel welcome.'

'Oh, they are,' I say. 'I'm really enjoying myself. It's so peaceful here; it feels as if we're a million miles from London.'

'Yeah, there's nothing like a long walk in the countryside to clear your head.' She looks down as she begins rethreading my other boot. 'I've been going through quite a stressful time with work lately; today was just what I needed.'

I seize on this disclosure hungrily. 'What is it you do for a living?'

'I'm a sales manager at an estate agent – or at least I used to be.' She sets the boot back down in front of me. 'There you go.'

I slip my foot inside the boot and stand up so she can tighten the laces. '*Used* to be?'

'Yeah, I got made redundant a few weeks back. The owner reckoned the business was top heavy. He decided to get rid of one of the managers and I drew the short straw.' She flips a hand in the air. 'Fuck knows why. I could comfortably be lobotomised and still do my job better than most of the people in that place.'

Her comment makes me giggle. 'Have you had any luck finding another job?'

She shakes her head. 'It's not a great time; the property market's not exactly buoyant at the moment. How about you – what do you do?'

'I'm a florist.'

'How fantastic,' she says, looking up at me. 'It must be so rewarding putting smiles on people's faces every day.'

Something inside me swells at Izzy's insightful comment. 'Yes, actually it is.'

'Have you been doing it for a long time?'

'Nearly fifteen years. I can't ever see myself doing anything else, to be honest. Floristry is in my DNA, it's more of a vocation than a job.'

'That's lovely to hear. So many people fall into careers by accident and then spend the rest of their lives regretting it.' She tightens the final row of lacing and begins tying a knot. 'Who do you work for?'

'No one. I have my own business.'

'Nice,' she says admiringly. 'Whereabouts are you based?'

'I have a shop in South East London.'

'I live south of the river. What's your shop called? Maybe I've heard of it.'

I rub the end of my nose. I very much doubt the Elliotts have mentioned me to Izzy – not when her birthday party is supposed to be a surprise – so there's no reason to think she'll work out the connection. 'Darling Buds. There's a website too.'

'Aww, that's an adorable name,' she says. 'I'll have to remember that the next time I want to send flowers to someone.'

Gazing over the top of her head, I see that the walk leader is on his feet and the others are starting to pack up their lunch things. 'I think we're about to get going,' I tell Izzy.

She pats the toe of my boot and stands up. 'That's you all sorted; fingers crossed you won't get any more blisters.'

'Thanks,' I say, picking up my rucksack. I'm not quite sure what happens now. It's like that awkward moment at the end of a date when you have to affect nonchalance because you don't want to risk rejection by showing how keen you are. Just because Izzy offered to help me with my footwear doesn't mean she wants me hanging round her for the rest of the walk. I'm sure there are plenty of other people here she'd rather spend time with.

'Well, enjoy the rest of the walk,' I tell her as I hook my rucksack over one shoulder.

She cocks an amused eyebrow. 'Don't tell me you're disappearing already. Why don't you come and meet my friend Maria? I can introduce you to a few of the others as well if you like.'

I can hardly contain my delight. 'Well, if you're sure you don't mind me tagging along . . .'

Generally speaking, I hate small talk, getting to know people in that fake way that guarantees you'll know less about them at the end of the conversation than you did at the beginning. But it's not like that with Izzy and Maria. Both women are so open and friendly, segueing rapidly from one topic to another, like guests at an all-you-can-eat buffet who can't bear to leave any dish untasted. I learn that they've known each other for more than ten years after meeting at a Pilates class and that Izzy's just bought a flat a hop, skip and a jump away from Maria in Greenwich. Izzy talks passionately about her love of foreign travel, while Maria regales us with amusing anecdotes about her job as a GP and talks lovingly about her husband and two kids. When I enquire, with faux innocence, about Izzy's own relationship status, she references her recent divorce and says she's enjoying playing the field for now.

Naturally, they have questions for me too. Because of my history I have to be careful, but my back story is well-rehearsed. I've told it so many times now that the details have acquired a kind of patina, like the strap on a leather handbag after repeated handling. I throw out a handful of innocuous tidbits and then it's easy enough to turn the spotlight back on to them. Like a lot of self-confident people, Izzy and Maria enjoy talking about themselves – and I enjoy listening to what they have to say. There's something so definite about them both, a solidity anchoring them to the world that I envy.

I'm so enthralled that the miles simply fly by, and before I know it, we're back in the village where we started. I'm hoping the group leader will suggest drinks in the pretty little pub we've just passed, but people are keen to make the next train, which leaves in eight minutes' time.

'Maria and I drove down,' Izzy remarks as the group troops along the high street in the direction of the church. 'Did you get the train?'

'I did indeed. I was in the quiet coach; it wasn't quite the bastion of silence I was expecting.'

Maria smiles and points to a sports car parked up ahead on the side of the road. 'I'd offer you a lift back to London, but I've only got a two-seater. My husband needed the SUV so he could take the kids to their swimming lesson.'

I feel a little spike of disappointment; it would've been nice to hang out with them a while longer. 'No worries,' I say, injecting a carefree tone into my voice.

Izzy reaches into the bumbag around her waist and pulls out her phone. 'Shall we swap numbers, Amy?' she says. 'Maybe we could grab a coffee some time.'

I feel a slight tremor as something comes to life inside me, like a match struck in the darkness.

'Yes,' I say, my hands feeling clumsy as I scrabble in the front pocket of my rucksack for my own phone. 'Yes, I'd like that.'

8

I wake in a panic, drenched in sweat. I was having one of my nightmares. A bad one that caught me by the throat. I'd almost fought clear of it once or twice, but then the weight of my own limbs had pulled me under again.

I glance at the clock on the bedside table. Five twenty-six. I might as well get up; I won't get back to sleep now.

When I check my phone, I see there's a text from Claire, sent just after midnight. She won't be coming in to work today. The camper van broke down on the way back from Cornwall and they're stuck at a Travelodge in Exeter. Meanwhile, the van is in a local garage, awaiting repair. She apologises profusely for letting me down at such short notice and assures me that if the garage can't fix the van today, Kyle can stay in Exeter and she'll get the train back to London. The last thing she wants to do is leave me in the lurch two days on the trot.

I text her back and tell her not to worry. The shop's usually pretty quiet on a Monday; I'm sure I'll be able to manage on my own. The only mildly annoying thing is that now there's no one to tell about the glorious Sunday I spent in East Sussex.

As I drink my coffee, I can't resist checking Facebook. Izzy has already posted a selfie from yesterday. She's standing in front of a stile, the rolling South Downs just visible in the background. Underneath it are several more photos from the walk: sunlight filtering through the branches of a tree, a caterpillar on a dog rose, a pair of feet (her own, I assume), clad in hiking boots, standing at the edge of a fast-flowing stream.

'Nature is cheaper than therapy,' reads the caption. Usually I find those sorts of feel-good slogans cringe-worthy, but on this occasion – perhaps because I shared the experience with her – it comes off as charming and rather inspirational.

After my shower, I blow-dry my hair instead of letting it dry naturally. If I'm going to be on show in the shop all day, I need to look presentable. When I've finished, I stare at my reflection in the dressing table mirror. I was hoping that some of Izzy's glamour and rampant good health would rub off on me. I think it's starting already; I can feel it settling on me, like delicate snowflakes. I move closer to the mirror, angling my head this way and that, wondering if anyone else will be able to see it.

I get to the shop just before seven. After checking the weekend orders on the Darling Buds website, I start making up the bouquets, stopping at eight-fifteen for the breakfast of buttered bagel I brought from home. It's nearly open-ing time, so I turn my attention to the pavement display. Sometimes, especially when we're busy, it can feel like a chore, but today I derive a good deal of satisfaction from arranging mason jars filled with sweetheart roses on the rungs of an old wooden ladder and packing our vintage pram full of blowsy orange marigolds.

There's the usual stream of smartly dressed commuters calling into the shop en route to the station to buy flowers for colleagues' birthdays and leaving presents. When things quieten down I decide to make myself a cup of tea. As I can't leave the shop unattended, I've brought the kettle in from the studio and set it up next to the sink in the corner. As it reaches a shuddering climax, Ewan arrives for his daily delivery round.

'Perfect timing,' I say, beaming at him. 'Fancy a quick cuppa before you start loading up the van?'

'Lovely, thanks,' he says, coming over to join me at the counter.

I pop a teabag into a second mug and reach for the kettle. 'The bouquets are all laid out on the workbench in the studio,' I tell him. 'I'll print out the delivery schedule for you in a mo.'

'Great, thanks,' he says, running a hand through his dark hair that's just starting to go grey above the ears. 'Is Claire in the studio?'

I shake my head. 'She's not coming in today. She and Kyle were at a festival over the weekend and their van broke down on the way back. They're stuck in Exeter until it's repaired.'

'That's a bummer for them,' he says. 'Will you be all right on your own? I can stick around after I've finished the deliveries if you need help with anything.' He gives a crooked grin. 'I'm not much cop at flower arranging, but I'm pretty good at fetching and carrying.'

'Thanks, Ewan, that's kind of you to offer.' I add milk to the two cups and hand one to him. 'Did you have a nice weekend?'

He leans against the doorframe, cupping his mug in both hands. 'Yeah, not bad. I didn't get up to much – just went fishing with my brother and had a few beers at the pub. How about you?'

'I went hiking in Sussex. Ten whole miles.'

'Nice one, who'd you go with?'

'My walking group,' I reply, enjoying the taste of the words on my tongue. 'It was the first time I'd been out with them, but I had such an amazing time.' I sigh dreamily. 'I can't stop thinking about it; it was the best day out I've had in ages.'

I catch something in Ewan's expression – amusement and pity fusing together in his eyes. He *knows*, I think to myself. He knows I'm a pathetic little person with no friends and that the hike was the first time I've done any proper socialising in months. *Years*, if I'm honest. A flare of embarrassment warms my cheeks.

'I do a fair bit of hiking myself,' he says. 'Me and a couple of mates climbed Snowdon last year.' He pauses to take a drink of tea. The gulping noise he makes in the back of his throat is unpleasantly loud. 'You should think about a trip to North Wales. The scenery there's spectacular. I can recommend a couple of good places to stay, if you're interested.'

'I don't know about that,' I say stiffly. 'I'm probably

not in your league, Ewan; I think I'm better off sticking to the Home Counties.' I go over to the sink in the corner and empty my mug so violently that tea splashes all over the draining board.

I turn to face him. 'Much as I'd love to stand around chatting all day, I really must do some work. If you pop back when you've finished loading the van, I'll make sure the delivery schedule's printed out for you.'

'Sure,' he says, looking faintly bewildered.

When he's gone, I start assembling an anniversary bouquet. My good mood has evaporated and I set about it the way a pit bull goes to a postman's leg – grim, ferocious, unsparing. I handle a long-stemmed rose so roughly I end up snapping its neck and immediately feel ashamed, as if I've just murdered one of my offspring.

During the post-lunchtime lull I take the opportunity to sketch out a design for a flower wall I'm doing for the opening of a new hair salon. I'm not usually short on inspiration, but today I can't seem to concentrate. My skull feels like a snow globe recently shaken, swirling with random ideas that I can't seem to gather into one coherent concept.

Ewan returns just after three. While he was gone, I thought about asking him to help me bring in the jardinieres from the pavement display. They're heavy and slightly awkward to manoeuvre on one's own. If I leave them out overnight, they'll only get vandalised – or worse still, stolen. In the event, I don't even get the chance to ask him, because he doesn't actually come into the shop – just sticks his head round the door to let me know the deliveries have been completed successfully and the keys to the van are hanging up in the studio.

'See you in the morning,' he says with a wave of the hand and then he's gone. I'm not surprised he doesn't want to spend any more time in my company than the terms of his employment contract dictate; I *was* rather abrupt with him earlier. Hopefully, he'll have forgotten my rudeness by tomorrow.

There's a steady trickle of walk-ins between four and five-thirty and then it's time for me to lock up and go home to my empty flat. As I turn the sign on the door to closed, I wonder if I should think about getting another cat; at least then there would be someone who was pleased to see me when I walked through the door.

A short burst of synth from underneath the counter heralds the arrival of a WhatsApp on my phone, an event I find faintly startling. Unlike most women of my age, I don't belong to any WhatsApp groups – of old school friends, or family members, or people I met at an NCT class. I can't imagine who it might be from. The only person I'm expecting to hear from is Claire, with confirmation that she's made it back to London. But now I come to think of it, Claire has never sent me a WhatsApp before; her preferred mode of communication when we're not standing next to each other is standard text. I guess this time she's broken with tradition.

I don't check my phone straight away. Instead, I busy myself with all the mundane tasks that Claire usually takes care of: emptying the trash, mopping the floor, drawing the window blinds. When I do finally check my phone, a wonderful surprise awaits me: the WhatsApp isn't from Claire after all, it's from Izzy.

Hey Ames, it begins.

Ames? Nobody's ever called me that before. I like it though. It feels . . . intimate. *Just wondered if you fancied getting together for a bite to eat on Friday eve. There's a great tapas place near me – that's if you can be bothered to come to Greenwich.*

I stare at the screen, my eyes pulling each word apart before putting them back together again. Is she kidding? Of *course* I can be bothered. I'd crawl over broken glass to get there if I had to. I'm actually quite shocked. I didn't think Izzy would get in touch so soon – if at all. I had a horrid feeling she might vanish, like a Polaroid photo left in bright sunlight, fading to a skeleton-grey silhouette, then gone.

Sounds great, I type back. *Shall we meet at the restaurant?*

The two ticks turn blue within seconds. I grip my phone tightly, almost forgetting to breathe as I watch the slow death march of the three little dots that tell me she's composing her reply.

It's not the easiest place to find. Probably best if you come to mine first. 36 Hyde Terrace SE10. Top floor flat. Is 7.30 ok? Gratifyingly, she's even added an x at the end this time.

My reply pings back immediately: *It's a date! Look forward to seeing you on Friday x*

After that I have to sit down, dizzy from the emotional whiplash of it all.

9

The bus journey is quicker than I anticipated and I arrive in Greenwich with twenty minutes to spare. Not wanting to get to Izzy's too early, I kill time by looking in the window of an antiques shop, wondering who on earth can afford to spend six grand on a refectory table.

Izzy's flat – a period conversion in a leafy street – is a short walk away. She buzzes me up straight away, but when she opens the door there's a phone at her ear. 'Hang on a sec, will you, El?' she says into the handset.

She presses the phone to her chest and beckons me in. 'Sorry, Amy, I'm just talking to my sister.' She flicks her eyes sideways, suggesting it isn't an experience she's particularly enjoying. 'The sitting room's in there, why don't you go on through? I'll be with you in two ticks.'

As I walk through the door that Izzy indicated, I reflect on the coincidence that I've caught the two sisters in conversation for a second time. It makes me feel uncomfortable and slightly underhand. If Izzy and I are going to be friends, I need to think of a way to bring my relationship with the Elliotts out into the open – and sooner rather than later.

The sitting room is well proportioned and has glorious views out across the park. The furnishings aren't as chic or expensive as the things in Eleanor's home, but the effect is nicer, more welcoming somehow. Izzy has an eclectic sense of style and an intriguing collection of knick-knacks. There's a bowl of smooth, river-rounded pebbles on the coffee table and the shelves flanking the chimney breast are dotted with exotic figurines: a soapstone Buddha, a trumpeting Ganesh and something Mayan, or possibly Aztec, its onyx teeth bared menacingly. I've just picked up a brightly painted Hindu goddess for a closer look when Izzy appears.

'Sorry about that,' she says, chucking her phone down on the sofa. 'I got rid of her as soon as I could.'

I can see she's made an effort with her appearance. A pretty tiered dress is teamed with thick-soled white trainers and lots of silver jewellery. Her hair is pinned up with a tortoiseshell clasp, accentuating the length of her neck, and her dewy make-up knocks five years off her age. I'm glad I nipped out for a blow-dry at lunchtime; at least I'm halfway presentable.

'No worries, I was early anyway.'

'Did you find your way here OK?'

'Yes, thanks. I decided to get the bus rather than driving; that way I can have a couple of drinks.'

'Ooh, goodie,' says Izzy, rubbing her hands together with exaggerated glee. 'I hate drinking alone.' She notices the statuette in my hands. 'I see you've found Durga – otherwise known as the protective mother of the universe.'

I turn the multi-armed goddess over in my hands. 'She's gorgeous – where did you get her?'

'My ex-husband bought her in Nepal; it was the first gift he ever gave me.'

'What was he doing in Nepal?'

'Travelling; we both were. I'd just graduated and Hugh was taking a sabbatical from his job in the city. We were staying in the same hostel and just hit it off. He was on his own, so he spent a lot of time hanging out with me and the friends I was travelling with.' She gives a small, static smile. 'I didn't know Hugh was interested in me romantically – not until he bought me *that* at a street market in Kathmandu. He'd seen me admiring it earlier in the day and he went back later to buy it for me. After that, we were pretty much inseparable and when we both got back to England three months later, he asked me to move in with him.'

I place the goddess carefully back on the bookshelf. 'It sounds ever so romantic.'

'It was,' she says, the words escaping from her like a sigh. 'Hugh's the only man I've ever been in love with. I really thought we'd be together for ever.'

'When did you guys split up?' I ask her, even though I already have a rough idea, thanks to Eleanor.

'Our decree absolute came through last month,' she says and I hear the catch in her voice. 'I won't lie to you, Amy – it's been tough. I'm still coming to terms with it, to be honest.' She gives her head a little shake as if trying to exorcise the thought. 'Anyway, I didn't invite you over for a pity party, so let's head to the restaurant, shall we?'

She bends down and scoops her phone up off the sofa. 'I haven't booked a table, but it shouldn't be a problem.'

When we get there, the restaurant is absolutely heaving – hardly surprising for a Friday night. 'It's awfully busy,' I say, as we make our way to the unmanned reception desk. 'Perhaps we should try somewhere else.'

'It'll be fine,' replies Izzy assertively. Her eyes cast around the room until they settle on a fit-looking waiter with a large tribal tattoo on his forearm. She raises a hand in the air as if hailing a taxi. A moment later the waiter spots her. Breaking into a smile, he tucks the empty tray he's holding under his arm and begins weaving his way in between the tightly packed tables towards us.

As Izzy leans in to me, I catch a waft of grapefruit-scented shampoo. 'Danny and I are fuck buddies,' she says out of the corner of her mouth. 'I'm sure he'll do his best to accommodate us.'

'Marvellous!' I cry, trying not to show how taken aback I am by this unexpected – and frankly, unnecessary – intimacy. Moments later, a table for two is magicked up.

'Thanks, darling,' Izzy purrs, stroking the side of Danny's jaw as she takes the seat he's pulled out for her. 'I might text you later on.'

He flashes a wolfish grin. 'Look forward to it.'

By this point my eyes are practically out on stalks. The air is so thick with pheromones, I can barely breathe.

'I'm glad you could make it tonight,' Izzy says once the

ever-obliging Danny has taken our drinks orders. 'I hate spending Friday nights alone.'

I offer a vigorous nod. 'Me too. Most of my friends are busy with their partners at the weekend, so I often find myself at a loose end.'

Izzy props her chin on her palm and gazes directly into my face. 'Are you single too, then? I don't think we discussed your love life on our walk the other day, did we?'

'No,' I say. 'That is to say, *no* we didn't discuss it, and *yes*, I am single; I have been for quite a while actually.'

I clear my throat awkwardly. In the wake of Izzy's admission about her trysts with the waiter, I feel under pressure to reciprocate with a confession of my own.

'My last boyfriend and I were together for six years,' I reveal. 'He left me for someone else.'

Her face puckers in sympathy. 'I'm sorry to hear that. Honestly, men are such bastards.'

'Oh, Rob wasn't so bad,' I tell her. 'And anyway, I have to shoulder some of the blame. I took him far too much for granted but by the time I realised that it was already too late.' I pause as a waiter – not the rampant Danny this time – arrives with a bottle of Zinfandel and fills our wine glasses before placing the bottle in a cooler.

'How do you find living on your own?' Izzy asks.

'I don't mind it actually. I like the fact I can do whatever I like without worrying how it looks to someone else.'

'What sort of things are we talking about here?' she says interestedly.

I think of some examples that aren't too embarrassing to divulge. 'Conducting full-scale operas in the shower, complete with multiple voices. Leaving the dishwasher unpacked for three entire days. Polishing off a family-size bag of Doritos while binge-watching a six-part documentary series about serial killers.'

Izzy grins and takes a sip – more of a swig, really – of her wine. 'But don't you miss the sex?'

I think for a moment, remembering how it used to be with Rob. Invariably with the lights off, straight to the relevant erogenous zones and nary a word spoken – he working diligently, I respectful of his concentration. And when it was all over, he would express satisfaction not so much at the mind-blowing quality of our respective climaxes, but at a job well done.

'I guess I miss the closeness,' I concede. 'But not so much that I'd go out looking for a one-night stand. I wouldn't even know how to go about finding one, to be honest.'

'Believe me, it's not that difficult.' Izzy's gaze drifts towards Danny, who's clearing plates from a nearby table, the topography of his groin alarmingly obvious in his tight-fitting jeans.

I pick up my wine glass and swirl the liquid around. 'How did you find out about your husband's affair?'

She throws me a sharp look. 'Who said he had an affair?'

I bite the inside of my cheek so hard I almost draw blood. I can't believe I just said that. It was *Eleanor* who suggested Hugh had embarked an affair, not Izzy.

'Sorry, I just assumed,' I say, back-pedalling frantically. 'I shouldn't have done. Just because my partner cheated on me doesn't mean the same thing happened to you.'

'No need to apologise, hon,' she says, reaching across the table and laying her hand on top of mine. 'You wouldn't be the first one to think it.'

'No?'

'My sister Eleanor was *convinced* Hugh left me for another woman. She's wrong, though. He just fell out of love with me. Simple as.'

'So why does your sister think there was a third party involved?'

Izzy shrugs, the gesture at odds with the intensity in her eyes. 'You'd have to ask her that. Maybe she just said it to be cruel.'

'Surely not,' I thrust back. If Izzy knew all the trouble Eleanor was going to for her fortieth, she wouldn't be saying that. 'Why would your own sister deliberately set out to hurt you?'

'I don't know. I think she just likes feeling superior.' She glowers at the wine cooler. 'She thinks I drink too much as well; she's always telling me I need to cut down. She doesn't seem to appreciate that my whole life has fallen apart and I need to wring every little bit of pleasure I can out of it.'

My mouth tightens a little. If I were in Izzy's position, I'd be counting my blessings, instead of feeling sorry for myself. Yes, she's lost her husband and her job, but she lives in a beautiful flat and she's getting a regular, no-strings seeing-to from a hot waiter. Still, this is going to be a very short-lived friendship if I come off as overly critical, so I keep quiet and smile in what I hope is an understanding manner.

The same waiter who brought our drinks comes over to ask if we're ready to order food. As I go to pick up the laminated menu, Izzy plucks it from my hands and puts it back down on the table. 'I know we haven't known each other very long, but do you trust me?'

'Yes,' I reply, without even thinking about it.

'Good, so let me order for both of us.'

She turns back to the waiter and reels off a list of dishes without referring to the menu once; I guess she must be a regular here. The waiter seems utterly mesmerised, his eyes sliding from her face, to her décolletage, and back to her face again. It seems like half the staff in this place are under Izzy's spell. I find myself wondering what it must be like to have so much sex appeal. Eleanor's a classic beauty, but Izzy's got something else: an indefinable charisma.

While the waiter tries to convince her to swap the *gambas al ajillo* for the chef's special, I mentally prepare myself for the delicate conversation that lies ahead. I need to get it out of the way soon, or I won't be able to relax. I take a big gulp of wine and then another, feeling it go straight to my head.

As soon as the waiter departs, I launch into my pre-prepared script.

'Is your sister married?'

'Yeah, James is a real sweetheart. He and I have always got along well.'

I'm careful to keep my features blank. 'Do they live in London too?'

'West Dulwich.' Izzy picks up the wine bottle, topping up her own glass first and then mine. 'They have an amazing church conversion; it's like something out of a movie.'

I frown, my lips twisting to the side as if I'm thinking. 'You're not talking about James Elliott by any chance, are you?'

Izzy's jaw goes slack. 'Yes,' she gasps. 'Don't tell me you know him.'

I gawp back at her, pretending to be just as amazed as she is. 'James is one of my corporate clients. I do the flowers for his office.'

'No way!' she says, thumping the table with the palm of her hand and making the cutlery jump. 'Does that mean you know my sister too?'

I take a sip of wine. Here's where it gets tricky. I can hardly confess my role in Izzy's fortieth birthday celebrations; Eleanor would never forgive me for ruining the surprise. 'We've only met once, very briefly, when I delivered some flowers to the house. I think it might have been her wedding anniversary.'

Izzy's hand goes to her mouth. 'Shit, I wouldn't have said all that stuff about her if I'd known.'

'Oh, don't worry about that,' I say quickly. 'I keep my personal and business lives very separate. Nothing you say this evening will go any further, I promise.' I hope she believes me. I don't want there to be any constraints on our relationship. I want her to be at ease with me, to feel I'm someone she can confide in. A true friend.

'That's good to know,' she says. 'Eleanor drives me mad, but she's still my sister. I wouldn't want her to find out I've been slagging her off behind her back.'

We exchange a meaningful look as understanding flows between us, a secret, intimate transmission.

'Do you have any more siblings?'

'No, it's just the two of us.'

'Are you both close to your parents?' There's a note of wistfulness in my voice, an acknowledgement that my relationship with my own parents has become increasingly distant over the years.

'It's just my mum now. Dad died when I was fourteen. He was an orthodontist and he had a massive heart attack one day in his surgery. Even though there were medically trained staff on site, they couldn't save him.'

'Oh God, that's awful,' I say, my facial muscles contorting into a gruesome rictus in an effort to convey an appropriate level of empathy. 'Losing your father at such a young age must have been tough for you and Eleanor.'

'It was hideous – and the situation wasn't helped by the fact that Mum completely fell apart and could barely function for the next six months.'

'So who looked after you two?'

She tucks a tendril of hair behind her ear. 'Mum turned down all offers of help from the family, so we pretty much looked after ourselves. I have to say Eleanor was brilliant during that whole period. She's two years younger than me, but she acted like she was the big sister. She'd make my sandwiches for school every day, remind me to brush my teeth, check to see I'd done my homework. I don't think I could have got through that dark time without her. It's probably the closest I've ever felt to her in my entire life.'

'How lovely,' I say. 'You guys must have a very special bond.'

'We might have done back then, but things are quite different now,' she says with a scowl.

Just then, the waiter arrives with our food. I watch hungrily as he offloads dish after dish from his tray until there's hardly any room left on the table. It all looks and smells amazing. I'm glad Izzy took control of the ordering; left to my own devices, I would never have been this adventurous. Before we tuck in, she points to each dish and lists the main ingredients. It turns out she knows a lot about Spanish cuisine, thanks to her extensive travels in the country. I love her worldliness, her sophistication, her willingness to share her knowledge. We've known each other less than a week, but I've learned so much from her already.

As I help myself to a thick slice of tortilla I see the longing look she gives the almost empty wine bottle. Catch the quicksilver thought crossing her mind: *is it too soon to order another?*

I make eye contact with a passing waiter. 'Could we have another bottle of the Zinfandel, please?' I say, thrusting my chin upwards and slightly to one side, the way Izzy does when she's talking.

Her face opens into a broad smile that warms me like the summer sun. 'You must've read my mind, hon.'

The rest of the evening passes in a pleasant haze of lively conversation and increasing inebriation. I find Izzy quite fascinating, the way she presents herself in so many different lights – sometimes serious and introspective, other times mischievous and playful – but always evincing strong emotion. Her intensity makes me think of one of those unexpected gusts of air that make windows fly open.

I, myself, am far more circumspect, giving over myself in pieces, slivers of truth, carefully edited anecdotes. It isn't necessary to bare my soul. Not yet. Pretending to be something you're not can be exhausting, but tonight I'm enjoying myself. I'm like a child enjoying a boat trip. I know that under the water there are all sorts of dangers: unpredictable currents, choking seaweed, predators with gaping jaws – but up there on the deck, all I can see is the sunlight glinting off the water.

We manage to sink two bottles of wine with our food and after a rather rich chocolate torte that I can only manage half of, Izzy persuades me to try an espresso martini.

'Be an angel and pop that in a box for my friend, will you?' she says to our waiter, indicating the torte.

Such an innocuous request and yet it thrills me. I, too, cannot stand waste. I remember Rob physically cringing when I remonstrated, quite forcefully, with a waitress at a French bistro who was refusing to bag up my leftover portion of cassoulet. She claimed the premises could be held liable if I stored it at home in sub-optimal conditions and subsequently gave myself food poisoning. A ridiculous argument, when I have a perfectly legitimate claim on the delicious food that someone vastly more culinarily capable than I has cooked and for which I have paid a considerable sum of money. Izzy and I are clearly on the same page in this regard and her rescue of my leftover dessert represents another generous deposit into our friendship account.

I smile my thanks at her. They've dimmed the lights in the restaurant and her pupils are dilated. She raises her martini glass in a toast. 'Thanks for a lovely evening, Amy. I've really enjoyed it.'

'Me too,' I say, as our glasses touch. 'We'll have to do it again some time.'

I am in a state of mild euphoria as I travel home on the bus. Even the obnoxious youths sitting on the other side of the aisle, who keep swearing and showing each other pornographic images on their mobile phones, can't take the shine off my evening.

I lean my head against the window and close my eyes as my mind works back over the last few hours – the laughter, the intimacy, the novelty of spending an entire evening outside the four walls of my flat.

It feels as if something tight and clenched has unfurled within me, like a fern releasing its fronds and stretching out into the light.

Now

10

WITNESS STATEMENT

This statement is true to the best of my knowledge and belief and I make it knowing that, if it is tendered in evidence, I shall be liable to prosecution if I have wilfully stated in it anything which I know to be false, or do not believe to be true.

Signature: *J. Hodge*

My name is Jennifer Hodge. I am a paramedic with the London Ambulance Service, based at Brixton. I qualified as a paramedic in 2011 and I have been in my current role since December 2015. I have made this statement whilst referring to my notes, which I completed on the day of the incident.

On 22nd September I started work at 0830 hours. My call sign for the day was Q217 and I was crewed with fellow paramedic Kelly Wilson. We were at our base when we got the call to go to The Sanctuary in Oakwood Road, West Dulwich at approximately 1145 hours. We were informed that the patient was a 36-year-old woman, who appeared to be unconscious. No further details were available.

On our arrival, we were met by a woman who said she worked as a cleaner at the property. She was quite distressed and unable to give us any information about the patient's condition, beyond the fact she wasn't responding to any stimuli.

The woman escorted us to a bedroom on the first floor. The door was only open by a few inches and through the gap I could see the casualty lying on the floor. The position of the body meant the door could not be easily opened, but as my colleague and I both have a slim build, we were able to pass through the gap.

On entering the room, I saw three adult females lying on the floor, all fully clothed, all apparently unconscious. Two had visible blood stains on their clothing. I also noticed a bloody handprint on the wall.

The room was in a considerable state of disarray. A shelf unit was lying on its side with children's toys scattered around it. A lamp had been knocked over on the bedside table and one of the curtains was hanging off the rail. I also noticed there were fresh flowers scattered all over the floor.

Concerned by what I saw, I radioed my control room and asked them to dispatch police to the scene immediately.

My colleague and I were fully aware that this could be a crime scene. However, our priority as paramedics was to evaluate the patients' condition and render any assistance necessary, even if it meant compromising evidence.

The first thing we did was triage the casualties to determine which of them required the most urgent treatment. The first casualty had sustained what appeared to be knife wounds in her right arm and chest. Her radial pulse was weak, she had a delayed pupillary response and she was showing signs of haemorrhagic shock. In my professional opinion, she was the most seriously injured of the three individuals and I judged her injuries to be life-threatening. While I was conducting my examination, I noticed that there was a blood-stained knife lying on the floor approximately two feet from the patient's head.

The second casualty was lying next to the first one – so close that their lower limbs were touching. She had a large contusion on her forehead; however in my opinion this was not caused by a knife as there were no visible skin lacerations. Her vital signs were good, but because she was unconscious, it was hard to assess the likelihood of any internal injuries.

The third casualty was lying approximately four feet away from the other two. She had two lacerations, consistent with a knife wound, in her chest and abdomen and had sustained significant blood loss. As I examined her, she started to moan and move her head, indicating that she was regaining consciousness. I asked her if she could hear me, but she didn't reply and her eyes remained closed.

It was clear to me and my colleague that all three individuals needed to be transported to hospital for emergency treatment. I radioed the control room on my radio and requested that two further ambulances be dispatched to the scene. I reiterated the need for police to attend as soon as possible and was advised that they were en route.

My colleague spoke to the cleaner, who was waiting outside on the landing, to ask about the possibility of there being any other injured parties on the premises. The cleaner informed my colleague that she couldn't say for certain, as she hadn't checked all the other rooms but that, to the best of her knowledge, there was no one else in the house.

It was clear that we were in a young child's bedroom and I was concerned that there may have been minors present when the incident took place, who might now be hiding and too frightened to come out. With this in mind, I looked under the bed and also opened the doors of the wardrobe, but I didn't find anyone.

My colleague and I had been at the property for ten to fifteen minutes when the first police officers arrived.

Having apprised them of the condition of the three patients, I continued to stabilise the most seriously ill patient, administering oxygen and applying pressure to her wounds, while my colleague attended to the other two patients.

Shortly afterwards, two more ambulances arrived. The three females were taken to hospital in separate vehicles. We were responsible for transporting the second casualty. My colleague drove, while I stayed in the back of the ambulance to monitor the patient. At one point her eyes flickered open briefly and she said something. I can't be 100 per cent certain, but it sounded like 'Amy'.

One Month Earlier

11

'You've been seeing a lot of this Izzy lately, haven't you?'

Claire's right. In the past fortnight, Izzy and I have met up twice more. On Saturday, at my suggestion, we had lunch on the South Bank, followed by a mooch around the Tate Modern. It was a splendid day. I've found that Izzy brings out the best in me, enables me to be the smartest, wittiest, most relaxed version of myself – a version I didn't even know existed. Then, last night, we went to a burlesque club in Covent Garden. I've just been showing Claire the photos Izzy uploaded to Facebook and the glowing comments I posted after she tagged me.

A friend of Izzy's was performing; she did some very inventive things with a hula hoop, and after the show she joined us for a drink at the bar. I was totally awestruck and couldn't stop fangirling over her fabulous costumes. She told me I had an interesting look (whatever *that* means) and said she teaches burlesque in Balham on a Tuesday night if I'm interested. I'm not (I've never been much of an exhibitionist), but I took one of her flyers anyway, not wanting to appear rude.

'Izzy's so much fun,' I say to Claire. 'I know we've only just met, but I really think we're going to be friends for life.'

Taking a step back, I cast a critical eye over the bouquet I'm working on. Normally, I prefer to work in the studio, but today I feel like company. The bouquet is a gift for someone who's just come out of hospital after a long illness and I've chosen its component parts with care: daisies for positivity, lavender for relaxation, gladioli for strength and lilies for new beginnings.

'It's great that you two have hit it off so quickly,' Claire says. She takes a break from sweeping the floor and rests her chin on top of the broom handle. 'Did you say Izzy was James Elliott's sister?'

'His sister-in-*law*,' I correct her.

'And you two met on a hike – right?'

'Yeah, I couldn't believe it when I found out she was related to James. Crazy, huh?' I pick up a sprig of restorative eucalyptus and add it to the bouquet, mainly so I can avoid looking Claire in the eye.

'Does she know you're doing the flowers for her fortieth?'

'No, it's a surprise party.'

Picking up my tweezers, I begin gently removing the anthers from a half-open Stargazer lily. It's a fiddly process, but so worth it. Not only does it protect the customer's clothing and soft furnishings from the dreaded pollen stains; it also lengthens the bloom time.

Claire bends down to pick up the dustpan. 'Sounds like the two of them are pretty close.'

'They used to be, but they aren't getting along too well at the moment. Izzy got made redundant recently and Eleanor doesn't think she's trying hard enough to find a new job.'

'Is she asking Eleanor for handouts then?'

'Not that I know of. I get the impression Izzy's reasonably well off. Her ex-husband was a trader in the City; he made a shitload of money betting against oil prices. I don't know all the details, but Izzy walked away from their divorce with enough cash to buy her flat in Greenwich outright. Job or no job, I don't think she'll be queueing for the food bank any time soon.'

'Lucky her,' Claire mutters. 'It'll be years before Kyle and I have enough saved up for a deposit – and in the meantime all we're doing is lining some greedy landlord's pocket.'

She carries the dustpan and broom over to the cupboard in the corner of the room and puts them away, out of sight. Claire knows how much I hate to have ugly, practical items on view; I want everyone who walks into the shop to feel they're in a lush, beautiful oasis, as far away from the real world as it's possible to be.

As I start wrapping a length of twine around the stems to hold them in place, I think back to the conversation Izzy and I had last night. I must admit that some of her criticisms of Eleanor struck me as rather unfair – and, not having siblings myself, it was hard for me to empathise. I was tempted to say something in Eleanor's defence, but of course I couldn't mention the upcoming party, and anyway, I didn't want Izzy to think me unsupportive.

As Claire walks back across the room she seems distracted, her head turned towards the street. The door to the shop is wedged open, the way it always is in warm weather. It's better for us – *and* the flowers; makes it easier for all of us to breathe. Catching my eye, she dips her head towards a tall man in a well-cut suit standing on the pavement outside. 'Speak of the devil . . .'

When I look again, I realise it's James. He's pacing in circles, a mobile phone clamped to his ear. My pulse starts racing, the way it always does when I see him. Instinctively, my hand goes to the butterfly clip that's holding my hair up. I yank it free, shaking my hair loose around my shoulders. I look much better with it down – younger, softer, prettier, although those are all relative terms.

As she watches me, the corners of Claire's mouth turn upwards; I think she knows I have a soft spot for James. She points to her right cheekbone. 'You've got some pollen from those lilies on your face.'

I drag the heel of my hand across my cheek. 'How's that?'

'It's still there.' She licks her thumb. 'Come here, I'll do it.'

I lean towards her, one eye still on the door, tilting my face upwards as Claire rubs away the burgundy stain.

'There you go, all gone now.'

As we break apart, James walks through the door. His jacket is draped over his arm and his phone is now nowhere to be seen. 'Good afternoon, ladies,' he says. Despite his cheery tone, there are bags beneath his eyes, as if he hasn't been sleeping well. It makes him look vulnerable and I have a sudden compulsion to take him in my arms and press his head against my breast.

Claire who, unlike me, is not lost in fantasy and can formulate a coherent sentence, goes towards him. 'Lovely to see you, Mr Elliott. How can we help you today?'

He smiles at her, before turning to me. 'I was working in the area. I thought I'd pop in and see if Amy fancied joining me for a spot of lunch.'

The invitation takes me by surprise and for a moment I don't know how to react. 'Just a quick sandwich,' he adds. 'There was something I wanted to discuss with you in regard to Izzy's party, but if you're too busy for lunch we can always chat here.'

'She's not too busy – are you, Amy?'

I turn to look at Claire. Her lips are pursed as if she's trying to keep a straight face. 'You go ahead, I can manage here on my own,' she says.

'Are you sure?'

'Course I am. I'll take my lunch hour when you get back.'

'Great,' James says. 'The vegetarian café next door looks nice. I had a quick look in the window when I walked past just now.' He smiles. 'Unless you're a confirmed carnivore?'

I smile back. 'No, veggie's good.' I untie my apron and

pull it over my head. 'Give me two ticks; I just need to grab my handbag from the studio.'

He gives a quick shake of the head. 'You won't be needing that; this is my treat.'

Shit. While I retrieved my bag, I was planning to run a brush through my hair and apply some mascara.

Feeling slightly flustered, I step out from behind the counter. We move towards the door at the same time and there's a tiny quick confusion as we both feint and hesitate, waiting for the other one to step through it first. James lightly touches the small of my back, encouraging me to go ahead of him. As I feel the pressure of his hand, I get a prickling sensation along my spine, like all the nerve endings have been suddenly brushed awake.

It feels funny, being with James outside one of our respective workplaces, but it isn't long before we've relaxed into our usual easy banter.

'I'm glad you could join me because if there's one thing I hate it's eating alone,' he says once we've ordered our food and settled into a table by the window. 'You'll have to forgive me if I seem a little preoccupied. I've just come from a meeting with a very demanding client.' There's a note of exasperation parcelled in his tone. 'I could have quite cheerfully wrung her neck at several points in our conversation.'

He unbuttons the cuffs of his shirt, rolls the sleeves up to his elbows. The fine gold hairs on his muscular arms catch the light streaming in through the window and I have an urgent desire to run my fingertips through them.

'Anyway,' he says. 'I didn't bring you here to talk about that. As I mentioned, I wanted to have a quick catch-up about the party. Eleanor tells me you were planning to come to the house the day before to assemble the floral arch.'

'That's right. Why, is it a problem?'

He pulls a face. 'We've gone and double-booked ourselves, unfortunately. I asked our gardener to come and do a tidy-up on the same day, not realising it clashed with your own plans.'

His feet shuffle under the table. I can feel the heat emanating from his knee where it almost touches mine. 'Eleanor and I were wondering if you could possibly do the arch on the morning of the party. It doesn't start till mid-afternoon. Would that give you enough time?'

Not really, I think to myself. Still, the Elliotts are important clients, I'd like to accommodate them.

'That should be fine,' I say after thinking about it for a moment. 'The metal frame for the arch comes in several pieces. I can work on the individual sections in my studio the day before, so that when I get to yours all I'll have to do is slot them together.'

'Thanks, Amy, you're a star. Sorry about the mix-up – my fault entirely. I should've checked with Eleanor before I went ahead and booked the gardener.'

'It's no biggie, I just want everything to run as smoothly as possible for you guys. I know how stressful these events

can be for the hosts, however much they're looking forward to them.' I clear my throat. 'Listen, James, while
we're talking about the party, there's something I need to
make you aware of.'

I break off as a waitress arrives with our food. James
thoughtfully moves the metal beaker of cutlery and the
tray of condiments to make room for her tray.

'The thing is . . .' I take a quick breath. I need to sound
convincing. If James knows I hunted his sister-in-law
down on Facebook, stage-managed an encounter, strained
every sinew to create a friendship with her, it would make
me look very . . . well, weird and slightly stalkerish. 'A
couple of weeks ago I ran into Izzy at a hiking event that
was advertised on Facebook. Of course I didn't know
it was *your* Izzy, not at first. But we got on so well, we
arranged to meet up again and that's when we discovered
the connection.'

He cocks an amused eyebrow. 'I already know.'

'You do?'

He helps himself to a knife and starts cutting his falafel
pitta in half. 'Izzy dropped me a text . . . some time last
week, I think it was. She told me she had a new friend who
was a very talented florist and gave me three guesses as to
who it might be.' He reaches up a hand to loosen his tie.
'I guessed right first time, which is hardly surprising since
you're the only florist I know.'

'Oh,' I say, feeling oddly deflated. 'Does Eleanor know
too?'

'Yup. She was a bit worried you might have said something about the party, but I told her that was highly unlikely.'

'I promise you I haven't said a word to Izzy,' I say staunchly. 'Please reassure Eleanor on that front.'

'I will,' he says, reaching for the pot of yoghurt dressing. 'You should come, you know.'

'Come where?'

'To the party – as a guest, I mean.'

'That's very kind, but I wouldn't want to impose.'

He lifts the pitta to his mouth. 'Why would you be imposing? You're one of Izzy's friends, aren't you?'

'Well, yes, I suppose I am.'

'In that case you must come; I'm sure Izzy would love to see you.'

As he says the words, my heart feels like a helium balloon, rising away from my body. 'Well, if you're sure.'

'I am. I'll get Eleanor to send you an invite, just so you have all the timings.' He looks directly into my eyes and it feels as if he's stripping through my layers like paint thinner, seeing much deeper than other people can.

Unable to hold his gaze any longer, I stare down at my plate, feigning delight at my beetroot and crispy chickpea sub.

12

A bubble of excitement wells up inside me as I approach the house. It's grander than I expected – a Victorian semi in a smart street, the sort of thing that could reasonably be described as a *villa*: three storeys, a covered verandah with a wooden bench seat and a gorgeous magnolia tree in the front garden. London GPs are clearly paid handsomely – or maybe Maria just married well.

Her text arrived two evenings ago. *Hi Amy, it's Maria from the walking group. Izzy gave me your number. Are you free on Saturday evening by any chance? I'm having a few friends round for dinner – just a kitchen supper, nothing fancy. Be great if you could join us. Izzy's coming btw x*

Naturally, I *was* free – and even if I wasn't, I would've cleared my diary without a second thought. I can't remember the last time I went to a dinner party. It was probably the one that Rob and I hosted when our relationship was in its dying throes; I can't say it was a huge success. An over-ambitious menu and the inexplicable disappearance of my only sharp knife put me on the wrong foot from the get-go. Then I managed to mislay my phone, which I had cunningly programmed with an array of alarms and reminders. As a result, I didn't have the faintest idea what I was supposed to do next. Meanwhile, Rob had conveniently absented himself from the kitchen and was busy drenching the bathroom with air freshener and building a pyramid of loo roll like some deranged doomsday prepper. By the time our guests arrived, I was an exhausted wreck in a *jus*-splattered blouse.

Fortunately, I'm a far better guest than I am a host and Maria's soiree will be an excellent opportunity to expand my button-sized social circle. And of course it means I get to see Izzy again.

I decided to drive; that way I don't have to worry about making the last bus home. The cars were parked nose to tail outside Maria's and the only space I could find was two streets away. By the time I arrive at her front door, sweat is pooling in my bra, and the new shoes I rushed out to buy this morning are starting to pinch.

'Oh Amy, that's so sweet of you,' she says as I hand her the ribbon-tied posy I knocked up in the studio yesterday. I don't know much about my hostess, having only met her once before, so I've hedged my bets with crowd-pleasing pink and cream roses.

'It's just to say thank you,' I reply as she closes the door behind me. 'For saving me from a microwaveable ready-meal-for-one and a date with Netflix.' As soon as the words are out of my mouth I wish I hadn't said them. I'm trying to impress these people, not make them pity me.

'Well, I'm very glad you could join us. It was such short notice I thought you'd probably have other plans.' She lifts the flowers to her nose. 'Gosh, they smell amazing – not like the roses you buy in the supermarket.'

The phrase 'if I had a penny for every time I've heard that' springs to mind. I dismiss it with a private smile. 'When it comes to roses, most commercial growers only have two concerns,' I tell her. 'Appearance and durability. Poor old fragrance doesn't even get a look in. It's no wonder that over time, the gene that switches on the scent enzyme has been completely bred out of many varieties. It's such a shame, because isn't that why most of us buy flowers for our homes – because of their gorgeous smell?'

She strokes the velvet petals with a fingertip.

'Absolutely . . . so much nicer than one of those plug-in aerosol thingies with all their chemicals.'

'It's the reason I only buy from growers who produce roses with their scent gene firmly intact, just as nature intended.'

'Is somebody getting married?' A man appears behind Maria. He's wearing knee-length shorts and an eye-catching Hawaiian shirt.

Maria turns to him, offering the bouquet up for inspection. 'Aren't they gorgeous?'

'Stunning,' he agrees.

'Amy's a florist, Izzy and I met her on the hike the other week.'

'Yes, I remember you telling me.' The man comes towards me. He has a distinctive jerky gait like a puppet, with extra joints and hinges in his limbs. 'Pleased to meet you, Amy, I'm Marcus, Maria's husband.' He leans forward to kiss me. It's a proper kiss where his lips actually connect with my cheek.

'This is for you as well,' I say, pulling a bottle of wine out of my messenger bag. I spent ages in the off-licence choosing it.

'A sparkling Shiraz; very nice too. Thank you, Amy.'

'Be a love and pop these in a vase for me,' Maria says, handing him the flowers. 'The nice yellow one we got from that gallery in St Ives. Oh, and check on the kids, will you? If Jake's still not asleep, he can listen to a story on the iPad . . . that'll send him off.'

Marcus touches his fingertips to the side of his head in a mock salute. 'Yes, ma'am.'

Maria reciprocates by blowing him a kiss. 'Come on, Amy,' she says, draping an arm around my shoulders. 'The others are in the garden; let's go and join them.'

She takes me to the kitchen, an appealing mash-up of heritage (slate flags, butler's sink, Aga) and contemporary (floor-to-ceiling cabinetry, mood lighting, huge, pastel-coloured fridge) and through the bifold doors to the patio where the other guests – two men and two women – are gathered.

Inevitably, it's Izzy who draws my eye. She's wearing a bright green dress that only someone with her colouring could get away with and her strawberry blond hair is torched into gold by the setting sun. She's talking to a man with flashy dark looks and black curls that hang over his collar. I was feeling a bit nervous about this evening, but the sight of her relaxes something inside me, vents a little anxiety from the pressurised chambers of my chest.

As soon as Izzy sees me she breaks off her conversation. 'Ames – at last! I was wondering where on earth you'd got to.'

'Slight difficulty parking,' I mumble, as everyone's eyes swivel in my direction.

'Yeah, sorry about that,' says Maria. 'Marcus keeps saying we should concrete over the front garden but I can't bring myself to chop down that lovely tree.'

I smile at her. 'My vote's for the magnolia too.'

Izzy comes over, folds me in a hug, her chunky necklace jangling between us, her hair pressed against my cheek. When she moves away, the vanilla scent of her perfume lingers in the air. 'Great to see you again,' she says.

'You too,' I reply, my tongue feeling clumsy in my mouth.

Maria introduces me to the other guests. There's a married couple, Ben and Niamh, and the man who was talking to Izzy earlier is a friend of Marcus's called Rafe. He's staying at the house for a few weeks while his own home in West London undergoes refurbishment. Maria asks him to pour me a drink before disappearing back inside the house, saying she needs to check on dinner.

'What can I get you?' Rafe asks, gesturing to a rattan table that's laden with bottles.

'Um, maybe just some sparkling water,' I tell him, spying a bottle of Pellegrino.

'I know you're driving, hon, but one drink won't hurt,' says Izzy. She looks at Rafe. 'She'll have a gin fizz.'

Rafe picks up a heavy glass jug filled with yellow liquid, sprigs of rosemary bobbing on the surface.

'And you can top me up while you're at it,' Izzy says, holding out her own glass.

When our drinks have been poured, we all go over to join Ben and Niamh. I ask them how they know Maria and it turns out they're both GPs and work at Maria's surgery. Izzy remarks how difficult it's been since the pandemic to get a face-to-face appointment with her own doctor and this leads on to a general conversation about the state of the NHS. It's not a subject I'm very knowledgeable about, but I manage a few pithy rejoinders.

After fifteen minutes or so, Marcus steps through the bifold doors with a plate of warm bruschetta. When he offers one to me, I take the opportunity to compliment him on his beautiful garden. 'That's a magnificent climber,' I say, indicating the vigorous specimen of clematis that covers half the boundary fence.

'It is, isn't it?' he replies. 'Unfortunately, I can't take any of the credit. Maria's the one with the green fingers.' He passes me a paper napkin. 'You've got a bit of tomato on your chin . . . just there.'

'God, that's typical me,' I say, dabbing at my chin. 'I once went an entire afternoon at work with mayonnaise on the end of my nose before a customer pointed it out.'

There I go again. Too much information.

It isn't long before Maria reappears and tells us that dinner's ready. We eat at a huge round table in the kitchen.

The conversation is animated and there are no awkward silences. Rafe talks at length about his property renovation. He's having the basement dug out, but there's some sort of issue with the underpinning, which means it's going to cost nearly double the initial estimate. Still, it sounds as if he can afford it because in the next breath he's telling us about the bespoke timber barn he's having built to house his classic car.

I don't know if Rafe and Izzy have met before tonight, but she watches him very intently as he speaks, suggesting she has designs on him. Whether her interest is purely sexual, or goes deeper than that, is impossible to know at this stage. Rafe isn't wearing a wedding ring, which speaks to his availability, and judging by the way he looks at her, with a hungry slide of his eye, the attraction is mutual.

As Maria asks Rafe if his decree nisi has come through yet, it occurs to me that one of the purposes of this dinner party – if not the *main* purpose – is to set him up with Izzy. Unease flexes inside me like a cramp. If the two of them embark on a relationship, there'll be less time in her life for her friends. Less time for me.

'What do you do for a living, Rafe?' I ask as Marcus clears away our starter plates.

'I'm a professor of molecular physics at Imperial College,' he replies. I wonder if he's joking. Physically, he's about as far removed from the stereotype of an academic as it's possible to be. Instead of being tweedy and bearded and slightly stooped, he's handsome and energetic and fashionable in his fine-knit grey sweater and designer jeans.

As none of the others are laughing, I decide he must be telling the truth.

Marcus opens the oven and takes out a Le Creuset casserole dish. 'Rafe and I were at boarding school together,' he reveals. 'Even then it was obvious to everyone – including our teachers – that he was destined for greatness.' He brings the casserole over and sets it down in the centre of the table. 'Not like me, who ended up wasting an expensive education and leaving halfway through sixth form to work in a car dealership.'

Rafe sweeps his hand through the air, indicating our comfortable surroundings. 'I'd say you've done pretty well for yourself, old chap.'

The rest of us smile and nod, signalling our assent.

'What are you working on at the moment?' I ask Rafe.

'I'm doing some research into wave-particle duality, but I won't tell you any more about it because I don't want to ruin a lovely evening by sending you all to sleep,' he says self-effacingly.

Izzy props her chin on her palm and gazes directly into his face with a look that says: *you are the most fascinating person in this room by a mile.*

'I think science is the new sexy,' she says, slurring her words ever so slightly.

'Perhaps you could tell that to my vice chancellor,' says Rafe, taking a slice of crusty bread from the basket. 'It might encourage him to direct a bit more funding my way.'

'I hated science at school,' I say. 'I just didn't have the right sort of brain for it. I have huge admiration for people like you who are pushing the boundaries and making new discoveries.'

Rafe tears off a piece of bread and rolls it between his forefinger and thumb. 'That's very kind of you, Amy, but scientists aren't as clever as people think we are. We're just good at solving problems, albeit quite complex ones. The trick is accepting you can't solve all of them at once.'

'How do you mean?'

'In any research project, there's always one overarching question – the big target, if you like. But if you think too hard about the sheer enormity of it, you lose focus. The key is to start small. Concentrate on solving problems you can answer. Start putting the pieces of the jigsaw puzzle together, edges first. And slowly, bit by bit, the mystery of the overarching question reveals itself. Think of it like one of those large-scale murals that are made up of thousands of tiny objects. Viewed close up, it doesn't make any sense at all. It's only when you step back that the bigger picture emerges.'

He pops the piece of bread into his cheek. 'How about you, Amy, what line of work are you in?'

'She's a florist,' Izzy says before I have a chance to reply. 'She creates these incredible floral installations.'

Ben's broad face is brisk with enquiry. 'I'm obviously hopelessly out of touch because I don't have the foggiest idea what a floral installation is.'

'It's rather a grand description for what is basically a large statement piece,' I explain. 'It can be anything from a simple column of roses to a themed display that covers an entire shopfront.'

Izzy picks a ladle up off the table and begins helping herself to slow-cooked lamb from the casserole. 'I loved what you did for that hotel launch in Clerkenwell,' she says. She looks around the table. 'Amy turned their lobby ceiling into an upside-down meadow with all these beautiful grasses and wildflowers.'

I look at her quizzically. 'How do you know about that?'

'It was on your Instagram, hon.'

I had no idea Izzy had looked at my social media. The thought makes my skin ripple with pleasure; it feels good to know she's as interested in my life as I am in hers.

'So what's your ultimate ambition, Amy?' asks Rafe.

'A royal wedding,' I reply.

Rafe laughs. He thinks I'm joking.

'I adore fresh flowers,' says Niamh. 'I buy them for the house as often as I can. I don't care if they only last a week; they're just so incredibly uplifting.' She takes the ladle from Izzy. 'Who was that famous artist who said "I must have flowers, always and always"?'

'Monet.'

She looks at me, clearly impressed. 'Do you know what, I think you might be right, Amy.'

I *am* right, but I resist the temptation to say as much.

Niamh starts transferring chunks of lamb to her plate. 'Do you have a business card, Amy? Only there are a couple of big birthdays coming up in my family.'

I smile at her. 'Sure, I'll give you one before I go.'

'I've got one of those,' says Izzy.

'A business card?' says Niamh, not understanding.

Izzy shakes her head. 'No, a big birthday; the week after next.' She pouts prettily. 'Forty years old, I can hardly believe it. It only seems like yesterday that I was giving my first boyfriend a hand job behind the cricket pavilion.'

As the entire table erupts with laughter, Izzy tilts her head kittenishly to one side, clearly enjoying the attention.

'How do you plan to celebrate?' asks Ben.

'I'm going to my sister's house for lunch; not very exciting, I know.'

'Just the family, is it?'

'My sister said I was welcome to bring a friend, so I asked Maria.' Izzy flutters her eyelashes and adds witheringly. 'One solitary friend . . . sooo generous of my little sis.' She glances at Maria. 'Of course, we could always give Eleanor's poxy lunch a swerve.'

Something pulls inside my chest, tight as a stitch. I have to take a drink of water so Izzy doesn't see the look of panic on my face.

'You've already accepted Eleanor's invitation; I think she'd be a bit cross if you pulled out now,' says Maria. 'You and I could always do something fun in the evening.'

'Hmm, maybe,' Izzy looks at me. 'Would you be up for a big night out on my birthday, Ames? Bar-hopping in the West End, and maybe a club afterwards?'

'For sure,' I say. 'It's been a good few years since I saw

the inside of a nightclub, but I rarely turn down an opportunity to relive my misspent youth.'

'Excellent!' says Izzy, apparently satisfied with this compromise.

As I take the dish of sweet potato mash from Marcus, I notice that Ben is looking at me rather fixedly.

'Just out of interest, where *did* you grow up, Amy?' he asks me. 'Only I've been trying to work out where that accent's from.'

I feel myself tense. I've gone to considerable lengths to cultivate a neutral accent that's hard to place. It usually only slips during moments of heightened emotion.

As I start to reply, Ben lifts a hand. 'No, don't tell me – let me guess.'

Niamh gives a little groan of protest. 'Sorry about this, Amy; it's one of Ben's party tricks. He's an army brat; he lived all over the UK as a kid. He's an expert when it comes to regional accents.' She pats her husband's forearm affectionately. 'Or at least he thinks he is.'

'Go on then, buddy,' says Marcus. 'Let's see how good you are.'

Ben's eyes narrow. 'I was leaning towards the West Midlands earlier on, but I reckon we're looking a bit further north – but not as far north as Sheffield or Manchester.'

Niamh sighs. 'Do get on with it, darling.'

'I can't narrow it down to one specific town or city, so I'll go with a county.'

He pauses, just long enough for Marcus to do a little drumroll on the table with his palms.

'Derbyshire.' Ben looks at me expectantly. 'Am I right?'

As it happens, he is. Bakewell to be precise. It's a pretty market town, on the edge of the Peak District. A lovely place to grow up, although the influx of summer tourists used to get on my nerves.

I pick up my napkin and dab the corners of my mouth. 'You should have stuck with your initial hunch,' I say calmly. 'Warwick.'

'Damn it,' Ben mutters as the others jeer at him good-naturedly.

I lean towards Maria, who's sitting next to me. 'Where's your loo?' I whisper.

'Just out in the hallway. We converted the cupboard under the stairs.'

'Back in a sec,' I say, pushing my chair away from the table.

Once inside the bathroom, I lock the door. I don't actually need to empty my bladder; it was simply a way of ending an uncomfortable conversation. Now that I'm here, I take a few moments to straighten my mind; scan for loose ends. I know I'm not in any real danger of being exposed, but still, I can't afford to let my guard down. I desperately want these people to accept me, which means they can never, *never* find out the truth.

Satisfied that all bases have been covered, I look in the mirror to see how my make-up's holding up. I used a new technique I learned from a YouTube tutorial. It's supposed to make hooded eyes look bigger and brighter and was surprisingly effective. Spotting a mascara smudge under my right eye, I dampen a piece of toilet paper and wipe it away. I wish I'd thought to bring the lipstick from my handbag because I'm badly in need of a touch-up. I might try to apply some discreetly when I get back the table.

When I open the door I almost run straight into Maria, who's loitering outside.

'All yours,' I say.

'It's OK, I don't need to go, I just wanted to have a quick word in private.' She lowers her voice. 'It's about Amy's birthday party. I helped Eleanor put together the guest list; she said you were going.'

'Yes, I can't wait,' I whisper back. 'My heart almost stopped back there when she threatened to cancel her lunch with Eleanor.'

'Yeah, I saw the look on your face when she said that; I thought I'd better put your mind at rest.' Her eyes flit towards the kitchen, as if she's worried we might be overheard. 'Much as we all love Izzy, she can be a little unreliable. That's why Eleanor suggested she bring a friend to lunch, knowing full well she'd choose me.'

'And your role is to make sure she turns up,' I say, as realisation dawns.

She nods. 'I've promised Eleanor faithfully that I'll get Izzy to the house at the appointed time, even if I have to drag her there by her hair.'

Just then, we hear the sound of the kitchen door opening. I half turn and see Izzy coming towards us. Judging by the way she's holding on to the wall for support, she's more than a little drunk.

'What are you two whispering about?' she says with a smile.

'I was just checking up on Amy,' Maria tells her without missing a beat. 'Us lot can be a bit loud when we get together. I wanted to make sure she wasn't feeling too overwhelmed.'

'Course she isn't, are you, Ames?' Izzy plaits her arm through mine and rests her head on my shoulder. I can feel the heat from her face, burning through the thin fabric of my top, branding me.

'No, I'm having a lovely time; you're all such interesting people.'

'It's a shame you're not drinking though. You can always crash at mine tonight, hon. I've got nothing planned for tomorrow. We could have a mooch round Greenwich Market in the morning, then maybe grab some lunch?'

I want to say yes more than anything, but unfortunately I have a prior engagement, one that I committed to weeks ago.

'Thanks, Izzy, but I can't. I've promised to help Janet creosote the fence tomorrow.'

Izzy's head snaps up. 'Who's Janet?'

'My upstairs neighbour; I'm sure I've mentioned her to you.'

'Probably, I've got a memory like a sieve. Can't you blow her out?'

I make a face. 'Not really. The fence at the front of the house is a shared responsibility. It desperately needs some TLC and neither of us wants to put it off any longer.'

Izzy's face betrays a flicker of annoyance. 'Suit yourself,' she says petulantly. The next moment she's pulling her arm away from mine and turning to Maria. 'You were right about Rafe,' she gushes. 'He's absolutely gorgeous. I really hope he asks for my number before I go.'

I feel a dull ache in the pit of my stomach. It's like that breathless sensation that follows a punch, before the pain sets in.

'I'm sure he will,' Maria says. 'And if he doesn't, I'll get Marcus to give him a gentle nudge.'

Izzy's mouth splits in a wide smile. 'Thanks, hon; you're the best friend a girl could ever have.'

Maria's face lights up, the way everyone's does when Izzy tosses out a handful of her fairy dust. 'There's no need to thank me; you deserve to meet someone nice after everything you've been through.' She smiles at us both. 'I don't know about you two, but I'm dying for pudding. Let's get back to the others, shall we?'

Back in the kitchen, Maria produces a homemade roulade and shop-bought sorbet. As we all tuck in, I divert attention away from myself by inviting Ben to tell us more about his peripatetic childhood. Every now and then I sneak a look at Izzy. Her chair seems to be getting closer and closer to Rafe's. By the time coffee is served, she's practically sitting in his lap.

After coffee, several liqueurs are proffered – expensive-looking varieties that are actually drinkable, not the sort of sticky-necked souvenirs from long-ago foreign holidays that languish at the back of my own kitchen cupboard. Since I'm driving, I abstain, but Izzy has two, one after the other, knocking them back like tequila shots.

As the alcohol takes effect, the mood around the table turns increasingly frivolous. Ben treats us to another party trick from his seemingly inexhaustible repertoire – the ability to name all US states in alphabetical order. It earns him more generous applause than he deserves. When Izzy suggests a round of truth or dare, I take it as my cue to leave. It's a puerile game and, for someone like me, fraught with risk.

'It's been a wonderful evening, guys,' I say, reaching under the table for my handbag. 'But I think I'm going to call it a night.'

Izzy gives a short laugh, harsh and off-key. 'Oh yeah, I forgot. Amy needs her beauty sleep. She's got a hot date with a tin of creosote in the morning.'

Marcus looks at me in puzzlement. 'What?'

'Just a spot of fence painting,' I explain. God, I sound boring.

As I say goodbye to them all, Izzy barely makes eye contact. She's too busy helping herself to another sly tot of Honey Badger. I consider asking if she wants to meet up mid-week, but decide against it, not wanting to sound needy.

'Would you like me to escort you to your vehicle?' Rafe offers chivalrously.

At this, Izzy looks up from her drink, the lines on her forehead pinching together.

'That's kind of you, Rafe, but I'll be fine – the streets around here are pretty well lit,' I say, not having the faintest idea if this is true.

As Maria walks me to the front door, I open my handbag and take out half a dozen business cards. 'For Niamh,' I say, pressing them into her hand. 'And anyone else who might be interested.'

She hugs me briefly and says she'll see me soon. I know it's one of those stock phrases people trot out without necessarily meaning it, but I really hope I do see her soon and I pray that in time Maria – Marcus, Niamh, Ben and Rafe too – will become very dear friends of mine, just like Izzy.

I'm almost at the car when I realise I've forgotten something – my scarf, a pretty, lightweight thing that was loosely knotted around my neck when I arrived at Maria's. When we sat down to eat, I took it off and draped it over the back of my chair. Sighing, I turn around and begin to retrace my steps.

As Maria's house comes into view I see that the light above the front door is on and the three men are sitting out on the front verandah. They're smoking cigars and talking in loud voices, the way drunk people do.

'Funny little thing, wasn't she?' The speaker is Rafe; I recognise his distinctive voice with its husky edge. I move closer, ears straining. 'How long has Maria been friends with her?'

Marcus blows a plume of smoke into the air. 'She only met her a couple of weeks ago – they belong to the same hiking group. She's Izzy's friend really; Maria didn't particularly warm to her the first time they met – she thought she seemed rather desperate. She only invited her tonight because Izzy asked her to.'

I turn sideways, so I'm shielded from view by the next-door neighbour's laurel hedge. It also means I can't see the men any more.

A third voice that must be Ben's. 'I wonder what Izzy sees in her; they're very different.'

'Oh, you know Izzy – she loves a project.'

'What does that mean?' asks Rafe.

Yes, Marcus, what *does* that mean?

'Don't get me wrong, Izzy's a great girl, but she likes to be surrounded by people who think the sun shines out of her backside – impressionable people that she can re-design so they're just the way she wants them.'

'Sounds like Rafe's house renovation,' Ben quips. 'A partial demolition, a bit of remodelling, the final fix, and then she'll be shiny and new.'

His comment detonates explosions of laughter. I turn around and start walking quickly away. I wish now I'd never gone back for that stupid scarf.

13

'I'm not too late, am I?'

Claire and I both look up from the jardiniere we're busy dragging back into the shop from outside. It's five twenty-five and Darling Buds is about to close for the day. Standing on the pavement a few feet away, looking lovely as ever in a knee-length halter dress and Grecian sandals laced to mid-calf, is Eleanor Elliott.

I let go of the jardiniere and stand up, horribly conscious of my messy hair and grubby apron. Although I haven't seen Eleanor since our initial meeting, we've exchanged a flurry of texts and emails in the interim. She's made several adjustments to the original scheme – increased the number of table arrangements, swapped out the foliage in the arch for more flowers (against my advice, but hey – it's her party), and changed the colour of the hydrangea posies from blue to pink and back to blue again.

It can be annoying when clients vacillate, but given how much Eleanor is paying for my services I've been more than happy to accommodate her. Besides, there's an awful lot riding on this party for me, personally as well as professionally.

'Hello, Eleanor, how lovely to see you,' I say, brushing my hair out of my eyes with the back of my hand. 'Were you after some flowers?'

She adjusts the position of the caramel leather handbag on her shoulder. 'No, I wanted to talk to you about the table arrangements for Izzy's party.'

'Oh? Do you need to change the quantity again?'

'No, it's not that.' She bares her teeth in an expression of pained regret. 'I've been looking at the sketches you sent again and it suddenly struck me that your designs might be too formal for the occasion. I wondered if perhaps we could change them for something a little more bucolic.'

I have to basket my fingers together to stop myself punching her. There's less than a week to go to the party – far too late to be making anything other than minor cosmetic tweaks.

'Bucolic,' I repeat, buying myself some time while I try to skim the sour off my expression.

'Yes. I wondered about a country hedgerow theme – daisies, cowslips, bluebells, that sort of thing.'

'Good luck finding bluebells in August,' Claire says under her breath.

I scrub a hand over my face. 'I'm sorry, Eleanor, but the flowers have already been ordered from my suppliers – they're being delivered in two days' time. Even if I placed a second order right now, the replacements would never arrive in time.'

Eleanor's expression suggests this is not within the range of answers she had expected. 'Oh well, never mind. I daresay I can live with them.'

Her comment cuts me like a razor blade. I don't want

people to 'live with' my creations. I want them to be dazzled, bewitched, blown away.

'If you like I can make the arrangements a little looser, a little more relaxed,' I offer. 'That should go some way towards achieving the look you're after.'

'Do whatever you think best,' she says curtly.

'How are the rest of your plans shaping up? Did you manage to get the waiting staff sorted?'

'Yes, thank you. I used one of the agencies you recommended.'

I feel the pressure of her gaze. There's something unflinching about it, a kernel of hardness.

'James tells me you'll be joining us for Izzy's special day.'

As she says it, the air around us seems to cool. Despite the warmth and spontaneity of James's invite, I had suspected Eleanor might not be quite as keen to include me in the festivities. The nature and tone of our communications thus far tells me that to her, I'm just the help.

'That is OK, isn't it? If you'd rather I didn't . . .'

'No, no, it's fine.' The detached quality of her voice tells me she doesn't mean it. Not even close.

Suddenly, her eyes narrow. 'It's an incredible coincidence, isn't it? A few weeks ago you and Izzy were complete strangers. I hire you to do the flowers for her fortieth birthday and the next thing I know the two of you are BFFs.'

There's an edge in her voice that makes me feel slightly nervous. She doesn't know I engineered the meeting with her sister; she can't do. And even if she has her suspicions, so what? My initial encounter with Izzy may not have been coincidence, but our friendship is real. Nobody can take that away from us.

I attempt a laugh, but it comes out as a cough. 'Just goes to show it really is a small world, huh?'

'Clearly.' She folds her arms in front of her chest. 'I won't keep you from your work any longer. I guess I'll see you on Monday then.'

'Yes, I'll be there bright and early.' I was going to tell her to trust me about the table arrangements, but it's too late – she's already walking away.

'So *that* was the legendary Mrs Elliott,' Claire says as we heave the jardiniere through the shop doorway. 'She's very beautiful, just the sort of woman I imagined James being married to. No wonder he's always in here, buying flowers for her.'

The words chafe. Eleanor *is* beautiful, and no doubt she *does* deserve to be lavished with bouquets of Desdemona roses and Gloriosa lilies at £8.50 a stem (and *that's* the wholesale price). But for some reason I can't help feeling that, despite her obvious charms, James deserves better.

'How are the two sisters getting along these days?' Claire asks. 'It could be quite awkward if they're shooting daggers at each other during the party.'

'I'm not sure. I haven't seen Izzy recently.'

'No? I thought you two were joined at the hip.'

I thought so too. I haven't seen her since Maria's dinner party and that was a couple of weeks ago now. We've exchanged a few texts, but when I suggested a mid-week meet-up, Izzy said she was too busy preparing for a job interview. I was a little disappointed, but pleased about her interview, and I wished her luck for it. She didn't suggest an alternative date and I didn't press her for one, knowing that we'll be seeing each other sooner than she thinks.

'I've had a lot on just lately,' I say. 'I feel bad that I haven't been able to make time for her, but we'll have plenty of time to catch up at the party.'

'Yes, of course you will. Is that other friend of Izzy's going, the one you met on the hike – what was her name again?'

'Maria. Yeah, she'll be there with her husband, Marcus.'

Thinking about them takes me back to that evening and the word Marcus used to describe me. *Desperate* . . . hardly the most flattering description. He's right though. I *am* desperate.

I've spent far too long with my nose pressed up against the glass of other people's lives, waiting to be let in. It's time for me to step out of the shadows.

14

When I arrive at The Sanctuary, it's Katya who comes to the door. She's dressed, but the ends of her hair are damp, as if she's just got out of the shower.

'Eleanor and James aren't up yet,' are the first words out of her mouth.

'Oh,' I say, feeling slightly deflated. On the short drive over here, I constructed a silly little fantasy. In it, I enjoyed a leisurely cup of coffee with James before I started work. Coffee that would no doubt be of barista quality and produced using one of those gleaming chrome machines that cost an arm and a leg. The two of us would sit on high stools at the granite breakfast bar and talk excitedly about the marvellous day that lies ahead; a day that will surely remain in our shared consciousness for years to come.

'No problem,' I tell Katya. 'I'll unload the van and then I'll start setting up in the garden, if that's all right with you.'

'As you wish,' she says with a languid shrug. 'The side gate's open for you.'

I go back to the van, where Ewan is waiting. Assembling a pre-decorated arch is a fiddly business. I could probably have managed it on my own, but it'll be much easier with two of us. Claire was my first choice but, as

I expected, she and Kyle already had plans. Fortunately, Ewan was available and grateful for the extra cash.

'Are we good to go?' he says through the van's open window.

'Yep, let's get the arch out first and leave the table arrangements in the van where it's nice and cool.' I glance up at the sky which, even at this early hour, is already a canopy of cornflower blue, the promise of a beautiful day ahead. 'We don't want them wilting before the guests have arrived.'

I go to the back of the van and open the double doors, pushing them all the way back.

'This shouldn't take more than a couple of hours,' I tell Ewan as I carefully slide out the first section of arch. 'I'm sure there are more exciting things you could be doing on a bank holiday Monday.'

'Not really,' he says, pushing the sleeves of his faded blue shirt up to his elbows. 'I'm yours for as long as you need me.'

The Elliotts' garden is immaculate, the lawn luminously green, the box hedges clipped to perfection. Underneath the gazebo, the tables and chairs have already been set up, and off to one side is a small raised stage, which must be for the band. The caterers won't be arriving for another couple of hours and until then Ewan and I should have the garden to ourselves.

The arch assembly proves more time-consuming than I had anticipated. Some of the flowers have been dislodged in transit, while others are damaged and have to be replaced. Even though Ewan doesn't know the first thing about floristry he makes himself useful, stripping the leaves from the spare stems I brought with us and cutting short lengths of wire to hold each one in place. Other than issuing the odd instruction, I don't say very much. When I'm doing an installation, I prefer to work in silence; otherwise it's easy to lose concentration and make a mistake. Ewan seems to instinctively understand this. He only speaks twice – the first time is to point out a badly bruised salvia I've missed, the second comes as the arch is nearing completion.

'Looks like somebody's just woken up,' he says.

My head turns towards the house. I'm hoping to see James, but it's Eleanor who steps barefoot through the French doors. She adjusts the belt on her knee-length robe and runs her fingers through her tousled hair.

'Morning,' she calls out as she makes her way across the lawn. 'Sorry I wasn't around when you arrived. We had a bit of a late one last night – a retirement party for one of James's employees.'

Wiping my hands on my apron, I go to meet her.

'That's OK, I thought it best to just crack on,' I say. 'My assistant and I are making good progress with the arch. Ten more minutes and we should be done.'

She peers over my shoulder. 'Mind if I have a sneak preview?'

'Of course.'

I watch as she goes over to the arch and walks slowly round it, looking it up and down, studying it from every angle. She was very enthusiastic about the sketches I sent, but it's always slightly nerve-wracking when a client sees an installation in the flesh for the first time.

'I've got just three words to say about this,' she announces when her inspection is complete. 'Wow, wow and wow again.'

I break into a smile. 'I'm glad it's lived up to expectation.'

'To be honest, it's even *more* beautiful than I imagined.' She reaches out to stroke a jewel-coloured amaranthus.

'You haven't said anything to Izzy, have you – about the party, I mean?' There's a sudden, sharp shift in her voice; a distinctly icy undertone.

'Absolutely not. The last thing I'd want to do is ruin the surprise for her.'

'Good, because if I find out you've even so much as hinted at it, I'll make sure you never work in this city again.'

Nausea creeps through my stomach and up into my throat. I very much doubt the Elliotts' social connections extend to the whole of London, but if Eleanor decided to bad-mouth me, she could certainly deal Darling Buds' reputation a serious blow.

'I haven't said a word to her, I swear.' I speak in a breathless rush, the words spilling over each other. 'I'd never breach a client's confidence like that; *never*.'

She waits a beat or two before responding. 'Oh, Amy, your face is a picture!' she says, hooting with laughter. 'Don't worry, darling, I'm only pulling your leg.'

I laugh too, when what I really want to do is slap her. Jokes like that are never funny when you're a small business owner who relies on word of mouth. 'That's a relief, you had me worried for a minute there.'

Spotting an errant bloom lying on the grass, she bends down to pick it up. 'I suppose I'd better go and get dressed,' she says, tucking the flower behind her ear. 'Is there anything you need to ask me before I go?'

'Just one thing. I'll be decorating the gazebo shortly – are you planning to put coverings on the tables or leave them bare?'

'I have the most gorgeous floral tablecloths; Katya spent most of yesterday evening ironing them,' she replies. 'I'll get her to put them on the tables when she's finished giving Toby his breakfast.'

'No need, we can do that.'

'Thanks, I'll tell her to bring them out to you.'

As she starts padding back towards the house, I look over at Ewan, wishing he hadn't been there to witness my discomfort at Eleanor's little 'joke'. I reach into the front pocket of my apron, feeling for my secateurs. 'I can finish this off on my own,' I tell him. 'Why don't you go and get the table arrangements from the van?'

Once the arch has passed my stringent quality control checks, I start collecting the debris. I'm halfway through the task when James emerges from the house. As he strides across the lawn with his athletic gait, I raise a hand to wave at him, using the other one to shield my eyes against the sun.

He's wearing jeans and a Pearl Jam T-shirt and there's a stack of tablecloths tucked under his arm. As he gets nearer I can smell his shower gel and the more animal scent of his skin underneath.

'Eleanor tells me you're working miracles out here,' he says, his eyes bright and playful. He turns to my creation. 'And I'm inclined to agree with her – that arch is quite extraordinary.'

'I'm so pleased you like it,' I say. 'It was a really fun project to do.'

He holds out the tablecloths. 'My wife told me to give these to you.'

'I'll take them, shall I?' says Ewan, who's just finished unloading the van.

'Are you Amy's new apprentice?' James asks him.

He gives a lopsided smile. 'No way, I don't know a begonia from a buttercup.'

'Ewan's our delivery driver,' I explain. 'He's just helping me out today.'

'Well, you're clearly very versatile,' says James as he hands over the cloths. 'Because from where I'm standing, you're doing a terrific job.'

Ewan gives a shy half-smile. 'Do you want me to put these on the tables for you?' he asks me.

'Yes, please,' I say, glad of an excuse to get rid of him. 'I'll be with you in a sec.'

*

Now that James and I are alone we can talk more easily, the way we do when he comes into the shop. He asks me how business is doing and if I'm still thinking about trading my Peugeot in for a VW. I'd forgotten I'd even told him I was in the market for a new car. I love that about James – the way he remembers everything I tell him and always seems so interested in what's going on in my life, even the small stuff. It makes me feel appreciated, special.

As we chat, I find myself becoming more animated, opening up to him the way a dahlia opens up to a bee. I'm always like that when I'm in the company of someone I admire; it's the same with Izzy. I'm so lucky to have both of them in my life; together, they fill a hole inside me I didn't even know was there. But all too soon James has to go, claiming he's only halfway through the list of chores his wife has assigned him. Given that Eleanor outsources the vast majority of her domestic responsibilities, I'm struggling to think what these tasks can be.

Thanking me for my hard work, James reaches out and touches my bare arm with the tips of his fingers. They're on my skin for an instant, but they send electricity coursing through me. I feel like I could spark and crackle with it.

As James starts off towards the house, I see Ewan out of the corner of my eye. He's standing underneath the gazebo, not doing anything, just staring at us. The expression on his face is cool and assessing. It looks very much like disapproval, but it passes so quickly I can't be sure.

Once I've positioned the table arrangements, I turn my attention to the hydrangea posies I've made for the living room wall niches. Together, they make an eye-catching display and will form a striking contrast to the putty-coloured walls. I'm making the final adjustments when the caterers roll up and suddenly the house is filled with people and noise. Eleanor flits between the kitchen and living room, looking slightly stressed as she tries to coordinate their activities. Time for Darling Buds to make an exit.

Even though it's wildly out of my way, I offer to take Ewan home, figuring it's the least I can do. He thanks me but asks if I can drop him at the station instead, saying he's going to visit a friend on the other side of the river. I could have sworn he told me earlier that he didn't have any plans for the rest of the day but perhaps I misheard him.

After taking the van back to the shop, I get in my car and drive home to get ready for the party. My Uber's due in half an hour – barely enough time to shower, touch up my make-up and change into the forgiving maxi dress I bought from ASOS three days ago.

I'm in such a rush I almost forget Izzy's birthday present – a cashmere pashmina in a soft shade of indigo – and have to ask the driver to wait while I run back into the house to get it. One thing I haven't forgotten is a plentiful supply of business cards. I'm attending the party as Izzy's friend, first and foremost, but a little self-publicity never did any harm.

By the time I get to The Sanctuary, most of the other guests have arrived. There's a palpable air of excitement as we huddle together in the garden, out of sight. Not knowing anyone else there, I hover self-consciously on the fringes of the group. After a minute or two, I spot Marcus and Rafe. As far as I'm aware, Rafe and Izzy hadn't met before Maria's dinner party. Their relationship must've come on in leaps and bounds for Maria to have convinced Eleanor to add him to the guest list. I do hope Izzy knows what she's doing; she can be rather impulsive. I wave at Marcus but he doesn't see me, so I train my gaze on the French doors instead, eager to catch my first glimpse of Izzy.

The moment, when it comes, is every bit as delicious as I'd imagined. As soon as Izzy sees us, she freezes in shock. I watch as different expressions scud across her face like high-speed clouds: bewilderment, disbelief, delight. I, too, am caught unawares by a powerful emotion. Seeing her again after two whole weeks without her is like shrugging off my winter clothes and stepping into the sun.

Delighted by the guest of honour's stunned reaction, everyone starts whooping and clapping. Some guests break away from the group and go over to extend their good wishes to Izzy in person. I follow in their wake, but there's so many people around her she doesn't see me. Never mind, I tell myself, there'll be plenty of other opportunities to snatch a private moment with her.

As ambient chill-out music starts playing through the outdoor speakers, waiting staff in smart black and white uniforms swarm on to the lawn with trays of drinks. I help myself to a glass of Prosecco and look around for Marcus and Rafe, but they're nowhere to be seen. A man who turns out to be Izzy's uncle comes over to introduce himself. He speaks painfully slowly, as if he's reading from a script in a different language, one he has to mentally translate each line of before uttering the words. I'm hoping he has some interesting anecdotes about Izzy's childhood to share, but it transpires that he was living in South Africa for most of it. Extracting myself without causing offence proves surprisingly difficult and it's three quarters of an hour before I manage to get away.

After refreshing my drink I spot Maria. She's talking to a tall woman who looks awfully familiar. I observe her for several minutes, trying to work out where I've seen her before. Then I realise she was one of the women in Christmas jumpers on Izzy's Facebook – a friend from university if my recall is correct.

I decide to go over and introduce myself. Maria looks pleased to see me, but the friend – who introduces herself as Tess – seems faintly irritated at the intrusion. The three of us start chatting and Maria compliments me on the floral arch, but after only ten minutes I have to excuse myself as my bladder is full to bursting point.

There's a queue for the downstairs loo. I think about looking for another bathroom but it seems impolite to venture upstairs. By the time I get back to the garden, Maria has vanished and Tess is standing with several other women, all of them shrieking with laughter, obviously terribly familiar with each other.

As the afternoon wears on, the air thickening with the day's accumulating heat, I enjoy a series of pleasant encounters with my fellow guests. It's not too difficult to bring up the subject of my job and point out my handiwork, before discreetly handing a business card to anyone who seems remotely interested.

I haven't managed to speak to Izzy yet. Every time I see her she's deep in conversation with someone. I'm dying to know what she thinks of the arch and find out if she's had a chance to open my birthday gift. I would have preferred to give it to her myself, but when I arrived Katya instructed me to leave it on the table in the living room, with all the other presents. I wonder if she's still annoyed with me for not staying the night after Maria's dinner party. I do hope not; I'd be disappointed if our friendship floundered now, after all the effort I've put into it. Bloody furious, actually.

In a rare moment when I find myself alone, I stand in the shadow of the gazebo, watching Izzy. She's on the other side of the garden, chatting with a group of girlfriends. She looks rather flushed; I'm not sure if this is down to the sun or the amount of alcohol she's consumed – certainly every time I've seen her she's had a drink in her hand. Despite the physical distance between us, we are still connected. It's as if there's a gossamer strand from her being to mine, a spider-silk tether that I could, if I wanted to, shorten millimetre by millimetre until we were cheek to cheek.

After a couple of hours, the band appears on stage. Feeling a sudden urge to take the weight off my feet, I flop down on one of the checked picnic rugs that have been spread out on the lawn. The band turns out to be rather good, with a broad repertoire that ranges from soul and Motown covers right through to grunge and hard rock.

Pretty soon, people start dancing. I don't usually dance in public, but after four and a half glasses of Prosecco I'm feeling brave, so after a while I get up and join them. As the band breaks into a Nickelback song I absolutely adore, I raise my hands in the air, swaying from side to side, eyes half-closed, totally lost in the music. This has to be one of the best parties I've ever been to. I can't remember the last time I enjoyed myself so much.

When the band finishes its first set to enthusiastic applause, James comes on to the stage and announces that food is being served. I've worked up quite an appetite, so I join the queue at a long trestle table that's groaning with a lavish buffet. Behind it, a man in chef's whites and a blue neckerchief is carving thick slices of meat from a spit roast; it smells divine.

After loading up my plate, I make a beeline for the seating area under the gazebo. The sun is still high in the sky and I'll be glad of some shade. As I scout around for somewhere to sit, I catch one of my fellow guests carelessly sweeping my table centrepiece aside to make room for his plate. Bristling with indignation, I deliberately jog the back of his chair with my hip as I walk past, making him spill his drink.

Just then, I catch sight of Izzy. She's sitting at a table with Marcus, Rafe, Maria and a couple of people I haven't met yet. I start walking towards them, but stop when I realise there are no free seats at their table.

In my peripheral vision, I see Izzy's uncle raise his hand and pat the empty chair next to him. I pretend not to notice and move quickly towards a table at the opposite end of the gazebo. It's occupied by two women, who turn out to be old colleagues of Izzy's from the estate agency – and very entertaining they are too. One of them tells me a funny story about the time Izzy let herself into a property to conduct a scheduled viewing, only to find the male tenant making himself a ham sandwich in the kitchen – *stark naked*.

I'm sure Izzy wasn't fazed in the slightest; in fact, she probably enjoyed the experience. If she liked what she saw, and hadn't been happily married at the time, I daresay she would've propositioned the guy.

I realise, somewhat belatedly, that I'm quite drunk. The alcohol has seeped into my bones, loosening my tongue and softening my limbs. I feel hyper-aware of everything around me: the sound of a plane flying overhead, the smell of lavender, the grass tickling my bare feet (I kicked off my wedges to dance; I must try and remember where I left them). I really ought to drink some water, or I'll have a banging headache later. I look around for one of the servers in their distinctive uniforms. A waitress with blond hair tied in a loose ponytail is clearing plates from the next table, but when I wave to her, she appears not to see me and walks away. Oh well, I think to myself as I raise my wine glass to my lips, more Pinot it is.

After the meal, Eleanor makes a short speech, in which she thanks us all for coming and asks us to raise our glasses in a toast to her 'beautiful and utterly unique' sister. Izzy seems very moved, almost tearful. I watch as she gets up from her seat and goes over to embrace Eleanor, the tension between them forgotten – for now, at least.

15

By the time a long, slow summer dusk, thick with bird-song, starts to fall, the party has thinned out considerably. The celebrations show no sign of ending, however. As the stone walls of the old church start to disappear into shadow, dozens of twinkling LED lights come on. They're wreathed around trees and hanging from the beams of the gazebo, making the garden look quite magical.

I still haven't managed to bag any one-on-one time with Izzy, but when I look around for her she's nowhere to be seen. She must have gone indoors – to use the bathroom perhaps. On impulse, I decide to go and look for her.

Inside the house, the living room lies still and empty. The last remnants of sun are shining through the rose window, the stained glass casting the living room in a kaleidoscope of reds and blues. I pause for a moment, enjoying the sensation of having the place to myself, even though I know that Toby is asleep upstairs. I saw Eleanor carry him off to bed a little while ago, his head lolling and heavy, like a rose on its stalk.

As I make my way to the downstairs loo, I find myself marvelling, yet again, at the way James has managed to preserve the sanctity of this special building, while cre-ating such a family-friendly living space. He really is an incredibly talented man; I hope Eleanor appreciates him as much as I do.

Finding the loo unoccupied, I retrace my steps and head towards the kitchen. It too is empty. I pick a mug up off the draining board and fill it with water from the tap, gulping it down greedily. Izzy must be outside after all. Perhaps she and Rafe have snuck off to enjoy a private moment together. After draining a second mug of water, I decide to rejoin the party. I won't waste any more time looking for my friend; I'll let her have her fun.

I've just reached the French doors when I hear it. A loud, sickening thud that seems to come from everywhere and nowhere. It surrounds me, ricocheting inside my head, filling the air around me. It even silences the birds.

Seconds later, someone starts to scream.

Unsure of what's happening, I step on to the patio. The first person I see is Izzy's university friend, Tess. She's pointing towards the house, at an unlit area of the garden a few metres from where I'm standing. Following the direction of her trembling finger, I see a dark shape lying on the patio. As my eyes adjust to the ambient light, I realise that the shape is a person and they're lying quite motionless, their limbs awkwardly splayed.

Several people start moving towards them, while others, including me, are rooted to the spot. On the other side of the garden, Maria springs from her seat under the gazebo and runs the full length of the garden. The sight of her jolts me into action and I start running too.

By the time I get there, Maria is already on her knees beside the casualty. She's in full-on doctor mode, checking for vital signs. She glances up briefly and asks someone to call an ambulance. I pat the pockets of my dress, thinking that my phone might be in one of them as I was using it to take pictures earlier, but they're empty. I must have left my phone on the table. It's all right though, Marcus is already dialling.

'Who is it?' Katya asks.

Maria tilts the casualty's head back and grabs their chin, pulling it down to open their mouth. 'Izzy.'

A plunge of horror goes through me. The force of it unearths something buried deep inside – a little hard seed of memory. I ball my fists with the effort of trying to push it back down.

All around me people are gasping and crying out. A woman who I'm pretty sure is Izzy's mother collapses to the ground.

'Has she fainted?' someone asks.

One of the waitresses points up at the bell tower that looms above Izzy's crumpled form. The glass roof extension lies in darkness, but a light is on in the second-floor room directly beneath it and both of the casement windows are wide open.

'I think she might have fallen from there.'

Just then, Eleanor appears from the passage next to the house, the one that leads to the side gate.

'What's going on?' she demands to know.

'Izzy's had an accident,' James tells her. He's standing right next to me and yet I've only just registered his presence. His cheeks are strangely flushed as if he's been working out.

'*What?*' she cries, almost sending me flying as she pushes past me. James pulls her back and holds her tightly, pinning her arms to her sides.

'It's OK,' he tells her firmly. 'Maria's giving her first aid.'

First aid, I think to myself. Surely it's obvious to everyone here that we're a long way past that.

As if to prove the point, Maria starts administering CPR, pushing down on Izzy's chest in forceful movements. The tear in my heart deepens, opening into a bloody fissure. The sensation is so vivid that I am genuinely surprised, when I look down, to see my cardigan with its mother of pearl buttons covering my chest.

I cast a furtive glance at Izzy's mother. She hasn't got up off the ground yet and she's being comforted by two other women.

'Does anyone else know CPR?' Maria says, already breathless from her efforts. 'Depending on how long the paramedics take to get here I may need someone else to take over.'

At this, Eleanor, who's still in James's arms, lets out a ragged cry.

Slowly, I start to raise my hand. A couple of years ago, a man at my gym had a heart attack while he was working out and almost died. Afterwards the gym hosted a series of

free 'lifesaver' courses. I signed up for one of them, thinking it might be a good way to meet people. I never thought
I'd actually get a chance to use the skills I learned and,
come to think of it, I'm not confident I can still remember
them. My hand gets to shoulder height when Izzy's uncle
speaks out.

'I do, I used to be a volunteer with the St John's
Ambulance.'

My arm falls back down to my side.

'Good, come and stand next to me,' Maria says. 'I need
you to be ready.' She glances at Marcus, who's still on the
phone to the emergency operator. 'Ask them where the
nearest defibrillator is.'

'There's one outside the library,' says an older man,
who I recognise as the Elliotts' next-door neighbour. 'I'd
offer to go and get it, but I can't drive – I've had too much
to drink.'

Rafe steps forward. 'I'm stone-cold sober; I'll drive if
you can show me the way.'

'Quick as you can,' Maria says tersely. 'The emergency
operator will give you the access code.'

Rafe nods, his face so tense the veins in his forehead
look like they're about to burst.

After that, everything happens very quickly. The ambulance arrives within minutes, even before the others return
with the defibrillator. As Maria hands over to the paramedics, James asks us all, terribly politely, to leave. Even

though there's nothing I can do to help, I'm reluctant to go, desperate to see how this plays out.

As the other guests start making for the French doors, I head in the opposite direction, to the gazebo, to retrieve my mobile phone. As I walk back towards the house I hesitate, watching with a morbid fascination as the paramedics start affixing the sticky pads of their own defibrillator to Izzy's chest. When Eleanor sees me standing there, she gives me a dirty look and makes a shooing motion with her hands. It's clear that my presence is unwelcome.

Once outside the house, I call an Uber and walk up to the main road to wait for it. I'm still there when the ambulance drives past, blue lights flashing and sirens wailing. As I watch it speed away, I can feel the fragile and precious reality I have inhabited since I met Izzy begin to evaporate.

The tears come then. I can't stop them. They spurt up in a rush, spilling out loud and ugly, my whole body shuddering with the force of them, the back of my hand against my mouth to hold back the messy tide of my emotions.

Now

16

'You have a beautiful flat; the light in here's amazing.'

I set two mugs of tea down on the low table between us.

She's right; my home *is* beautiful. I used to love coming back here after a long day at work, but it feels different now. All that wonderful positive energy gone, replaced by an uneasy stillness. I find myself walking softly across the stripped pine floorboards, as if wary of disturbing someone below, even though I know there's no one there. But how do I even begin to explain that to my visitor?

I paste a smile on my face, as if she's an old friend I haven't seen for ages and I'm trying to put a brave face on things. 'Thank you. This room is south facing; it gets bags of natural light. It was a big draw for me when I was looking at places to buy – that and the size of the kitchen. Mind you, I had to rip the whole thing out before I moved in. The previous owner was an elderly gent; I swear some of the appliances were older than he was.'

This makes her laugh a little. 'How long have you lived here?'

'Seven months or so. I came here after my husband died; I felt I needed a change of scene.'

'Too many memories?' she says gently.

I give a small nod. 'Something like that.'

She smooths her skirt across her lap. She's very feminine: softly spoken, shoulder-length hair, nails painted a delicate shell-pink. Not what I was expecting at all.

'Was Amy Mackenzie already living in the ground-floor flat when you moved in?' she asks, indicating that it's time to get down to business.

'That's right. I remember being pleased when the estate agent told me there was another single woman living downstairs. I'd got on very well with the neighbours at my previous home and I hoped the two of us would become friends.'

'And were you?'

I think back to the only two occasions that Amy and I socialised together formally. A few days after I moved in, I knocked on her door and invited her up to mine for coffee. The conversation was strained, even for people who'd only just met, and there was something off about her; something I couldn't quite put my finger on. Then, a month or two later, when the weather was warmer, she asked if I'd like to join her in the garden for a drink. I thought it only fair to give her another chance, but ended up wishing I hadn't. I drank a glass of wine and then, as soon as I felt it was polite to do so, scuttled back to my flat. She asked me round two or three times more, and on another occasion suggested a trip to the cinema. However,

I was always armed with a ready excuse and eventually she stopped asking.

DI Kilner is looking at me expectantly and I have a drink of tea to give myself time to formulate a response. I know *I'm* not the one who stands accused – but still, I don't want to portray myself in an unflattering light.

'We were on friendly terms, but I wouldn't describe us as friends. I did try with her when I first moved in, but it didn't work out.'

'No? Why do you think that was?'

'We just didn't gel. I don't know . . . perhaps it was the age difference, although there are only twelve years between us. I found her quite hard work, to be honest.'

'In what way?' she persists.

I rub a hand along my brow. 'Amy was very guarded; she didn't like talking about herself. It was fine if you asked her about something work-related – I could tell that floristry was something she was very passionate about – but every time I asked her a personal question, even quite an innocuous one, the shutters would come down. In the beginning, I thought it was shyness, but I don't think it was, because she was very assertive in other respects – *aggressively* so at times.'

She picks up her tea, takes a dainty sip. 'Can you think of an example?'

'Uh, give me a second, will you?' This interview is more challenging than I thought it was going to be. It's like sitting the French oral exam, the teacher giving me heavy-handed hints that I need to be more expansive with my answers if I'm going to pass. Thankfully, it doesn't take long before a suitable incident comes to mind.

'She once took a courier to task when she caught her chucking a parcel over the fence, instead of coming up to the door and ringing the bell. I happened to be hoovering the communal hallway at the time; I witnessed the whole thing. Amy was apoplectic – she demanded the girl's name, said she was going to report her. You could see the courier was terrified; she was barely out of her teens. She apologised profusely, but that didn't seem to appease Amy. She was still ranting as the girl got back in her van. When Amy came back in the building, I asked her what was in the parcel, thinking it must be something terribly valuable – or at the very least, fragile.' I shake my head despairingly. 'It was only a set of tea towels, would you believe?'

DI Kilner looks slightly disappointed; I think she was expecting something juicier. 'Anything else?' she enquires hopefully.

Something else rears up in my memory that may be relevant. 'I had a very strange encounter with her on the evening of the August bank holiday – although she wasn't so much aggressive on that occasion as hysterical.'

'Tell me about that,' she says in a coaxing tone.

'I spent the day at the coast with my sister and her family and when I got back, around seven-thirty, I noticed that none of the lights were on in Amy's flat. I naturally assumed she wasn't home. I'd bumped into her in the communal hallway earlier on, when we were both on our way out. I thought she seemed quite different to her usual self.'

'In what way?'

'Very buoyant; almost hyper. Usually when I saw her she was quite . . .' I think for a moment, wanting to be fair to Amy. 'Not dour exactly, just a bit flat.'

'Did you speak to her?'

'Only a few words. She told me she was going to a birthday party for a very good friend of hers. I asked her if it was a breakfast party – it was a tongue-in-cheek comment because it was so early in the morning. She laughed and explained that the party didn't start until much later, but that she was providing the flowers for the event and she had to get there early because it was going to take her a while to arrange them.'

'Did she say anything else about the party?'

'I don't think so. She got in her car then and drove off.'

She nods slowly, absorbing this information. 'And what happened after you got home?'

'I'm not sure exactly what time Amy came back because the sound-proofing between our flats is pretty good – and anyway, I had the TV on – but I must've been home for a couple of hours when I heard this ghastly noise coming from the rear of the building.' I draw the two sides of my cardigan together across my chest, feeling a sudden need to warm myself.

'At first, I thought it was foxes. We've had trouble with them in the past, foraging in the bins and making an awful mess. I went into my bedroom, because the window overlooks the garden and the side of the house, where the bins are kept. That's when I saw her.'

'Amy?'

'Yes. It was starting to get dark but the security light had come on outside – it has a motion sensor – so I could see Amy quite clearly. She was in the middle of the lawn, kneeling in I guess what you'd call a prayer position, with her head touching the ground. Obviously she's entitled to do whatever she likes in the privacy of her own garden, but it did strike me as rather odd. I wondered if perhaps it was some sort of yoga routine, although I'd never seen her do anything like that in the past. Just as I was about to draw the curtains, Amy suddenly lifted her head up and made this dreadful keening sound – the same sound I'd heard a few moments earlier. It was really chilling; I didn't even know it was possible for a human being to make a noise like that. It went on and on and on. Some of the other neighbours must've heard it too because it was loud enough to rouse a corpse.' I give a little shudder to convey the way it made me feel.

'Were you concerned about Amy at that point?'

'*Very* concerned – so much so that I knew I wouldn't be able to relax until I'd checked to see if she was OK.' I look down at my lap. It's only a small lie, and hardly a significant one in the grand scheme of things. The truth was, I seriously considered letting Amy get on with whatever personal crisis she was having and returning to my television programme. I even went back into the living room with that very intention in mind. It was only when I'd sat down and watched a few minutes of TV that I thought better of it. I like to think of myself as a Christian, and in that moment I reminded myself that ignoring someone in their hour of need was hardly Christian behaviour.

'I thought about opening my bedroom window and calling out to her,' I go on. 'But she seemed so distressed, I thought it was best if I went down to the garden. I knew she never locked the side gate, which I always thought was a bit of a mistake from a security point of view. By the time I got to the garden, Amy had stopped the dreadful wailing and she was lying on her side in a foetal position.'

'How did she react when she saw you?'

'She didn't. Not at first. I said her name and asked her if everything was all right, but she didn't reply; she just kept staring blankly ahead.'

'What did you do then?'

'I bent down and touched her on the shoulder and said, "Come on, Amy, let's get you indoors", or words to that effect. It was chilly out there; I could feel it through my fleece top and trousers and she was only wearing a thin summer dress and a short-sleeved cardi.'

'Did she react then?'

'She most certainly did. She showed me her teeth, *bared* them at me, like an animal, and said – and I think I'm quoting verbatim here – "I don't need your help, so piss off, you interfering old cow."' My toes curl as I recall her cutting tone, her sharp little words, burying under my skin like poisonous darts. 'I wasn't going to stay where I wasn't wanted, so I did what she had asked and went back to my flat.'

'Did you see her again that evening?'

'No. I did glance in the garden when I went to bed, around ten-ish, but she was nowhere to be seen. After that, I made up my mind to give her a wide berth, as she was clearly unstable. But then, two or three days later, I opened my front door and found a bunch of flowers lying on the mat. Of course I knew straight away who they were from.'

My mouth softens at the edges as I speak. It was quite a small bouquet, but absolutely gorgeous, one of the nicest I've ever received. It contained flowers I'd never even seen before and their fragrance was heavenly.

'There was a card as well.' Leaning forward, I pull open a drawer in the coffee table. It only takes a few seconds to find what I'm looking for.

'This is it,' I say, holding it up so she can see the word *Sorry* in pink printed letters on the front.

'Did she write anything inside?'

I open the card and read aloud. '*Please forgive my rude behaviour the other night. I'd just had a very traumatic experience and I wasn't in my right mind.* She didn't bother signing it.'

'How did you feel when you read that?'

I give a mental eye roll. First the French oral; now I'm in therapy.

'I was grateful for the apology. It meant I didn't have to keep on avoiding her for fear of another confrontation.'

'Did you and Amy discuss the incident the next time you saw each other?'

'No. I thanked her for the flowers and then we started having a conversation about the spots of mildew that had appeared above the dado rail in the communal hallway. After that our relationship was back to the way it had been: cordial but not close.'

'So you never asked her about the traumatic experience she referenced in the card?'

'I didn't think it was any of my business.'

'You must've been curious, though.' Her eyes are cool and level, with the careful blankness of a poker player.

'I suppose so, but if she'd wanted to talk to me about it, then presumably she would've done.'

DI Kilner hooks her hair behind her ears. 'OK, Janet, I'd like to take you back to three days ago, the twenty-second of September.'

A thin seam of cold opens up in my chest, even though I knew this was coming. Naively, I thought I was going to enjoy it – sharing my recollections, making a useful contribution to the investigation, helping the guilty to be brought to book. But now that the moment's here, I find that I just want it to be over as quickly as possible.

'No doubt you already have some knowledge of what happened that day.'

Oh yes. I've seen the TV news reports, visited the true crime chat rooms, scoured the internet for the gory details (and hated myself for it afterwards). I've had interview requests from journalists pushed through the letterbox and been waylaid by reporters outside my home. To date, I haven't spoken publicly on the matter; I'm not interested in my fifteen seconds of fame.

'An awful lot of what has been said in the media is pure

speculation, so I'd be grateful if you could set all of that aside and just focus on anything that you yourself may have seen or heard.'

'Understood.'

'Did you see much of Amy in the days leading up to the twenty-second? I'm just trying to get a sense of her state of mind during that period.'

'I'd seen her a couple of days earlier, on the Tuesday. I'd just had an Ocado delivery and I'd asked the driver to leave the carrier bags in the hallway. I'd already made one trip upstairs and I was going back down for the rest of my shopping when I saw Amy coming out of her flat. Her hair was all over the place and her skin was very blotchy. She looked so awful I actually thought she might be coming down with something.'

'Did you speak to her?'

'I said hello and asked her where she was off to. She said she was going for a walk because if she stayed in her flat for a moment longer she was going to kill someone.'

DI Kilner rears back on the sofa. 'Those were her exact words?'

'Yes. I didn't think she actually meant them, though. I assumed it was one of those overly dramatic turns of phrase that millennials are so fond of.'

In my mind's eye, I can see Amy's strained expression and her eyes that were hooded and blinking madly. Perhaps if I'd shown more sensitivity, asked her if everything was all right, offered to join her on her walk even, then maybe I could have stopped it from happening.

'I didn't see her again until the morning of the twenty-second,' I go on. 'I was outside, putting some rubbish in the outside bin, when she came running out of the house. She flew past me without saying a word and jumped in her car. Her face was flushed and she seemed rather agitated.'

'Did you notice if she was carrying anything?'

I exhale softly. I think I know what DI Kilner means. A weapon. Was Amy carrying a *weapon*?

'Just her mobile phone, I think, although she did have a jacket on and it's possible there was something in the pocket. She drove off at high speed and that was the last time I saw her.' I pluck at a loose thread on the arm of my chair. 'Would it be all right if I asked *you* a question, DI Kilner? Only there's something I'd really like to know.'

'Go ahead. I might not be able to answer it, mind you. As you'll appreciate, this is an ongoing investigation and there are some things I can't disclose.'

'Of course.' I gird myself before I say the words, preparing for the worst.

'Amy . . . is she still alive?'

Two Weeks Earlier

17

Ten days have passed since Izzy's birthday party and I'm still trying to make sense of what happened. One minute I was having the time of my life, the next my whole world was pulled out from under me. There was no proximity alert, no warning sign; no time to brace or cover my eyes.

When I arrived home I was in quite a state – and it wasn't just shock that I felt, but something with a harder burn. A dirty feeling of shame and guilt.

After getting out of the Uber, I didn't go into my flat. What was the point when there was no one there to console me? I went to the garden, to be among the plants I have nurtured so lovingly they almost feel like friends. Bits of me were flapping about and I needed to gather the edges back together, sew up all the seams.

I kneeled down on the lawn and rested my forehead on the ground in a futile prayer. I wanted the earth to be absorbed into my body and replace me, molecule by molecule. If I couldn't be replaced, I wanted to dissolve and be washed away by the next rain shower.

Of course, neither of those things occurred. What happened instead was that Janet from upstairs came out to ask, not unreasonably, what the fuck was I doing – except she put it rather more kindly than that. Having taken me by surprise, she got caught in the crossfire of my emotions. I did apologise with some flowers a couple of days later, but I daresay she'll be avoiding me from now on.

It was nearly midnight when I finally let myself into the flat. I had a hot shower and went to bed. It took me ages to get to sleep and when I finally did, I slipped into an exhausting dream where I was trapped in an endless, illogical series of tasks. In one of them, I was lost in a maze where all the walls were made of steel. Every time I thought I'd found a way out, a shutter would come down, cutting off my escape route. I think my subconscious mind was trying to tell me something, but I didn't have the mental bandwidth to work out what it was.

When I woke up the next morning, the first thing I did was send Maria a text: *Any update on Izzy?*

I wasn't stupid, I knew it was touch and go – I'd seen her crushed skull and the crimson pool around her head – but I still had a crumb of hope.

That hope was dashed when Maria's brief reply came through: *So sorry Amy, I'm afraid she didn't make it.*

At the risk of sounding cruel, perhaps it was for the best. As Maria explained to me, even if Izzy had survived, she would've been severely brain damaged and unable to communicate. What sort of life would that have been for someone like Izzy – someone so vibrant and energetic?

Maria and I have kept in contact and I'm grateful to her for keeping me in the loop. She was the one who told me the police were interviewing everyone who'd been at the house that night. I was glad of the heads-up and by the time a pleasant young PC came to see me, my story was well rehearsed.

'Did you notice any changes in Izzy just before she died?' he wanted to know.

'I hadn't seen her for a couple of weeks beforehand,' I told him. 'Not since a friend's dinner party.'

'How did she seem?' he probed.

'Her usual self. Funny, lively, gregarious.'

'She wasn't down or out of sorts then?'

Of course, I knew full well what he was driving at. 'Not in the slightest. She had a bit of a moan about her ex-husband – apparently he was refusing to hand over some artwork that she said belonged to her, but I would never have described her as suicidal, or even mildly depressed.'

I thought it prudent to add a caveat. 'To be fair I hadn't known Izzy for very long. I'm not so naive to think I was privy to all of her innermost thoughts and it's quite possible there were things she'd chosen to keep from me.'

'Can you think of any reason she might have gone to the bell tower?' he asked me a little later.

My ears pricked up when I heard that. 'So it's true,' I said. 'She did fall from the window.'

He nodded a yes.

'But how can you be sure?' I needed to know if it was

one of those 'balance of probabilities' scenarios, or if they had actual proof.

'The forensics don't lie,' was all he would say.

He had a few more questions about the day of the party, but I wasn't able to offer much in the way of insight, except to point out that Izzy had drunk a considerable amount of alcohol that evening and the last time I remembered seeing her she'd been noticeably unsteady on her feet.

I asked the officer a few carefully worded questions of my own, hoping to get a steer on where the investigation was heading. Annoyingly, he wasn't giving anything away. Neither are the Elliotts.

As soon as I found out Izzy had died, I sent James and Eleanor a sympathy card and a beautiful mixed bouquet in muted colours. When that failed to elicit a response – even a simple thank you – I sent Eleanor a text, asking if there was anything I could do to help. She didn't respond, which I guess is understandable; the poor woman must be in bits.

I was hoping to get the chance to speak to James in person when I made my regular delivery to his office, but there was no sign of him. The receptionist told me he was on compassionate leave and had yet to provide a date for his return.

I did think about taking a few days off work myself, but I was worried Claire and Ewan wouldn't be able to cope on their own. I told them what happened and they've both been very kind and understanding. Claire, in particular, has really put herself out – offering to come in on her day off and telling me that if I ever want to talk to someone, she's there for me. I doubt I'll take her up on it. Izzy's death is a deeply personal matter and not something I want to discuss with someone who never even met her, but it was still nice of Claire to offer.

I'm grateful that today it's been so busy in the shop I haven't had any time to dwell on Izzy. First, I had to do a rush order of table flowers for a restaurant who'd been let down by their regular supplier. Then Claire went home early because she wasn't feeling well, meaning I had to abandon the paperwork I was catching up with in the studio and work front of house. Usually, I enjoy helping customers make their selections, but today I was unenthusiastic and lacking in energy. I hope I haven't caught whatever it is Claire's got.

I'm locking up at the end of what has felt like a *very* long day when my phone pings. Wrestling it free of my apron pocket, I find a text from Maria. She wants to know if I'm free for a drink this evening. I'd love to see her, but I'm absolutely shattered. When I ask if we can make it another time, her reply comes back straight away: *Please Amy, it's important.* Thinking there might have been a new development in Izzy's case, I agree to meet her in an hour's time at a wine bar in Blackheath Village, not far from her surgery.

When I arrive she's already there, sitting at a table in the corner, a glass of red wine half-drunk on the table in front of her. She stands up to greet me, but when we hug, her body feels stiff and unyielding.

I sit down and ask her how she is.

'I'm coping – just about,' she says, her chin buckling slightly. 'Most of the time I feel as if I'm just going through the motions.'

'Same here,' I tell her. 'It still doesn't seem real. I keep looking at my phone, expecting to see a missed call from Izzy. The worst thing is not knowing what happened – how she ended up falling through that window.' I break off to order a glass of sparkling water from a passing waitress. 'I wish I could've been more helpful when the police came to see me. I racked my brains for anything that might have been remotely relevant, but there really wasn't much I could tell them.'

'You didn't see anything when you were in the house, then?'

Everything goes very quiet and still inside my head. 'What do you mean?'

'Marcus said he saw you coming out of the house; right after Izzy fell.'

'He can't have done. I mean, I *was* in the house just beforehand – I'd nipped in to get a drink of water – but when she actually fell I was standing outside. I remember the awful sound of her body landing on the patio.'

Even as the words leave my lips, I'm already doubting myself. The truth is, the minutes leading up to Izzy's death are a bit foggy – a combination of post-traumatic stress and the fact I'd had a lot to drink myself.

'Whatever,' says Maria, a tad impatiently. 'The point is you might have seen Izzy while you were in the house.'

'No, I'm guessing she was already in the bell tower by that point.'

Maria fixes me with a stern look, the one she probably reserves for patients who have been neglecting to take their medication. 'Did you see anyone else?'

'No.' I'm silent for a few moments, trying to gauge what she's thinking. 'Are you saying you don't think Izzy's fall was an accident?'

'I don't know, but it's certainly a possibility – and one I'm sure the police are looking into. I mean, what was Izzy even doing in the bell tower? You know how she loved to be the centre of attention; why would she suddenly decide to sneak off to a little-used guest bedroom without telling anyone?'

'Perhaps she popped in there to change, or freshen her make-up.'

'What – and then she opened the window for a bit of fresh air and accidentally fell out?' I can hear the note of challenge in her voice.

'Don't forget, Izzy *was* pretty drunk that night.'

'We all were,' she sighs. 'That's the problem – nobody's memory is a hundred percent reliable when they're intoxicated.'

The waitress arrives with my water and Maria orders a second glass of wine. Keen to hear the latest on Izzy's case, I give her a gentle prompt.

'Have you heard from Eleanor lately?'

'Yes, we're in contact almost every day. She's doing remarkably well . . . considering.'

'That's good to hear.' I wait a few seconds, but she doesn't volunteer any more information. 'Has there been an update from the coroner's office?'

'They haven't found any evidence to indicate that Izzy committed suicide. That's as much as I know.'

'So how does that impact on the police investigation?'

Maria gives me a half-raised eyebrow as if she finds my questions unseemly. I can't think why – my curiosity is perfectly natural when you consider how close I was to Izzy.

'I suppose it means they're exploring other theories.'

She clamps her lips together, unwilling to elaborate. Whatever she wanted to talk to me about, it clearly isn't Izzy.

In an attempt to shift the focus on to a more cheerful subject, I enquire about her son, Jake, who I know has recently started school. Maria's reply is oddly stilted and the ensuing conversation is awkward, sticking in our throats like the bowl of complimentary nuts that came with Maria's wine. Nervous energy radiates from her like static. I sense she's feeling uncomfortable, I just don't know why.

'What's wrong?' I ask her after a while. 'I mean, apart from the fact you've just lost one of your best friends. You seem a little on edge.'

She bites her lip, takes a breath. 'Actually, there is something I wanted to address with you.'

'O-K,' I say slowly, noting the formal language.

She pushes her wine glass to the side and rests her forearms on the table, hands folded as if in prayer. I imagine it's the same pose she uses when she's preparing to deliver bad news to a patient.

'I went round to see Eleanor yesterday. She wanted to talk to me about Izzy's funeral.'

'Are you helping with the planning?'

'No, but Eleanor's asked me to deliver one of the eulogies.'

'That's nice. Has a date been set for the funeral, then?'

'Yes,' she says – but doesn't tell me when it is.

Another red flag.

'While I was with her, Eleanor said something that I found very troubling.' She sucks her cheeks in. 'I won't beat around the bush – she thinks you're having an affair with James.'

My disbelief catches in my chest like something I need to cough up. 'What?' I splutter.

'She knows about your secret rendezvous. She found a receipt in James's jacket pocket when she was taking his suit to the dry cleaner's. It showed that he'd bought lunch for someone at the café next door to your shop. Eleanor put two and two together.'

'And came up with five,' I say indignantly.

She frowns. 'So you *didn't* have lunch with James?'

My cheeks flare, even though I've done nothing wrong. 'No, we did have lunch together, three or four weeks ago, but I can assure you there was nothing secret about it. James was in the area on business and he popped in to the shop to discuss the arrangements for Izzy's party. We spent a total of forty-five minutes in each other's company and both of us remained fully clothed throughout.'

Judging by the look on Maria's face, my attempt at a joke has fallen flat.

'So why didn't he mention it to Eleanor?'

'No idea. Do *you* tell Marcus every time you talk to a member of the opposite sex?'

I feel the fierce, hard heat of her gaze. 'So you're denying it then – the affair?'

'Of course I'm bloody denying it!' A couple at the next table stop talking and turn round to stare at me. I lower my voice. 'And I'm sure James has denied it too.'

'Eleanor hasn't asked him about it.'

'Why not? If she thinks she has evidence her husband's cheating on her, then surely she'd want to confront him with it.'

'She'd only just found the receipt when I went round there. I could see she was upset the minute I arrived, but I thought it was because of Izzy. When I went to give her a hug, she broke down and the whole thing came spilling out.' She pauses, takes a sip of wine. 'I must admit, I was a little surprised she was so willing to confide in me when we hardly know each other. I'm guessing she just couldn't hold it in any longer.'

I press a hand to my forehead. I can't believe what I'm hearing. I know Eleanor must be out of her mind with grief – not sleeping properly, unable to think straight – but this . . . this is utterly ludicrous. Any rational person would think the same. So why is Maria looking at me like I'm a spillage someone has forgotten to clear up?'

'C'mon, Maria, you can't seriously think I'm sleeping with James.' I spread my arms wide. 'I mean, look at me. Do you think for one second a man like him would be interested in someone like me?'

There is a long see-sawing moment.

'No,' she says at last. 'No, I don't.'

Her words are a barb, grazing the thin membrane of my confidence. Still, I'm grateful for her honesty. I break into a relieved smile.

She doesn't smile back, shifts awkwardly in her chair.

The evening suddenly feels ruined, as if oil has seeped into the clean water of the river and slicked the feathers of all the ducks until they drowned. It's a familiar feeling, since I am well practised in ruining things. If ever I'm feeling at a low ebb, my mind will pounce, dragging me backwards through the rubble of my life. I scramble and flail, clawing my way through the scree back up to the top of the mountain, but the views on the way down are horrific.

'I hope you assured Eleanor her suspicions were entirely without merit.'

'I told her it was highly unlikely, but she didn't seem wholly convinced.'

'Did she ask you to have it out with me?'

'No, that was my decision. I wanted to hear your side of the story.'

'Well, now you have it,' I say primly.

I take a sip of water, wishing it was something stronger. 'I was thinking,' I say, desperate to salvage something from the evening. 'Perhaps I could help you with your eulogy.

I didn't know Izzy as well as you, obviously, but I have one or two anecdotes you might want to incorporate.'

She makes a meaningless little sound in the back of her throat. 'I'm not sure, Amy. I don't think Eleanor would like that.'

'Fine,' I say and regret it as soon as I hear the sharp way in which it issues from my mouth.

We stare at each other wordlessly for a few seconds. It's as if some pivot has shifted between us, some relentless mechanism that is moving us slowly apart.

Maria reaches across the table but her hand stops short of my own. 'I hope you'll be OK, Amy,' she says and it feels like a goodbye. There's a softness in her face, but something hard and metallic behind her eyes.

She picks up her glass and drains what's left of her wine. 'I really need to get going now; I promised the kids I'd be home in time to read them a bedtime story.'

When I get back to my flat, I find I can't settle. There's a sour taste pooling on my tongue and a hot, hollow spot under my ribs. I make some cheese on toast, eat a couple of mouthfuls and throw the rest in the bin, realising I've completely lost my appetite. I sit down on the sofa and stare into space for a while, as my mind works back over what Maria said.

I can't figure out why Eleanor is so convinced I'm sleeping with James. A receipt for two sandwiches is hardly a smoking gun. I cast my mind back, trying to recall any occasion when she might have seen us together – if perhaps there was something in my behaviour or body language that gave away my undeniable attraction to him. There was the brief conversation we had in the garden on the morning of the party, but Eleanor was in the house. Even if she'd been watching us from a window I don't think she'd have seen anything that raised her hackles. Later, when the band was playing their second set, James came and danced with me – but then again, he danced with lots of female guests.

I'm not denying that over the years I've had many sexual fantasies about James – some of them quite torrid. But I'd never have an affair with him, or any other married man. I get that Eleanor doesn't know me very well, but even if she doesn't trust me, surely she trusts her own husband. But then again, if she trusted James, she wouldn't have suspected him of cheating in the first place.

Eventually, my brain grows weary of thinking about it. I open my laptop and scroll through a few websites, trying to distract myself with mindless videos of animals doing funny things and people falling off skateboards and almost castrating themselves in the process. Then, almost without realising I'm doing it, I'm logging in to Facebook.

I've gone to Izzy's page several times since her death, to read the dozens of tributes left by her distraught friends, each word raking across my skin like my own personal form of flagellation. I haven't contributed anything myself, unable to find the right words. It occurs to me now that this might have made me seem rather uncaring. I really ought to write something, however clumsy or mawkish.

I think for a few moments, fingers poised above the keyboard. Then I start typing.

> *A true friend is never truly gone. Their spirit lives on in the memories of those who loved them – and I count myself extremely lucky to have made so many happy memories with Izzy in the short time I knew her.*

Pleased with what I've written, I slide the laptop on to the sofa beside me and reach for the TV remote. I flick through the programme guide, eventually selecting a nature documentary. I'm totally absorbed by the sight of a Siberian tiger crunching his way through a snowy forest when I hear a sound from my laptop, signalling a Facebook notification.

Glancing at the screen, I'm surprised to see that someone has commented on my post already. Assuming that one of Izzy's friends has been moved by my words, my first reaction is one of gratification. But then, when I read what they've written, my blood turns to ice.

> ***Amy Mackenzie*** *Enough of your fake sentiments about my sister. When are you going to stop pretending and tell the truth about what happened at the party?*

Eleanor's words hit me like a spray of bullets: one at a time but in rapid succession, each one compounding the pain of the previous hit. I slam my laptop shut, as if by removing the post from my field of vision I can make it disappear.

I get up off the sofa and start pacing round the room. I can feel myself growing warm, not from the movement, but from the steady beat of fear inside me as the implication of Eleanor's words hits home.

First she accuses me of seducing her husband and now, unless I'm reading this all wrong, she's implying I know more about Izzy's death than I'm letting on.

Another chirp. Someone else has commented on my post. I glance at my laptop. Part of me doesn't want to read it, in case it's Eleanor spewing more bile, but I can't just ignore it. If people are talking about me, I need to know what they're saying.

I return to the sofa and open my laptop. It's not Eleanor; it's Tess, Amy's old university friend.

*OMG!! Are you serious, **Eleanor Elliott**? Do you really think **Amy Mackenzie** had something to do with Izzy's accident?*

So it isn't just me who thinks Eleanor's pointing the finger. I'm still digesting Tess's post, when Eleanor's reply pops up.

*I don't think this is an appropriate forum to air my views on the subject. Let's just say that **Amy Mackenzie** isn't who people think she is.*

I stumble backwards, catching my heel painfully on the coffee table. It feels as though the ground beneath me is beginning to open, revealing a vast sinkhole that's been there the whole time. Eleanor is out to get me. If I didn't know it after my meeting with Maria, I know it now.

Fury rises in me, filling me to the brim.

It makes me want to lash out.

Hurt someone.

18

Ewan comes over to the workbench. 'I know you didn't ask, but I thought I'd make you one anyway,' he says, putting a mug of tea down in front of me.

Mumbling a thanks, I continue scrolling through the sales records I downloaded earlier from Darling Buds' website.

'How are you doing?' he says, pulling out a stool.

'Not bad,' I reply, too absorbed in my task to really stop and think about it.

He takes a slurp from his own mug of tea. 'Is there a date for the funeral yet?'

I realise then that his previous question was less of a general enquiry and more of a desire to know how I'm coping in the wake of Izzy's death.

'It's next Thursday,' I tell him, glancing up from my laptop. 'We're doing the flowers for the after-party.'

Hurtfully, I haven't been invited to the funeral, but yesterday I received a phone call from James's PA, Rachel, asking if Darling Buds could provide the flowers for Izzy's wake. The request confused me at first, because clearly I've fallen out of favour with the Elliotts – a fact I would have expected any half-decent PA to know. But then Rachel mentioned she was only a temp, filling in while James's regular assistant was on a training course. My heart quickened when I heard that. It's an unexpected stroke of good fortune and one which, with a bit of imagination, can surely be wielded to my advantage.

'Mr and Mrs Elliott have their hands full with the funeral, so I've been drafted in to help with the arrangements for the wake,' Rachel explained. 'I know you do the office flowers, so I figured you'd be a safe pair of hands.'

I didn't disagree with her.

The wake is being held at The Sanctuary. A simple affair, Rachel said, just finger food and a few cases of good wine. She added, rather indiscreetly I thought, that the Elliotts were well aware that staging the wake at the house where Izzy had sustained her fatal injuries might be considered in bad taste by some. However, her accident had garnered unwelcome publicity (let's face it, it's a good story: 'Beautiful sister-in-law of millionaire architect dies in fall from church bell tower') and due to concerns about media intrusion, the couple had decided that a public venue was best avoided. They're probably right. I know from first-hand experience that journalists are a persistent bunch, especially the tabloid variety.

'As far as the flowers go, I don't think we want anything too showy or elaborate,' Rachel said. 'Just a couple of simple bouquets. They'd need to be delivered to the house on the morning of the funeral. Would that be all right?'

A more principled person would doubtless have pretended they had no availability and recommended some alternative florists. Suffice to say I am not that person.

Instead, I told Rachel I'd be delighted to do the flowers. I even offered to pop in to Cole & Elliott with my portfolio, so she could pick out some suitable arrangements. Our meeting is scheduled for later on today and, with James still on compassionate leave, there's zero chance of running into him.

I pick up my mug of tea and take a sip. It's too hot, so I put it back down again.

'Can I ask you something, Ewan?' I say.

'Sure, boss.'

I turn back to my laptop, scrolling up the page until I locate the sales record I highlighted earlier.

'Do you remember making this delivery?' I turn the screen towards him. 'March twenty-eighth. A Rhapsody in Pink bouquet, delivered to a Miss Victoria Williams in Bermondsey.' I point to the screen. 'That's the address.'

What I don't tell him is that the bouquet was ordered from Darling Buds' website by James Elliott. While James always chooses his wife's flowers in person, none of the other beneficiaries of his floral favours have received such personal treatment. Most of his online purchases have been gifts for members of his family. I know this because either their name was Elliott too, or the personalised message made it obvious – there'd be a reference to 'Darling Granny', or 'My favourite aunt'. But a couple of times James's relationship to the recipient hasn't been clear. Those are the purchases I'm interested in – the most recent being the bouquet for Victoria. A romantic confection of Cafe Latte roses, asclepias, limonium and phlox, the

Rhapsody in Pink bouquet is one of Darling Buds' best sellers. The message that accompanied it was disappointingly anodyne: *Happy Birthday, Vicki, may your day be as wonderful as you are, love James.*

If Victoria was a relative or a family friend, then presumably James would have gifted the flowers from Eleanor as well. There's a possibility she's a business contact – however, if that was the case, wouldn't James have sent the flowers to her place of work, rather than her home address? That doesn't leave many other options. It's a small but intriguing mystery and one I'm very much hoping Ewan can help me solve.

After reading the address he shakes his head. 'Sorry, I've done a ton of deliveries in Bermondsey over the past few months and this one isn't ringing any bells.'

Disheartened, I let out a puff of air. Then I remember something.

'But you would've taken a photo – wouldn't you?'

'Yeah, I always do.'

The photos were a thing I introduced at the beginning of last year. We had some issues when Ewan's predecessor, Davey, was in the job – a handful of customers complaining that their flowers hadn't arrived and asking for their money back. Davey always insisted the orders had been properly delivered, so either the customers were lying, or Davey had broken one of my cardinal rules and left the bouquets lying unattended on the doorstep, where they could easily have been stolen.

After that, I got him to take a photo every time a delivery was made. It had to show the flowers in an open doorway – either at the addressee's home or, if they were out, at a neighbour's. There weren't any more complaints after that, and when Ewan took over I asked him to do the same.

'Do you still have it?' I ask him.

'I'm not sure. I might have deleted it; I don't tend to keep the photos for more than a couple of months; they take up too much memory.'

'Do you mind checking for me?'

He pulls his phone out of his jeans pocket and spends a couple of minutes prodding and swiping the screen. 'What was that date again?' he asks.

'The twenty-eighth of March.'

'Yep, found her,' he says eventually, pushing his phone across the workbench. I look down at the screen. The photo shows a young woman in her early twenties, wearing a short nightie and furry bootee slippers. She's slim and pretty with a sheet of silky blond hair.

'I remember her now. It was my first delivery of the day and she took ages to answer the door; I'm pretty sure I got her out of bed.'

I touch the screen to enlarge the image. 'I wish I looked like that first thing in the morning.'

Ewan laughs softly. 'I'm sure you look just fine.'

I study the photo, hunting for clues. The woman doesn't look at all self-conscious about being snapped in her nightwear, clutching a bouquet of flowers. Behind her, I can see a laminate floor extending into a living room that looks a little untidy. To her right is a console table – quite a basic piece, the sort of thing you'd get in Ikea – and above it a film poster in a simple acrylic frame.

I hand the phone back to Ewan. 'Can you send this to me?'

He touches the screen. 'Done. Why are you so interested in this woman anyway?'

'It's a long story.' I turn back to my laptop. 'Thanks for the tea, Ewan, but I mustn't keep you from your deliveries.'

While Ewan busies himself loading the van, I navigate to the second of James's online purchases that caught my eye. It dates back to May of last year, when Davey was still doing the deliveries. Even in the unlikely event he still has the photo, we didn't exactly part on the best of terms so there's no point reaching out to him.

The recipient on that occasion was Miss Milli Nye-Browne. The bouquet – another Rhapsody in Pink – was sent to a residential address in Wandsworth and accompanied by an enigmatic message: *Just because . . . J x.*

With a name as distinctive as that it doesn't take me long to find Milli's Insta – an envy-inducing chequerboard of outdoor yoga, pristine flat lays of luggage and a rescue bulldog who balances treats on his nose. Milli is a tall, elegant brunette, who looks a similar age to Victoria.

She's in a relationship with someone called Guy who has a Mercedes convertible and a penchant for premium knitwear. I keep scrolling, hoping to see a picture of James, but there isn't one.

I head back to Google to see if I can find Victoria's social media. Her name is frighteningly common, however, and since I don't have ten hours to spare sifting through all the possibilities, I decide to call a temporary halt to my investigations.

I'm not sure where I'm going with this. I just know I can't stand by while Eleanor tosses out wild accusations that could seriously impact my professional, as well as my personal, reputation. What I find especially hurtful is the fact that, three and a half days after she posted her vile slur, I still haven't heard a peep from James. He's friends with Izzy on Facebook, so I assume he's read his wife's posts. Why hasn't he contacted me to offer reassurance; to let me know he's put Eleanor straight about the purely platonic nature of our relationship? Unless, of course, he and Eleanor are acting in concert to try and smear me. It's an unsettling notion, but one I'd be stupid not to give serious consideration to.

I definitely think there's something a bit phoney . . . a bit staged about this whole situation. First, Eleanor discusses her fears that James and I are having an affair with Maria – a woman she's met less than half a dozen times. Then she broadcasts her suspicions on social media. I know she's not the first person to air a grievance online, but still, it seems grossly out of character for an upper middle-class woman like Eleanor to wash her dirty linen in public. If she genuinely believes I had a hand in Izzy's death, why isn't she heading straight to the police, or to the highly paid solicitor she no doubt has on retainer? The more I think about it, the more this whole thing feels like a set-up.

But why would the Elliotts want to blacken my name? The most likely explanation is that they're trying to deflect suspicion away from themselves. Which means – and the thought is utterly horrific – that one, or potentially both of them, were responsible for what happened to Izzy. But if that *is* the case, how do I even begin to go about proving it?

Last night, when I was lying in bed, I had a flashback to the dinner party at Maria's, specifically the conversation I had with Rafe about science and problem-solving. Rather than agonising over the big question – namely, how did Izzy come to fall from the bell tower window? – I need to start small. Use the resources I already have at my disposal. Build the jigsaw, starting at the edges, and work my way methodically towards the centre. And then, if I'm lucky, the big mystery will reveal itself.

The first task I've set myself is to find out as much about Eleanor and James as I can. There's surprisingly little about them online. Just their respective social media accounts, James's LinkedIn and a handful of articles in architectural digests, none of which hints at any reason they might have had for wanting to harm Izzy. While Eleanor might have disapproved of some of her sister's lifestyle choices, it seems an unlikely motive for murder – especially as they seemed to be getting along so well at the party. That's why I'm focusing on James instead.

For the next few hours I push the Elliotts to the back of my mind, freeing up space to concentrate on the bridal bouquet I need to complete for tomorrow's wedding. The time simply flies by, the way it always does when I'm working with flowers, and before I know it, it's time to head out to my appointment with James's PA.

When I arrive at Cole & Elliott, the receptionist (I'm pleased to see it's the nicer half of the job-share this time) tells me Rachel's taking dictation with one of the junior associates and will be with me very shortly. Setting my portfolio down on a chair, I wander round the generous reception area, admiring the framed photographs that line every wall. Most appear to have been taken at prestigious industry awards ceremonies. Everyone's in evening attire and grinning for the camera, flushed with success after scooping yet another accolade for the firm. One picture in particular catches my eye. James is centre stage. He's holding an etched glass award and flanked by a dozen or so of his co-workers. I squint at the caption: *Cole & Elliott. Winner of Abode Magazine's Sustainable Small Home of the Year (London & the South East)*. It's an impressive achievement; no wonder James looks so smug.

My attention turns to his colleagues. I spot the woman I've just been talking to, barely recognisable in a floor-skimming gown. The firm's other receptionist is there too – the one with the attitude. She's posing with her right leg thrust forward, hands on her hips, like it's all about her. I derive a stupid amount of satisfaction from the fact I can see the bottom of her Spanx through the thigh-length slit in her dress.

Standing on James's other side is Adam Cole in a conservative black tux (I'm pleased to see he's trimmed his problematic nasal hair for the occasion). He's shoulder to shoulder with a pretty young woman in a form-fitting asymmetric dress.

Frowning slightly, my hand reaches for the zip on my messenger bag. I pull out my phone and go to my text messages, quickly finding what I'm looking for. As I look from the screen back up to the photo on the wall, my lips form a tight little smile.

It's her. Victoria Williams. She's one of James's employees.

It's strange that he chose to send the flowers to her home address and not to the office. I wonder if he had to go through her personnel file to find out where she lived. As an employer myself, I know there are strict regulations governing the use of people's personal information and I'm pretty sure that sending them flowers on their birthday doesn't qualify as a reasonable justification. I look over my shoulder to the receptionist.

'I can't believe how many awards you guys have won.'

'Impressive, isn't it?' she says, coming out from behind the desk. 'We have an amazing pool of talent at Cole & Elliott; it's part of the reason I enjoy working here so much.'

I let my gaze wander over the photos. 'I bet those award ceremonies are great fun, aren't they?'

'Absolutely,' she says, walking over to me. 'It's the only time these days I get to wear my glad rags.' She points to a picture on the top row. 'That's me, in the silver dress. My husband nearly had a heart attack when he found out how much it cost.'

'I'd say it was worth every penny; you look absolutely stunning,' I gush, laying it on thick. 'All of you ladies do.' I point to the photo of Victoria. 'I love this woman's dress; I've actually been looking for something similar myself.' I pat my waistline. 'Not for me; I'd look like an over-stuffed sausage in that. It's for my niece – a graduation present.' I let my head list to the right. 'I don't suppose your colleague's in the office now, is she? Only I wouldn't mind asking her where she got it.'

'Sorry, Victoria doesn't work here any more. She's an architecture student; she did a three-month internship with us in the spring.' She smiles. 'James is very good at nurturing upcoming talent. We get dozens of applicants for our internship programme, far more than we can possibly accommodate. James is very hands-on in the selection process; he insists on interviewing the shortlisted candidates personally.'

'Is that so?' The wheels in my brain spin, drawing me

ever closer to the one conclusion I didn't want to reach – even though, when I think about it, it was obvious from the get-go.

'Wasn't Milli Nye-Browne an intern here too?' I say casually.

She looks at me in surprise. 'That's right. Milli was in last year's intake. Why, do you know her?'

'Not personally, but her mother's one of my customers. She happened to mention that Milli had done a work placement at Cole & Elliott when we were chatting in the shop recently.'

The receptionist frowns. 'I'm sure Milli said her mother lived in France.'

'She did for a time, but she's back in the UK now.' I turn back to the wall. 'Is Milli in any of these?'

'She should be here somewhere, let's see . . . ah yes, there she is.'

She indicates a picture I haven't had a chance to scrutinise. There are six people in shot. Adam is in the centre, holding a pyramid-shaped trophy. To his right are two older colleagues. To his left are James and Milli, who I recognise from her Instagram. Despite her sophisticated off-the-shoulder dress and spike-heeled sandals, she looks very young. *Too* young.

I notice that everyone in the picture is looking straight ahead. Everyone except Milli, that is. She's not looking at the camera, or even at Adam. She's looking at James. There's an electric shimmer to her eyes, a kind of ravenous admiration. Her glazed pink lips are slightly parted and I can see the cavity of her mouth, dark and moist.

I'm not usually a betting woman, but I'd put money on the fact that when this photograph was taken, Milli and James were having a sexual relationship.

I turn my head towards the receptionist, wondering if she sees what I see. Her expression gives nothing away. Even if she knows that her boss has been gorging himself on a rolling buffet of interns – young, beautiful, impressionable women who would be easy prey for someone as charming and well connected as James – I bet she'd never tell. What loyal employee would?

Before I can fully process the implications of my discovery, a middle-aged woman emerges from a nearby office.

'You must be Amy,' she says. 'I'm Rachel. I'm so sorry to have kept you waiting.'

I take the hand she's offering. 'No need to apologise. Actually, you've done me a favour.'

'Oh?' she says, peering over the top of her half-moon glasses.

'You've given me a chance to check out this fine rogues' gallery.' I give a cool half-smile. 'It really has been eye-opening.'

Rachel proves to be refreshingly decisive when it comes to making her floral selections. A mere half an hour later I'm driving back to the shop, chewing over what I've just learned. Although there's no concrete proof, the circumstantial evidence suggests James was engaged in inappropriate relationships with at least two of his interns – and odds are, there were others before them.

Even though it wasn't me he cheated on, I still feel hurt and angry. James has betrayed his wife and taken advantage of at least two young women. It doesn't matter if Milli and Victoria were willing participants; he still abused his position of power.

Then there's the question of how he managed to dupe me. Make me believe he was the perfect man: respectful, kind, scrupled, when really he was anything but. And to think he had the gall to use Darling Buds to facilitate his grubby dealings!

It's like looking into the still waters of a lake. One minute you have the perfect view, right down to the bottom, but then something stirs the silt and all of a sudden the water turns dark and putrid.

My mind returns to the jigsaw I'm trying to build. How do all the pieces fit together? James's affairs, Izzy's death, Eleanor's clumsy attempt to implicate me. By the time I pull up outside the shop, a plausible theory is starting to take shape. What if the tension between the two sisters wasn't just down to Izzy's drinking or her self-absorption, but something darker, more destructive? What if Izzy and James were having an affair?

I don't think it's too much of a stretch – not when you take into account James's wandering eye and Izzy's tendency to flirt with every man who entered her field of vision. And now that I think back, didn't Eleanor half-hint at it, the first time we met, when she described how Izzy was always her best self whenever James was in the room? I don't think for one second she knew for sure (what woman throws a birthday party for her husband's mistress?) – but perhaps she had a vague suspicion. A suspicion that quickly took root, wrapping itself around her entrails like poison ivy. And while Eleanor might have been able to tolerate James's indiscretions at work, a relationship with her own sister would require swift and decisive action.

It might not be the case that she *meant* to kill Izzy. It could have been an accident, an argument that got out of hand. Perhaps Eleanor saw something at the party, something she didn't like. It could've been quite innocuous – an intimate look between her husband and sister – or something much more incriminating. She took Izzy into the house to have it out with her. The bell tower would be the perfect place – out of earshot of a sleeping Toby, or any guest who ventured into the main body of the house. The conversation quickly became heated. A furious Eleanor gave Izzy a shove, whereupon her drunken sister stumbled backwards, toppling through the open window on to the unforgiving paving slabs below.

Although some of my recollections from that evening are a little hazy, one thing I do know is that Eleanor wasn't in the garden with the rest of the guests when Izzy fell. I distinctly remember seeing her appear from the side of the house a couple of minutes later – certainly enough time for her to come back downstairs, let herself out through the front door and re-enter the garden via the side gate. She appeared to be bewildered, wanting to know why everyone was gathered around the patio with shocked looks on their faces. Could she really be that good an actress? After the disgusting way she's behaved towards me, I wouldn't put anything past that woman. I've long believed there is a latent violence in every human being. It lies in the dark folds inside us, waiting for something to draw it out into the light. Why should Eleanor be any different?

I'd hazard a guess that at some point – and I haven't quite worked out when or how – James became aware of his wife's involvement in Izzy's 'accident' (I'll give Eleanor the benefit of the doubt for the time being). Riddled with guilt (as he should be) and desperate to protect his wife from a murder charge (suggesting his relationship with Izzy was nothing more than a dalliance, which just makes me despise him even more), he helped her devise a smoke-screen – a way to draw attention away from the real culprit and turn the spotlight on to an innocent florist who just happened to have had the misfortune to cross paths with them. The more I think about it, the more it all makes perfect sense.

I'm assuming that when the Elliotts are confident they've built up a sufficiently strong case against me, they'll deliver my head on a silver platter to the authorities. I'd like to think the police are sensible enough to see through their tissue of lies – but if they don't, I'm in deep doo-doo. Mind you, it wouldn't be the first time.

I need to be proactive, get one step ahead of them, find concrete evidence to support my own theory – evidence the police can't ignore. But how?

I lock myself away in the studio for what's left of the afternoon, turning the problem over and over in my mind, like a pebble, considering every plane of its surface, its weight and heft, until finally I have a plan.

Now

19

Transcript of interview between DS Gareth Pearce and Peter Donaldson.

GP: Can you state your name and address for the tape, please.

PD: My name is Peter Donaldson and I live at Springfield House, Oakwood Road, West Dulwich.

GP: How long have you lived there?

PD: Coming up to six and a half years.

GP: Who lives there with you?

PD: Just my wife. We have two daughters, but they're both away at university.

GP: And your next-door neighbours at The Sanctuary – James and Eleanor Elliott – do you know roughly when they moved in?

PD: It must be what . . . two and a half years now. They'd bought the property quite a long time before that, but the place underwent a substantial renovation before they moved in.

GP: Are you friendly with them?

PD: Oh yes, very friendly. My wife and I know the Elliotts well. We've had dinner at each other's houses on several occasions and I usually play golf with James at least once a month.

GP: Were you and your wife at home on the morning of September the twenty-second, between eight a.m. and nine-thirty.

PD: My wife left for work around seven forty-five, but I was at home.

GP: Did you notice anyone entering or leaving The Sanctuary during that time frame?

PD: Yes. Just after eight o'clock I was letting the dog out for a wee when I noticed a car pulling up to the kerb.

GP: Can you describe the vehicle?

PD: It was a dark grey SUV – a Peugeot. I'm afraid I didn't make a note of the registration number. A woman got out of it and started walking up the Elliotts' drive. I recognised her straight away – we'd met a few weeks previously, at a birthday party the Elliotts hosted for Eleanor's sister, Isabel. The one where she had her, er . . . accident. Terrible business, that. My wife and I feel dreadful for James and Eleanor. Have you worked out how it happened yet?

GP: I'm afraid that's not something I can discuss with you at the present time.

PD: Yes, of course. I'm sorry, I shouldn't have asked.

GP: Do you know the woman's name?

PD: Yes, my wife and I spoke to her briefly at the party and she gave my wife her business card. I've actually brought it with me, if you'd like to see it.

GP: Yes, please.

PD: Here you go – Amy Mackenzie, Darling Buds.

GP: For the benefit of the tape, Mr Donaldson is handing me a business card. What was your impression of Miss Mackenzie when you met her at the party?

PD: I found her perfectly pleasant. We had quite an interesting conversation about houseplants; she gave me some useful advice regarding my aspidistra.

GP: Did you speak to Miss Mackenzie when you saw her again on the twenty-second of September?

PD: No. I was going to say hello, but then I thought better of it.

GP: Why was that?

PD: She seemed rather agitated and she looked rather . . . well, strange.

GP: In what way?

PD: Very dishevelled. Her hair obviously hadn't been brushed that morning and her clothes were very creased – almost as if she'd slept in them. It was obvious from her body language and the look on her face that she was upset about something. I watched her approach the front door of The Sanctuary and ring the bell. Then she hid.

GP: *Hid?*

PD: That's what it looked like to me. She went and stood behind a pot plant – a bay tree, I think it was.

GP: What happened then?

PD: Katya – she's the Elliotts' au pair – opened the door and Amy stepped out from behind the bay tree. The two of them exchanged a few words. I couldn't hear what they were saying, but I could tell from the expression on Katya's face that she wasn't very happy about Amy being there. After a few moments, Amy pushed past her and walked straight into the house.

GP: When you say 'pushed past her', can you be more specific? Was there any violence involved?

PD: I wouldn't describe it as 'violence', but Amy did make physical contact with Katya. I guess you'd call it a shoulder charge.

GP: How did Katya react?

PD: She looked shocked.

GP: Not scared then?

PD: I suppose she could've been scared. It was hard to tell from where I was standing. I wish now I'd called out to her, asked her if everything was all right – but as Amy was already known to the family, I didn't think there was any cause for concern. I saw Katya go back inside the house and close the front door behind her. That was another reason I wasn't unduly worried – if Katya had feared for her physical safety, I doubt she would have shut herself inside the house with that woman.

GP: What did you do then?

PD: I called to my dog and we both went back inside

the house. The first indication I had that anything was amiss next door was when the first ambulance pulled up outside.

Four Days Earlier

20

It's the day of the funeral. I've been up since five, my mind not on Izzy, but on all the things I need to accomplish today. By seven-thirty I'm in the studio, working on the flowers for the wake. I was feeling confident earlier but now, as I trim delicate stems of fragrant freesia to a uniform length, I start to question myself. There are too many variables; too much is out of my control. I'm paddling away from the beach into a vast ocean and with every passing hour the currents get stronger. I can't turn back now though; I'm already in too deep.

Still, I'm as well prepared as I can be. I used my meeting with James's PA to grill her about the funeral arrangements and I have a good idea of the Elliotts' schedule for today.

It's just after eight-thirty when Claire sticks her head round the door of the studio.

'How are you?' she asks me.

In truth I feel as if I'm on the verge of disaster. I can sense it now – a landslide bearing down on me.

'So-so,' I reply. 'Let's just say I'll be glad when today's over.'

'I don't blame you. Funerals are awful at the best of times, but it must be so much worse when it's somebody young, like Izzy. Still, it will be nice for you to say a proper goodbye to her.'

I never explicitly told Claire I was attending the funeral; I just let her assume it.

'I don't suppose the family are any closer to finding out how it happened, are they?' she adds. 'My heart really goes out to them; they must be desperate for closure.'

I shake my head. 'The police are still investigating. In the absence of any witnesses, I guess there's a chance we might never know the truth.'

I stare down at the Queen of Night I'm holding. It's a type of tulip, a striking species whose petals are such a deep shade of maroon they almost look black in certain lights. A fitting choice for a wake.

As I lay the flower tenderly back down, a rush of emotion catches me unawares. I miss Izzy so much it's like a wound. I can feel the outline of it, a desperate fiery ache that starts in my throat and ends under my sternum.

'Are you sure you'll be all right in the shop on your own?' I say to Claire. 'I'm hoping to be back by mid-afternoon at the latest.'

'Absolutely – and if you don't feel like coming back to work after the funeral, then for heaven's sake don't.'

'Thanks, Claire,' I say, blinking hard as tears prickle

behind my eyeballs. 'I don't know what I'd do without you.'

I told Rachel I'd deliver the bouquets to The Sanctuary in person, also offering to supply the vases and arrange the flowers in situ. I gave her an ETA of eleven a.m., since I know the hearse is collecting the Elliotts at ten-thirty. The caterers would let me in, she said; she'd tell them to expect me.

As Ewan has the van, I use my own car, parking it a little way down the street from the house. The catering company's vehicle is parked in the driveway and two employees are removing plastic pallets of food from its depths. The front door is wide open so I walk straight in and make my way to the kitchen, where I find more staff hard at work. It's not obvious who's in charge, but I introduce myself as the florist and they all smile and nod. As I set down the flowers and go to fill the vases at the sink, nobody gives me a second look – just as I had hoped.

It doesn't take me long to choose a couple of suitable locations in the living room for the vases. As I start to arrange the flowers, I wonder if James and Eleanor will recognise my handiwork. They'll probably be too focused on their guests to give it much thought – and even if they do, it will be too late by then.

Catering staff are still traipsing through the house, ferrying stuff from their van to the kitchen, so I fuss with the flowers for longer than I need to. It's only when I am alone and unobserved that I begin to move towards the staircase in the corner of the living area, stealthy as an assassin.

The first room I enter clearly belongs to Toby. It's as stylish as any two-year-old's bedroom can be, with matching white-painted furniture and a sea-themed mural covering one wall. I notice a small camera on the bedside table, facing the bed. I'm careful to stay out of its field of vision; the Elliotts mustn't know I was here. Its positioning means I can't check out the wardrobe or the chest of drawers, but it doesn't matter – the Elliotts aren't likely to stash the kind of material that interests me in a room to which their au pair has unrestricted access.

Next door to Toby's bedroom is a family bathroom and next to that another bedroom. It's rather untidy, with clothes draped over every piece of furniture. I know it belongs to Katya, even before I spot the foreign language novel and the long, dark hairs in the brush on the dressing table. Confident I won't find anything here either, I continue down the landing, past a recessed bookcase, and on to the final room. I'm hoping for an office, complete with fully indexed filing cabinet and a locked desk drawer whose key can conveniently be found in the pen tidy, or duct-taped to the underside of the desk. I'm disappointed when the door opens to reveal a guest room with a small en suite.

Tastefully decorated in shades of grey and lavender, it's simply furnished with a double bed, matching side tables and lamps. There's also a built-in wardrobe with sliding doors. One half of the wardrobe is empty; the other half is full of winter clothes. Another dead end.

My next port of call is the bell tower. Or it would be if I could find it. There's no other staircase in sight; no door that hasn't been opened. My heart sinks as I consider the possibility that the rooms in the bell tower are accessed not from the first floor, as I had assumed, but from the ground floor. If that's the case, I may as well call it a day. There's no way I can start poking around down there, not with all the catering staff milling around. The risk of drawing attention to myself is simply too great.

I think for a moment and then retrace my steps. Back to the bookcase. The upper half is lined with shelves that are filled with vintage books, the sort you can buy by the metre, while the lower section is wood panelling. Mounted on one of the panels, at approximately waist height, is a door-knob. It's painted the same delicate shade of duck egg as the panelling, which is probably why I didn't notice it before.

I grip the knob and give it a yank. The bookcase obligingly pops out of the wall and swings smoothly to one side. It's all I can do not to high-five myself.

Rising up in front of me is a spiral staircase. It's made from cast iron, with barley sugar spindles decorated with rosettes, and intricately designed treads and risers, all very Gothic. Turning my gaze upwards, I count three full revolutions; God knows how the Elliotts got their furniture up there. I'm guessing it's original because, even for someone with James's contacts, it would be next to impossible to find another staircase that fit this space so precisely. Leaving the bookcase-slash-door slightly ajar, I grip the handrail and start to climb.

At the top of the first flight I emerge on to a small landing with a single door leading off it. As my hand makes contact with the brass doorknob, I feel a small pulsing in my chest, like the beat of an invisible pacemaker. Now that I'm here, I'm not sure I want to go in. This, after all, is the room where Izzy met her death.

I roll back my shoulders and tell myself not to be so silly. I don't believe in ghosts; there's nothing behind that door that can possibly hurt me.

The room is small, with white walls and a three-quarter-sized bed with a broderie anglaise cover. Eleanor has accessorised it well with colourful abstract artwork, scented candles and a Lloyd Loom chair with velvet cushions. Despite the pretty trimmings, there's a peculiar heavy silence in here, as if the walls are holding their breath.

I go towards the windows, walking softly, as if wary of disturbing someone. They're the casement variety – a pair of latticed panes in wooden frames, each around four feet tall. Unusually, they aren't recessed, but fitted flush to the wall. The absence of a sill, together with the windows' low positioning, means it would be very easy for someone to fall through them. The windows wouldn't even need to be open. All you'd have to do is lift the stays up off the pins that hold them in place and wait for your unwitting victim to get into position. Easy.

Given how high up we are, I'm surprised James didn't think to fit the windows with some kind of restrictor to limit their range of movement – or, if that wasn't possible with period windows like these, a guard rail on the exterior. Clearly, aesthetics took precedence over safety on this project.

Bitterness stings my throat. It didn't have to be this way. Izzy might still be here if only . . . I bite down hard on my lip, almost drawing blood. What's the point of if onlys? What's done is done and I can't change the past. There's nothing more to see here and so, with one last, lingering look around the room, I head for the door.

The stairs that lead to the top floor are clearly a modern addition – a minimalist steel spiral with one and a half effortless twists that lead directly into the master bedroom. Size wise, it's fairly modest, but what it lacks in space it makes up for in wow factor. Three of its four walls are made of glass, the structure daringly overhanging the side of the original bell tower, giving it fifty percent more floor space than the room directly beneath it. I'd love to take a moment to admire the far-reaching views, but it's already eleven-twenty and, based on my calculations, the family will be back from the crematorium around midday.

I take a few moments to check out the en suite, which has a lux hotel vibe with his-and-hers sinks and a slipper bath made of copper. It's absolutely immaculate, with no smudges on the mirror, or hairs clogging up the plughole in the sink. I open the medicine cabinet to see if there's any prescription medication. I'm looking for sleeping tablets, diazepam, Prozac – something that might indicate an anxious mind, or explain Eleanor's erratic behaviour. But there's nothing, not even an aspirin.

Back in the bedroom, I go to a tall chest of drawers. There's a broadband router sitting on top of it; I guess you'd need more than one of them in a property of this size. I open a few drawers, careful not to disturb the contents too much, but all I find are neatly folded undies and nightwear. I forage in a pair of matching wardrobes, but they too yield nothing of interest. I drop to my knees and look under the bed, but there's only a single earring and a crumpled tissue.

A scratchy veil of fatigue irritates my eyes. I haven't slept well in days; not since Izzy died. I sit down on the bed, unwilling to accept that my reconnaissance mission has been a waste of time. I'm not sure what I was expecting. A diary filled with lurid details of James's sexual conquests perhaps, or some explicit selfies of him and Izzy. Something that would show Eleanor had a very real motive for wanting to harm her sister. But now that I think about it, wouldn't James be far more likely to keep any incriminating material in his office, rather than here at home?

As I rise from the bed something catches my eye; the hard corner of an electronic device. It's lying on the floor, in between the bed and the nightstand, attached to a plug socket by its charging lead. Bending down to pick it up, I see that it's an iPad in a smart leather case, embossed with the initials EE. I pull the lead out and sit back down on the bed, resting the iPad on my knees. I'm not holding out much hope as I press the power button. When the device comes to life, I expect to see a passcode prompt appear – but I don't. In a massive stroke of luck, the screen lock's been disabled.

The photos folder seems like an obvious place to start. I scroll down for what feels like forever until a series of holiday snaps catches my eye. James in shorts and snorkel mask, knee-deep in the turquoise ocean. Eleanor on a yacht, laughing as the wind whips her hair across her face. The two of them drinking cocktails on a plumbago-filled terrace at sunset. Anyone looking at these pictures would think they had the perfect life, the perfect marriage. But I know different. I know that just below the well-manicured, perfectly level surface lies an underground ants' nest. It's probably been there for years, waiting for someone like me to disturb it.

As I continue scrolling, I turn James's dirty little secret over in my mind, warming myself with its exotic heat. Why *do* men have affairs, I wonder – especially men like James, with young children and beautiful, intelligent wives? Boredom? Biological imperative? Insecurity? Adventure? Or, and something tells me this is the most likely scenario in James's case, just because they can.

He's such a bastard; that man deserves everything that's coming to him.

Feeling suddenly sickened by the Elliott family album, I turn my attention to Eleanor's email. It looks as if she's had a clear-out fairly recently because her messages only go back a couple of months. I wish I had half her discipline. Inbox zero is a faraway goal for me, as unachievable as losing the extra ten pounds I'm carrying, or learning to play the piccolo. I scrutinise the senders' names, hoping to spot Izzy's among them, but I'm out of luck. Instead, I find messages of condolence (some eloquent, others cloying), a reminder from the Audi dealership that Eleanor's car is due for a service, several invoices for online purchases and the usual plethora of marketing junk.

Exiting her email, I cast my eye over the apps on the screen. The name of a well-known home security system jumps out at me. I'm a little confused at first, as I didn't notice any CCTV cameras on The Sanctuary's exterior, only a burglar alarm. But when I tap on the app it isn't the outside of the property that appears, but Toby's bedroom. It's the baby monitor, that's all.

I check my watch again: eleven thirty-eight. Just enough time to examine Eleanor's browsing history, which should offer a useful insight into her current preoccupations.

I see parenting forums, an interior design blog, some high-end fashion retailers, a website offering eulogy-writing tips and multiple Instagram log ins (clearly, Eleanor is not so devastated by her sister's death that she hasn't found time to update her followers). Going back further, there are several funeral directors' websites, and a string of rather gruesome Google searches ('head injuries after a fall', 'brain death', 'what to do when someone dies'). When I spot a search for 'NHS organ donation', I experience a small thrill. It hadn't occurred to me that some of Izzy's organs might have been used to help someone else; that a part of her might still live on. I don't know if she was a registered organ donor – she and I never discussed the subject – but I think it's what she would've wanted.

I keep going, past the date of Izzy's death, just in case there's anything to suggest the attack on her was premeditated. But there are no red flags, no searches for 'how to make a murder look like an accident', or anonymous Mumsnet confessions along the lines of 'My sister is sleeping with my DH and I want to kill her. AIBU?'

Disappointed, I go to close the pane. But then I stop, my finger poised in mid-air. I've spotted something in the history I missed before. It's the name of a local newspaper; one I'm very familiar with.

A streak of something close to panic forks downwards from my brain, branching out along my limbs, making them tingle. *Breathe,* I tell myself as my heart punches a savage rhythm in my chest. *It might be nothing to do with you.* But even as I'm saying the words in my head, I know this can't be coincidence.

I check the date the article was viewed. The sixth of September; eight days after Izzy's fall and two days before Eleanor accused me on Facebook. Half of me doesn't want to read it; the other half needs to know.

As the page loads and I read the headline, the past comes roaring up at me like a fire-breathing dragon woken from a deep sleep. I feel weak with the heat and the force of it.

Derbyshire Tribune, 9th April 2014

Mother Speaks Out on 10th Anniversary of Daughter's Death

Louise Bellamy's 15-year-old daughter Frances died in a tragic drowning accident in the spring of 2004. Ten years later, the Bakewell mum is still seeking answers, as she revealed in an exclusive interview with the *Tribune*'s Tanya Savory.

'It may be ten years since Frances died, but the pain of losing her is still raw,' she revealed. 'It's like a bomb went off that day and changed our lives for ever. What makes the agony even worse is that we still don't know exactly how it happened.'

Louise struggled to contain her emotions as she shared her memories of that tragic day in April. 'Around lunchtime I got a text from Frances saying she wouldn't be coming straight home after school, as she and her best friend Sophie were going into town to buy a birthday present for a friend. I texted her back, reminding her to be home by six at the latest, because her grandma was coming round for tea that evening.'

When Frances failed to return at the agreed time, Louise called her daughter's phone, but there was no answer. 'In the beginning I wasn't too worried,' she explained. 'I thought she'd probably just lost track of time and that she and Sophie were still mooching round the shops. I didn't have Sophie's phone number, so I waited another half an hour and then, when Frances still wasn't home, I called Sophie's mum.'

To Louise's surprise, Sophie's mother revealed her daughter had been home for several hours already. 'When Sophie came on the phone, she denied making arrangements to go shopping with Frances,' Louise said. 'She insisted she had no idea where my daughter was, even though the two of them were supposed to be best friends.'

With the shops now closed and darkness starting to fall, Louise and her husband Ian called the police to report Frances as missing. A search was launched, with dozens of Bakewell residents turning out to help comb the local streets, parks and beauty spots.

When Frances's mobile phone was found on a bridge that spans the River Wye, less than half a mile from her home, concerns for her safety grew. Police refocused their search efforts on the river and twenty-four hours later, the teenager's lifeless body was recovered from the water, a mile downstream from the bridge.

'I'll never forget the moment two police officers came to my door to tell me they'd found her,' said a tearful Louise. 'I couldn't believe I'd never get to hug my little girl again, or tell her I loved her, and I was desperate to know what Frances was doing in the river. At that stage, the police had no way of knowing, but they promised me they'd conduct a thorough investigation.'

A post-mortem examination confirmed that Frances, who had never learned to swim, died of drowning. With no injuries on her body and no witnesses who'd seen her fall into the river, the police concluded that her death was a tragic accident. The river was unusually high that spring after several weeks of heavy rain and it's thought Frances may have been walking along the parapet of the bridge when she lost her balance and fell.

'It didn't make sense to me then and it still doesn't make sense now,' said Louise. 'Frances was afraid of the water. There was no way she'd have attempted to walk along the top of that bridge. I know the police did their best, but I'm convinced there were people living in Bakewell at the time who knew more about my daughter's death than they were willing to say.'

One person who came under particular scrutiny during the police's three-month investigation was Frances's best friend, Sophie Douglas. Sophie, who was also 15 at the time, stuck to her claim that she hadn't seen Frances after school that day and police never found any evidence to suggest otherwise. However, there were many in the local community who believed the teenager was withholding vital information. Even now, ten years on, the rumours still persist.

Louise Bellamy is reluctant to discuss her own feelings on the matter. 'I'm not going to point any fingers, but what I would say is that if there's someone out there who has any information about my daughter's death, however small or insignificant they think it is, it's not too late to come forward. I'll never be at peace until I know exactly how Frances ended up in that river.'

Anyone with information relating to Frances Bellamy's death should contact Derbyshire Police directly.

The article is accompanied by two photos. The first was taken by the *Tribune*'s photographer at the time of the interview in 2014. It shows Louise Bellamy and her husband, Ian. They're both wearing set expressions and Louise is holding a framed picture of Frances with her pet cat, which must have been taken shortly before she died.

The second photo shows Sophie Douglas, as she was in 2004. She's wearing school uniform and smiling self-consciously. She's quite a plain thing with a slightly crooked nose and nondescript brown hair, but there's a fierce energy lurking behind her eyes.

My nose has been fixed and my hair's a little darker, but I really haven't changed that much. Certainly, if you laid a recent photo of me beside this one, you'd see the similarities.

Looking at my old school photo brings back a rush of memories – none of them happy ones. The tears silently rolling down my father's face, the cracked vinyl seat in the back of the police car, the white pinstripes on my solicitor's blue suit, the catch in my voice as I doggedly stuck to the story I'd told Frances's mum on the phone.

Those images fade as questions rain down on me from all directions. How does Eleanor know about Frances? It's true that her death and the subsequent police investigation were covered in several national newspapers, but it all happened a long time ago. In any case, Eleanor was only a teenager herself at the time, so I doubt she paid much attention to the news. How has she made the connection between me and Sophie Douglas – a connection that no other person of my acquaintance in almost twenty years has managed to make?

Frances. The sibilance of her name is like a whisper, calling to me across the desert. Something inside me, some important part, is stuck, snagged on the day she died, like the loop of a jumper caught on a bramble, forever pulling me backwards. I did my best to forget what happened. Relocated to the other side of the country. Changed my name. Became a successful businesswoman. A decent, law-abiding member of society. A colour-changing chameleon hiding in plain sight. Who can blame me? Wouldn't we all rewrite the past, if it meant it could change our future?

But now it's all gone to shit. Everything's falling apart around me. I can feel myself slipping through the protective net I've painstakingly sewn around myself.

A sensation rushes in around me with sickening familiarity: the compulsion to lie down and never get up again. But I can't do that – the Elliotts will be back shortly and my work here isn't done.

I put the iPad back where I found it, remembering to reattach the power cable, and spend a few moments smoothing the duvet cover. Then I go to the router and turn it round, exposing the password on the back, before pulling my phone out of my jacket pocket. Seconds later, I'm hooked up to The Sanctuary's WiFi and making for the door.

As I wend my way back down the spiral staircase, my head's all over the place, but I try to keep my feelings in check. Now, more than ever, I need a sense of clarity.

After pushing the bookcase door shut behind me, I go to my phone again. It doesn't take me long to download the relevant home security app but, when I attempt to pair my phone with the camera in Toby's room, I discover that a password is required for Eleanor's account. Not willing to give up just yet, I tap the 'forgotten password' link and am given the option to answer a security question instead. It's a question which, amazingly, I know the answer to: *What was your father's occupation?*

O-r-t-h-o-d-o-n-t-i-s-t, I tap out, taking care to spell the word correctly. I'm not sure what, if any, use the baby cam will be – but right now, with the odds stacked against me, I need to do anything I can to give myself the advantage.

As the connection completes, I hear the sound of a door slamming, followed by the low rumble of voices. Thinking it's just the catering staff, I'm not unduly concerned. If anyone sees me coming down the stairs, I'll simply say I was using the loo. But then I hear something that makes my stomach lurch: the plaintive cry of a young child. It can only mean one thing: the Elliotts are home.

Shoving my phone back in my pocket, I tiptoe towards the top of the stairs. The voices are louder now; it sounds like they're right underneath me.

'I'll get Toby a snack, shall I?' someone says in heavily accented English.

'Yes, please, Katya,' comes Eleanor's reply. 'Nothing sugary though. Maybe some hummus and breadsticks.'

I risk a quick peek over the banister and catch sight of an older woman I recognise as Eleanor's mother. She's elegantly dressed in a navy-blue trouser suit and white pussy-bow blouse. 'I'm going to need a quick freshen-up before our guests arrive,' she announces. Her voice sounds gravelly, as if she's been crying.

'No problem, Mum,' says Eleanor. 'Why don't you use the upstairs bathroom?'

I mutter an expletive under my breath. I've miscalculated the timings; I thought they'd be out of the house for an hour and a half at least.

Eleanor's mother speaks again. 'Do you have any anti-histamine tablets? My eyes feel so puffy; I must look an absolute fright.'

'There should be some in the medicine cabinet upstairs. I'll get them for you in a sec, I just need to check on the caterers.'

I start backing away from the stairs. Even with the pretext of the flower delivery, it's going to be very difficult to explain my presence. Pretending I was looking for the loo won't wash with Eleanor. If she finds me up here, it's only going to give her more ammunition to use against me. Exactly what I *don't* need.

There's only one thing I can think to do now.

Hide.

21

The child-sized furniture in Toby's room offers limited opportunities for concealment, so I head to the guest suite instead. I can't hide under the bed, as it has a divan base – which only leaves the wardrobe. I choose the side with the clothes in, parting two long wool coats to make room for myself on the floor. After drawing the coats back in front of me, I slide the wardrobe door shut, leaving a narrow gap, so I'm not sitting in total darkness. The pointed toe of a boot is digging painfully into my backside and the smell of mothballs is nauseating. The situation is so ridiculous it's almost funny. If I wasn't so damn frightened, I might have laughed out loud.

Barely a minute later I hear footsteps coming up the staircase's stone treads. They're followed by a soft suck of air; the sound of a door being opened. Through the gap I watch in horror as Eleanor's mother appears. She takes off her jacket and lays it down on the bed, before walking out of view.

Another few minutes pass and then I hear more foot-steps, followed by Eleanor's voice.

'Here you go, Mum. They're the one-a-day kind; non-drowsy. I brought you some water too.'

There's no reply, but I can hear someone sniffing.

'Are you OK, Mum?'

'I've just buried my daughter, I'm about as far away from OK as it's possible to be.'

'I'm sorry, it was a stupid question.'

A long, mournful sigh. 'No, it's me who should be apologising. I shouldn't have snapped like that. I'm sure you're feeling every bit as wretched as I am.'

'Mmm, the funeral service was tough. I'm glad it's over.'

'So am I. At one point I felt so light-headed I thought I was going faint.'

'Oh, Mum, why didn't you tell me?'

'I couldn't, it was while you were delivering your eulogy. It was very good, by the way, and so was that other woman's . . . Izzy's doctor friend. What's her name again?'

'Maria. She's coming to the reception; I'll introduce you if you like.'

'That would be nice.'

The mattress springs exhale as someone sits down on the bed.

'I almost wish we weren't having a wake,' says Izzy's mother. 'I really don't feel in the mood for socialising.'

'Me neither, but it's what Izzy would've wanted – you know how she loved a good party. You don't have to stay until the bitter end, though. Why not show your face for half an hour and then slip back upstairs? You could even have a lie-down if you wanted to.'

'Good idea, I might just do that.'

I catch a glimpse of Eleanor through the gap as she joins her mother on the bed.

'You don't have to go back tonight, you know. You're welcome to stay here. I can always lend you a nightdress and we have spare toothbrushes.'

'Thank you, sweetheart, I appreciate the offer, but I think I'd rather go home.'

'Up to you, Mum.'

'Do you think the coroner got it right?'

The question is so abrupt, so out of context, that at first I think I might have misheard it.

Eleanor seems similarly nonplussed. She gives an awkward laugh. 'What are you talking about, Mum?'

'Ruling out suicide so quickly. I know he spoke to a few of Izzy's friends and so on, but I can't help thinking he jumped the gun.'

'But he couldn't find any evidence to indicate Izzy was thinking of harming herself. What other conclusion was he supposed to draw?'

I sense a frown even if I can't see one. 'I just think he should have probed a little deeper . . . turned over a few more stones.'

'Do *you* think she killed herself?'

'We both know Izzy could be rather mercurial – it's perfectly possible that something, or even some*one,* tipped her over the edge.'

A sharp intake of breath from Eleanor. 'I had no idea you felt that way, Mum. I wish you'd said something sooner.'

'I was scared to; I didn't want to be accused of interfering in your marriage.'

'What's my marriage got to do with it?'

The older woman snaps her tongue against the roof of her mouth. 'Oh, Eleanor, don't tell me you didn't know – or at least suspect.'

'Suspect what?' Eleanor's voice is shrill. Defensive.

I hear the approach of heavy footsteps. Both women fall silent.

The next voice I hear is James's.

'I've brought your handbag up, Valerie; I thought you might need it.'

'How terribly thoughtful of you.' Her tone suggests otherwise.

'Where would you like me to put it?'

'Anywhere you like.'

There's a protracted silence. You can cut the atmosphere in the room with a knife.

'I'm sorry, am I interrupting something?' James says.

'Not at all,' Eleanor replies. 'Mum and I were just—'

'I was just telling Eleanor that I think there's a chance Izzy took her own life.'

'But the coroner said—'

Now it's James's turn to get shut down. 'The coroner wasn't *at* the party; he didn't see what happened. All he can do is make an educated guess.' There's a steely strain in Valerie's voice, the thinness of a violin string about to break.

'With all due respect, Valerie, you didn't see what happened either. None of us did.'

'No, but I did see *something* that night. I haven't told anyone about it, but now I think perhaps I should've done.'

'Really?' James says doubtfully. 'Would you care to share it with us now?'

'Can we discuss this later?' Eleanor says in a pleading tone. 'Our guests will be arriving any minute.'

'If your mother's got something to say, I think she should get it off her chest.'

'Very well then,' Valerie says. 'I saw you and Izzy dancing together, at the party, to a slow song.' There's a heavy emphasis on the word *slow*.

'I danced with a lot of people that night,' James says. 'It's called being a good host.'

'And does a good host always fondle his guests' buttocks?'

I'm so shocked I rear back instinctively, catching my head on the metal buckle of a belt. I silently mouth a four-letter word.

Through the gap I see Eleanor put a hand to her forehead. 'Mum, please . . .'

'I *saw* him, Eleanor. His hands were all over your sister, and worse still, she seemed to be enjoying it.'

Suddenly, James comes into view. He stands with his back to the wardrobe, blocking my view of Eleanor. He's so close I can almost reach through the gap and touch the charcoal grey fabric of his trousers.

'If I wanted to grope my sister-in-law, don't you think I'd choose to do it in private, rather than in the middle of a crowded dance floor?'

'You weren't on the dance floor. You were behind the stage where you thought no one could see you.'

He makes a dismissive noise in the back of his throat. 'I think you must have me confused with someone else. You *were* rather drunk that night, Valerie. I seem to remember you falling into a flowerbed at one point; didn't one of the waiters have to help you up?'

There's a nastiness in his tone I don't recognise. A blackness swelling beneath the surface. I wonder why Eleanor isn't saying anything. If I were in her position, I'd be outraged at any suggestion of inappropriate behaviour between my husband and my sister.

Unless, of course, I already knew.

'Don't turn this back on me, James,' Valerie bites back. 'Yes, I was a little tipsy, but I wasn't rendered temporarily blind.'

She pauses briefly and I imagine her puffing her chest out, gathering her courage in both hands. I'm sure this can't be easy for her.

'I'm going to ask you a question, and I want you to give me an honest answer.'

'Knock yourself out.'

James seems very cocksure, which strikes me as odd. Most men in his position would be crapping themselves, as it's clear where his mother-in-law is going with this.

'Were you and Izzy having an affair?'

'No, we were not.' The denial spills from him as easily as blood from an open vein. 'Eleanor knows that, don't you, darling?'

His wife offers no response.

'Eleanor?' Her name sounds heavy in his mouth, like a warning.

'Of course they weren't having an affair, Mum,' she says after a beat too long. She sounds robotic, her tone lacking in emotion; a void where the feeling should be.

Valerie makes a tutting noise, her disdain obvious.

'Well, if that's the way you want to play it, good luck to you both. But I'm warning you, James, if I find out you're lying to me, I'll be straight on the phone to the police. If they knew you and Izzy were sleeping together, it would put quite a different spin on their investigation, don't you think?'

James's fists are inches away from my face. I watch as they slowly clench and unclench. 'That would be a very foolish move on your part, Valerie.' The words are spoken with softness but enunciated as precisely as a knife-cut across the wrist. Valerie hears it too.

'Are you threatening me?'

'No, he isn't,' says Eleanor. '*Are* you, James?' she adds pointedly.

'It's a friendly piece of advice, Valerie, nothing more. I just don't want you wasting the police's time – or your own.'

Downstairs, the doorbell rings.

'That'll be our guests,' says Eleanor.

'We'd better go and let them in then, hadn't we?' says James.

'You go on, I'll be down in a second.'

'Fine,' he snaps at her. 'But don't be too long.'

James disappears from view and now I can see Eleanor again. She's still sitting on the edge of the bed. I peer out between the coats, scrutinising her expression. She wipes her mouth with the back of her hand as if there's an unpleasant taste on her lips.

'Sorry about that, Mum. James isn't his usual self at the moment; he's under a lot of stress right now.'

Something's not right here. Eleanor's behaviour isn't normal. Now that they're alone, why isn't she quizzing her mother about what she saw at the party – or, at the very least, asking her why it's taken her so long to disclose it?

'Aren't we all?' Valerie replies. 'Your husband is so full of bullshit. I don't know why you can't just admit it.'

The doorbell goes again.

'I'd better go downstairs; it'll look rude if I'm not there to greet the guests. We'll talk about this later, Mum, just you and me – OK?'

'I suppose it'll have to be.'

Eleanor gets up and I hear her leave the room. After a few moments, Valerie goes into the en suite; I hear the sound of the extractor fan as she turns on the light. She isn't in there for very long. When she comes out she goes over to the bed and picks up her jacket. The next thing I know she's sliding back the wardrobe door – but luckily, it's the other one. As it comes barrelling towards me on its runner, I draw my head back just in time. Another millisecond and I could've been decapitated. That would've left the Elliotts with some awkward explaining to do.

I watch, heart pounding, as Valerie's hand reaches into the wardrobe for a coat hanger. When she returns it to the rail a couple of seconds later, her jacket is draped around it. She shuts the sliding door and then I hear the fusillade of her heels going down the staircase.

I remain in the wardrobe for another fifteen minutes or so, reluctant to leave my hiding place until the wake is in full swing. That's when I'll have the best chance of slipping out unnoticed.

As I wait it out, counting the rings on the doorbell, the breath in my lungs is being replaced with something denser, heavier. I'm so confused I don't know what to think or feel. If Eleanor's mother is telling the truth about what she saw at the party – and I can't think of any good reason why she'd make something like that up – it's powerful evidence that James and Izzy were, as I suspected, having an affair.

Disgust thickens in my throat. James is not the person I thought he was – and nor is Izzy. The knowledge of their betrayal leaks away inside me, like alkali seeping from a battery. I can feel it spreading through my bloodstream.

I bet Valerie's disgusted too. It didn't sound like she was remotely convinced by James's protestations of innocence. She seems to think his affair with Izzy might have prompted her daughter to kill herself, but that doesn't ring true to me. The lovers appeared perfectly happy when she spotted them smooching at the party. Why would Izzy throw herself out of a window just a short time later? Even if she and James had argued after Valerie saw them, I can't see Izzy killing herself after one little tiff, especially not at her own birthday party. No, that's not what happened. I'm sure of it.

Before I came here today, I'd all but convinced myself that Eleanor was responsible for Izzy's death, but now an alternative hypothesis presents itself. What if it was serious – for one of them, at least? Is it possible that Izzy, giddy with alcohol and emboldened by that natural sense of entitlement I always found slightly unattractive, gave James an ultimatum that night? Leave your wife for me, or else I'll go public about our relationship? I'm guessing that for James, who'd already cheated on Eleanor with at least two of his interns, the affair was just a bit of fun. In which case, wouldn't Izzy's threat have given him a pretty strong motive for wanting to shut her up? *Permanently*.

Eleanor isn't in the clear, though. She's involved in this too, right up to her pretty little neck. The unemotional way she reacted to Valerie's revelation tells me she already knew about the affair. I suspect she also knows James killed her sister and, for some unknown reason – perhaps because she doesn't want the father of her child locked up for life – she's protecting him. But in order to do that effectively, she needs to focus the police's attention elsewhere. That's where I come in.

Credit where credit's due, Eleanor has clearly done her homework. I don't know how she worked out that Sophie Douglas and I are one and the same person, but once she did, she must've realised I was the perfect fall guy. After all, I've already been linked to one unfortunate 'accident' involving a close friend. And while the police didn't have sufficient evidence to charge me with anything in relation to Frances's death, I might not be so lucky second time around. Somehow, I've got to dig myself out of this hole. But first, I need to get out of this house without anyone recognising me – and for that, I'm going to need a disguise.

When I emerge from the wardrobe, I'm wearing a man's leather aviator hat. With the earflaps down, it covers half my face. It isn't the sort of thing one would normally wear to a wake, but it's the best I can do with the limited options available.

Nursing a killer case of pins and needles, I hobble out on to the landing and lean over the banister. The room below is packed; there must be at least fifty people there, although the atmosphere is rather subdued. I spot Eleanor on the far side of the room. She's holding Toby on her hip, stroking the little boy's hair lovingly as she chats to Valerie and Maria. There's no sign of Maria's husband, Marcus; perhaps he didn't come. James is standing by the French doors, gulping red wine as he talks to a man with cropped white hair and a ruddy complexion.

I walk down the stairs as quickly as I can, chin glued to my chest. As I start weaving my way in between the guests, I don't look left or right. I'm halfway across the room when I'm waylaid by a waiter who offers me a glass of wine from a tray. I could seriously use a drink right now, but I give a small shake of my head and keep on walking.

When I get to the entrance hall, I make the mistake of lifting my head, thinking I'm home free. It's then that the door to the downstairs WC opens and a woman steps out.

A silvery chill snakes down my spine when I see that it's Katya. We make eye contact and her forehead crinkles. It's as if she knows I look familiar but can't quite place me. Or maybe she's just startled by the sight of my unusual headgear. She looks as if she's about to say something, so I forestall her by rushing past her into the loo with a mumbled 'sorry'.

When I open the door a few minutes later she's gone. I let myself out through the front door and walk briskly down the street to my car, pausing only to drop the aviator hat into a neighbour's wheelie bin.

As I slip into the driver's seat, the tension in my shoulders loosens. It's been a very trying morning and I'm looking forward to getting back to the peace and quiet of my studio. Reading that newspaper article has unsettled me more than I care to admit.

While the rational part of me has always known my old schoolfriend Frances was dead, there are many times over the years when I've felt her presence. She's the hairs standing up on the back of my neck, the dark edge of a shadow, the suffocating feeling that's always there, like an invasive weed, choking everything in its path.

22

I wake with a ringing in my ears and a tangle of unease in my chest. When I open my eyes, a snapshot from the previous day at the Elliotts' home floats in front of my eyes like an absurd little hologram. More images follow in quick succession, one superimposed on the next. As I press my fingertips into the pressure points at my temples, a strange kind of foreboding descends on me, a hot, kinetic tremor radiating out from my solar plexus.

I don't usually have a problem getting up in the morning but today it feels like a mammoth effort. I put on my dressing gown and go to the kitchen, hoping I'll feel better after some toast and hot coffee. When I don't, I text Claire to tell her I may be coming down with something and won't be in till lunchtime – if at all. My assistant is her usual solicitous self and forwards a recipe for an immunity-boosting green juice she swears by. The list of ingredients alone is enough to turn my stomach. Still, it's nice to know she cares. When all this is over, I might see if Claire fancies going out for a drink one evening after work. Until now I've always avoided socialising with my employees, but my friendship cup doesn't exactly runneth over, especially now that Izzy's gone and Maria's stopped responding to my texts.

I make a second cup of coffee and take it into the living room, where I watch breakfast news for a while. My body feels uncomfortable. My clothes are too tight; my internal organs seem to be rubbing up against each other, unhappy sharing the same space. Upstairs, I can hear Janet vacuuming. Usually the sound doesn't bother me, but today it makes my nerves jangle. I'm tempted to grab a broom and rap it on the ceiling, but our relationship is already hanging by a thread after that unfortunate business in the garden; I can't afford to alienate her even more.

By late morning, I've decided that I will go into work after all. I still feel out of sorts, but not so unwell that I won't be able to make myself useful.

I'm doing my hair in the mirror above the fireplace when the buzzer goes on the shared front door. I go to the intercom and pick up the handset.

'You can leave it on the step, thanks,' I say, assuming it's a courier with the anti-redness concealer I ordered on Amazon three days ago.

I've barely put the handset back in its cradle when the buzzer goes again.

'Yes?' I say, not bothering to mask my impatience.

'It's the police. Can you let us in, please?'

There's a smeary, indistinct feeling in my head as I press the button to release the communal door. A sense that I should have foreseen this. Should be better prepared than I am.

By the time I open my own front door, two officers in plainclothes – one male, one female – are already standing there.

'Amy Mackenzie?' the man says, showing me his ID.

'That's right.'

'We were wondering if you could accompany us to the police station, Miss Mackenzie. We're investigating a serious crime; we believe you may be able to assist us.'

'Oh? What crime's that?'

The female officer gives me a long stare and I feel like I'm about to shatter into pieces. I tell myself that if I can just keep every muscle perfectly taut and not show any weakness, then I'll be fine.

'We'll be able to tell you more down at the station,' she says. 'Hopefully it won't take too long. We can drop you back home afterwards.'

I think about telling them I have some urgent business to attend to and offering to drive myself to the police station later on – but what's the point? It'll only be putting off the inevitable. I gather everything I have left inside me and force a smile: 'No problem, I'll just get my handbag.'

Transcript of interview between DI Kate Kilner and Amy Mackenzie

KK: We appreciate you agreeing to come in and talk to us today, Amy. I'm calling you 'Amy', but that's not your real name, is it?

AM: Actually, it *is* my name. I changed it by deed poll eighteen years ago.

KK: Sorry, I didn't phrase that very well. What I should've said was, it's not your birth name.

AM: That's correct, I was born Sophie Douglas.

KK: And you grew up . . . where?

AM: Bakewell in Derbyshire.

KK: Any siblings?

AM: No, I'm an only child.

KK: Changing a birth name isn't something most people do lightly. What made you take such a drastic step?

AM: If you've looked me up on your police database – and it sounds very much as if you have – then you probably already know the answer to that question.

KK: Maybe so, but I'd still like to hear it from your mouth.

AM: Fine. When I was fifteen, my best friend Frances drowned in the River Wye. The police think she fell off a bridge, but nobody knows for sure how she ended up in the water.

KK: I remember when that happened. The incident received substantial media coverage as I recall.

AM: Yes – the town was besieged by journalists for weeks on end. They door-stepped everyone who knew Frances. Some of them were quite aggressive, they just wouldn't take no for an answer. Sorry . . . is this too much information?

KK: No, you're doing fine.

AM: The police brought me in for questioning – mainly because on the day she died Frances told her mother we were going shopping together after school. I don't know why she said that. Frances and I hadn't made any such arrangement; we hadn't even discussed it. It took a bit of time for the police to do all the necessary checks, but eventually they were satisfied I was telling the truth.

KK: So you were completely exonerated.

AM: Yes, I'm sure it's all there in black and white on your database. That didn't stop people speculating, though. Even after the coroner recorded a verdict of accidental death, there were still people in the community who thought I had something to do with Frances's death. A rumour started going round that we'd fallen out over a boy we both liked and I'd pushed her off the bridge, knowing she couldn't swim.

KK: How did that make you feel?

AM: Sick to my stomach. People wrote dreadful things about me on social media. Every day at school was a nightmare. There was a lot of name-calling – kids would whisper 'murderer' every time they passed me in the corridor. There was physical abuse too; I lost count of the times I was pushed or tripped in the playground. Nothing was done to protect me; I think some of the teachers believed the rumours as well and thought I was only getting what I deserved. It wasn't just me either; my parents were targeted too. Someone sent my mum a poison pen letter saying it would've been better if she'd aborted me. My dad had dog mess smeared over his car door handles more than once. Friends they'd known for years started giving them the cold shoulder and certain shopkeepers in the town refused to serve them. They stuck it out for a while, mainly because they didn't want those people to think they'd won, but eventually it just got too much for them. When I was 17, we relocated to Essex. A year later, just before I went off to art college in London, I changed my name.

KK: Because you didn't want the other students to make the connection between you and the tragic death of Frances Bellamy?

AM: Because I didn't want to be Sophie Douglas any more. I wanted to be someone else. Start afresh. Like a snake shedding its skin.

KK: I don't blame you. It sounds like you and your family went through the mill.

AM: We did, and it took me a long time to get over it. I think it still affects me today, if I'm honest.

KK: In what way?

AM: I'm not very good at making friends. I think it's because I spent so long avoiding other people, I kind of lost the knack. And then, when I was ready to socialise, I was overly enthusiastic – almost as if I was trying to make up for lost time. Even today, I can sometimes come across as a bit intense. It can be off-putting for people who don't know me very well.

KK: Another friend of yours died recently, didn't she – Isabel Harkness?

AM: Yes, that was a horrible accident.

KK: Is that what you think it was – an accident?

AM: I don't know. You'd have a better idea about that than me. Is that why you brought me here – to talk about Izzy? Because if it is, I've already given a statement to one of your colleagues. I really don't think there's anything more I can add.

KK: Why don't you let me be the judge of that? Can you tell me where you were yesterday evening, between the hours of eight-thirty p.m. and ten p.m.?

AM: I thought this was about Izzy.

KK: If you could just answer the question, please.

AM: I got back from work just after six-thirty and I was at home for the rest of the evening.

KK: Was there anyone with you, anyone who can verify that?

AM: No, I live alone.

KK: Did you leave your flat at any point, even for just a short time?

AM: No.

KK: So you were nowhere in the vicinity of West Dulwich?

AM: No, but I was there yesterday morning. I'm a florist, in case you weren't aware. I was delivering some flowers to a residential address in Oakwood Road.

KK: Which address is that?

AM: The Sanctuary.

KK: The house owned by James and Eleanor Elliott?

AM: That's right. It was Izzy's funeral yesterday. I did the flowers for the wake.

KK: What time did you arrive at the property?

AM: Eleven-ish. When I got there the family had already left for the crematorium, so the caterers let me in.

KK: You actually went *into* the house, then?

AM: Yes, the customer wanted me to arrange the flowers in situ.

KK: The customer being the Elliotts.

AM: Yes. Well, indirectly. James had asked his PA, Rachel Trevelyan, to organise the event. She was the one who actually hired me.

KK: I see. But presumably the Elliotts knew you'd be at their home that day.

AM: I'm not sure. You'd have to check with Rachel.

KK: We'll certainly do that. While you were at The Sanctuary did you see James Elliott at all?

AM: No, the family wasn't back from the crematorium by the time I left.

KK: What time was that?

AM: I want to say eleven forty-five but it may have been a little later. I wasn't really paying attention to the time, to be honest.

KK: And where did you go then?

AM: Back to my shop in Forest Hill.

KK: You didn't attend the wake?

AM: No.

KK: Why not? I thought you and Izzy were friends.

AM: Because I wasn't invited.

KK: Why do you think that was?

AM: Rachel said the Elliotts were worried about media

intrusion. I assumed they'd deliberately restricted the number of guests attending so they could keep a tighter rein on things.

KK: You hadn't had any sort of disagreement with the family, then?

AM: No.

KK: The reason I ask is because James Elliott was brutally attacked last night, at a recycling facility close to his home.

AM: Oh my goodness, that's awful. Is he all right?

KK: Not really. He was stabbed in the neck. A few millimetres to the left and it would have severed his jugular vein. Mr Elliott is extremely lucky to be alive. He's in hospital right now, seriously injured but stable. Are you all right, Amy? Only you've gone rather pale.

AM: Yes, I'm just a bit shocked, that's all. Do you have any idea who attacked him?

KK: We're working on several lines of enquiry at the moment. You and James were pretty friendly, weren't you?

AM: Reasonably so.

KK: Was your relationship strictly platonic?

AM: Yes. Why – has someone suggested otherwise?

KK: Just to remind you, Miss Mackenzie: my job is to ask the questions, your job is to answer them.

AM: Sorry.

KK: Would you have liked your relationship with James Elliott to have been on a more intimate footing?

AM: Absolutely not. I'm not denying I found James attractive, but I would never have propositioned him – or responded if he'd made a move on me. I'm just not interested in married men.

KK: Do you own a pair of secateurs?

AM: What?

KK: It's a very simple question. Would you like me to repeat it?

AM: No.

KK: No, you don't want me to repeat it, or no, you don't own a pair of secateurs?

AM: The first one. I'm a florist – of course I have secateurs; numerous pairs. They're an essential tool of my trade.

KK: I'm talking about a specific type of secateurs. The type that's made from carbon steel, with two straight blades that end in sharp points. They look more like scissors than the traditional garden secateurs, which have curved blades. Are you familiar with that variety?

AM: Yes, I am. Florists call them 'snips'; they're used for precision work.

KK: Do you own such a tool?

AM: What do *you* think? Sorry, I know . . . it's your job to ask the questions. Yes, I do own some snips.

KK: The reason I'm asking you this, Amy, is that a pair of secateurs, like the ones I've just described, was used to stab James Elliott.

AM: You're kidding me.

KK: Unfortunately not. One of the notable features about this attack is the fact Mr Elliott didn't have any defensive wounds. That suggests one of two things – either he was taken by surprise, or he knew his attacker and felt comfortable enough in their presence to allow them to get close enough to stab him.

AM: Oh.

KK: Is that all you've got to say?

AM: I don't think I want to answer any more questions until I've spoken to a solicitor.

KK: Very well. In that case, I am terminating this interview. The time is two thirty-five.

23

By the time a stony-faced female constable takes me back home, I'm absolutely shattered. It's one in the morning, but I'm too wired to sleep. When my interrogation resumed, it was under caution, with DI Kilner making no attempt to hide the fact she thinks *I'm* the person who attacked James last night. She conducted the entire interview in a state of controlled passive-aggression, trying to strike me in my tender spots, but never once demeaning herself by showing anger.

I answered 'no comment' to all her questions, as per the duty solicitor's advice. In the circumstances, I feel it was the right thing to do. Once I began talking, it would be the start of a fatal unravelling, like a single dropped stitch that ruins the entire knitting pattern.

Despite the stress I was under, I acquitted myself well. The fact it wasn't my first time in a police interview helped, of course. I wasn't tearful or panicky. I kept my chin up and my voice level, determined not to show any sign of weakness.

Eventually, they had to let me go, as they didn't have enough evidence – or *any* evidence for that matter – to charge me. It seems everything hinges on the secateurs and my lack of a verifiable alibi. A circumstantial case, and not even a very strong one. All I have to do is hold my nerve; stick to my story. Just like I did last time.

I allowed them to swab the inside of my cheek for DNA before I left. I could've refused, but how would that have looked? I don't think I have any cause for concern; I'd be surprised if they found my DNA on those snips. *Very* surprised.

As sleep isn't an option, I make myself a cup of chamomile tea and carry it through to the living room, not bothering to turn the light on. Despite my bravura performance at the police station, I feel like someone attempting to put themselves back together and not quite sure how all the pieces fit. I sit in the dark, trying to slow my breathing as my thoughts move in large, loose loops.

After I've drunk my tea, I position a cushion at one end of the sofa and lie down. When I close my eyes, I can see Izzy so clearly, as if she was stamped on my retinas, like the black shadows that have been roaming across my field of vision for as long as I can remember. I had such high hopes for our relationship; it's a shame things didn't work out the way I planned.

After a little while the image blurs and Izzy's face is replaced by a different one. At first I'm not sure whose it is, but then as it sharpens I realise it's Frances. I can see her pale skin, the freckles spilling over the bridge of her nose, the soft hazel of her eyes – but the whole picture is nebulous and shifting, as though I'm watching her underwater.

It might just be exhaustion, but I feel quite peculiar. Something strange is happening inside me: a blizzard of emotion, feelings criss-crossing, misfiring, different parts of my life colliding and merging in a way that makes my head spin.

The next thing I know, weak sunlight is streaming in through the window, forcing my eyelids open. Groggy and disoriented, I get up off the sofa and immediately feel dizzy, my vision pixellating. I stumble into the kitchen, where the digital display on the oven tells me it's 07:03, later than I thought. I'd better text Claire. After yesterday's no-show, she'll be keen for an update. I really don't feel like going in to work, but Claire will struggle to manage on her own for two days in a row – and anyway, I need something to help take my mind off things.

I pick up my phone from the mantelpiece. I haven't checked it since yesterday lunchtime. There are no missed calls; no friendly WhatsApps. Just a single push notification from the gym. I don't think I've ever felt quite so alone before – and this from someone who enjoys their own company. The pleasure I usually take in my solitude and self-containment has evaporated, vanished into thin air as if it had never been anything but a flimsy delusion.

I take my phone into the kitchen, where I send Claire a text, telling her I'll be at the shop within the hour. As I fill the kettle and set it to boil, my thoughts turn to Eleanor. I picture her all alone in her massive bed, sobbing gently, but still managing to look absolutely gorgeous. Eyes like two misted pools, cheeks prettily tear-stained: misery cushioned in a velvet-lined box. What I wouldn't give to be a fly on the wall in that house right now – and maybe I can.

Picking up my phone again, I search for the home security app I downloaded at The Sanctuary yesterday. On opening it, I'm greeted by the live feed from Toby's bedroom. The camera is trained directly on the bed and the little boy is fast asleep. His hair's tousled and his cheeks are slightly flushed. The device has audio too and I can hear the sound of his breathing, soft little snuffles that tug at my heartstrings. As I watch him lying there, so small and vulnerable, it suddenly occurs to me that if James had been killed, Toby would be all Eleanor has left. *And* her mum, of course – but let's face it, Valerie won't be around for ever.

Underneath the image are four directional arrows, arranged like the face of a compass. When I tap the top arrow, the camera lens tilts upwards, so that now I'm look-ing at the wall above Toby's bed. After tapping the bottom arrow to bring the lens back down, I hold my finger on the right-hand arrow and the camera obligingly tracks across the room. It moves past the wardrobe and a low toy chest and across the wall with the underwater mural. When it gets to the door, I lift my finger from the screen and the camera stops. I was hoping the door would be open, offer-ing me a tantalising view of the landing and any passing foot traffic, but annoyingly it's closed. Oh well, it'll be time for Toby to get up soon. I'll check the camera after I've had my shower. Maybe I'll catch a glimpse of Eleanor then.

I touch the left-hand arrow and wait for the camera to track back to its original position. It's almost there when I see something very strange. Something that makes me sit bolt upright – an object I noticed, but didn't fully register, when the camera performed its first sweep of the room.

At first, I think it's just my overworked mind seeing things. A scratch across vinyl – my brain skipping over the grooves, jumping to the wrong conclusion. Just to be sure, I pincer my fingers on the screen to make the object larger.

A rush of bile slides up my throat and suddenly it's hard to breathe. It feels like there's a strong hand around my neck, squeezing my throat, constricting my airways.

I wasn't seeing things. This is real. This is worse than anything I could've imagined. This is something so dark and monstrous it doesn't fit into any known shape in my mind. I know it wasn't there yesterday morning when I was in Toby's room; I would've noticed it for sure.

With trembling fingers, I navigate to the app's settings, looking for the footage from the previous twenty-four hours. But when I find it, I see to my frustration that the camera was trained on Toby's bed the entire time. The object of concern is on the other side of the room, well out of the camera's range. Scanning through the footage, I see Katya coming into shot around eight-thirty to put Toby to bed, but other than that there's no sign of movement in the room.

Pushing my chair away from the table, I punch out another text to Claire. *Sorry, change of plan. Forgot I had an urgent appt in West Dulwich. I'll be in asap.*

The rush hour in this part of London starts ridiculously early. I barely get five minutes down the road before I find myself stuck in a queue of slow-moving traffic on the South Circular. Even though I've only had a few hours' sleep, I feel hyper alert. Anxiety pulses through my flesh and bones, traces routes across my scalp. I'm caught up in something I don't understand. It feels like a runaway freight train and I'm not sure there's anything I can do to stop it – except stand on the tracks and wave my arms. And even then, there's a good chance it will simply run straight over me.

It's just gone eight by the time I arrive in Oakwood Road. Despite the bright September sunshine, a grey shroud seems to hang over The Sanctuary. The rose window looks duller, the bell tower more forbidding. Even the pair of gargoyles flanking the entrance portico seem more contemptuous than usual.

Although all the curtains at the front of the house are drawn, the window in the downstairs loo is open a few inches, suggesting that at least one of the occupants is up. I ring the bell, holding my finger down for several seconds, then dive behind a bay tree so I can't be seen through the peephole. If Eleanor knows it's me, she might not answer.

A few moments later, Katya comes to the door. Seeing no one there, she steps over the threshold and looks around. As I come out from behind the bay tree, she stares at me in an irritated sort of way.

'Oh, it's you,' she says flatly. 'What are you doing here?'

'I need to speak to Eleanor.'

'She's still in bed and I don't want to wake her because she's been up most of the night.'

'At the hospital?'

She frowns. 'You know what happened to James?'

'Yes, it's dreadful, isn't it? How's he doing, do you know?'

A mulish expression settles on her face. 'You'll have to ask Mrs Elliott.'

'I'll do that, but first you have to let me in. Please, Katya, it's really important.'

'Sorry, I can't, I'll get into trouble. You'll have to come back later.'

She turns around, momentarily distracted. From somewhere behind her, I hear the sound of a child laughing. A wave of relief crashes over me. I'm not too late after all.

Seizing my chance, I barge past the au pair and into the house.

'Hey, where are you going?' she yells after me.

Ignoring her, I stride across the living room, past Toby, who's playing on the floor with a plastic train set, heading for the stairs. I hear the front door slamming shut and then Katya's footsteps coming after me.

When I arrive on the landing I head for the bookcase door, but before I can get to it, it swings open. I stop dead, my heart hammering wildly in my throat, still unsure of how I'm going to play this.

A moment later Eleanor emerges. She's wearing cream silk pyjamas and fluffy slipper socks. She looks how I feel: red-eyed, ashen, as if a nightmare is loitering at her shoulder.

'What the hell?' she says when she sees me standing there. 'How did you get in?'

'I tried to stop her, but she pushed past me,' says Katya as she appears, breathlessly, at the top of the stairs.

Eleanor gives me a look of pure hatred. 'You've got some nerve showing up here. If you don't get out of my house right now, I'm calling the police. I can't believe they haven't come for you already – and when they do, I hope they lock you up and throw away the key. That way you won't be able to hurt anyone in my family ever again.'

My neck starts to burn, hot curls of shame, licking up my face. 'Please, Eleanor, just hear me out. Five minutes, that's all I'm asking for.'

Stranded on his own in the living room, Toby starts to wail. Sighing, Katya sets off back down the stairs to see to him.

Eleanor takes a step towards me. My insides crumble beneath the weight of her stare.

'I'm not interested in anything you've got to say. You're a psychopath, plain and simple. You deceive and manipulate everyone around you.'

My jaw flexes. 'I know how it looks, but you have to

believe me when I say I had nothing to do with what happened to James last night.'

'Just like you had nothing to do with Izzy's fall?' The words are delivered like the rapid staccato gunshots of a firing squad.

'Izzy was my friend,' I say, my voice splintering. 'I'd never have done anything to hurt her.'

Eleanor closes her eyes briefly, as if the sight of me is more than she can bear. 'Your little Miss Innocent act might have worked twenty years ago when the police were investigating the death of Frances Bellamy, but you don't fool me. You pushed that girl to her death from a bridge, didn't you, Amy – or should I say "Sophie"?'

Having seen the *Tribune* article on Eleanor's iPad, it's a line of attack I was anticipating. 'No, that's not true. If you know about Frances's case, then you'll also know I was cleared of any involvement in her death.'

She acts as if she hasn't heard me. 'Was James starting to get suspicious of you? Is that why you tried to kill him too?' The fury in her voice is so powerful it's like an earthquake. I can feel my limbs shaking from its force. 'You won't get away with it this time; the police are on to you. I just wish I'd gone to them sooner; maybe then my husband wouldn't be lying in hospital right now, unable to speak and drugged up to his eyeballs.'

My head is starting to throb, a dull beat at the base of my skull. I'm tempted to turn around and walk out of here, but I know I can't. If I don't go through with this,

I'll only find myself snared in one of those endless cycles of regret I've become so familiar with. I have to find a way to take control of the situation – and fast.

'You know, Eleanor, it's really quite ironic that you're blaming *me* for what's happened to your family, because up until an hour ago I was convinced you were the one who attacked Izzy and James.' Her face fills with the kind of horror that can't be faked – confirmation, in case I needed it, that my instincts were correct.

'Let's face it, you've got much more of a motive than me,' I say, taking advantage of her stunned silence. 'Being betrayed by two of the people you love most in the world . . . it's a pretty bitter pill to swallow, isn't it?'

The cords in her neck stand out; I can see I've struck a nerve. 'James and Izzy were having an affair, weren't they?' I press on. 'I wonder if you've told the police about *that*. I'm guessing not . . . after all, it would kinda make you the chief suspect, wouldn't you agree?'

'That's an outrageous suggestion,' she hits back, but her voice lacks conviction.

'Don't worry, Eleanor, I know it wasn't you. And do you know *how* I know?'

'No, but I expect you're about to tell me.'

'It seems to me that you love your son a great deal. While you might have had some very dark thoughts about your selfish sister and your adulterous husband, I don't believe you'd ever hurt Toby.'

'Of course I wouldn't hurt him,' she snarls.

'Unfortunately, there's someone out there who has no such compunction.' I can see from the horrified look on her face that my words have met their target.

'What are you trying to say?' she says slowly.

'Give me those five minutes and I'll tell you everything I know. Deal?'

She sighs, a long, heavy exhalation that makes her shoulders sag. She walks past me and looks over the banister to the living room below. 'Katya? Do you mind taking Toby out for a little while? The two of you could have hot chocolate at the café in the park.'

The au pair's voice drifts up to us. 'I thought you said he wasn't allowed sugary drinks.'

'I'm willing to make an exception, just this once.'

'Are you sure you'll be OK?' She doesn't actually articulate the words 'with *her*', but that's what she means.

'Yes, but bring me my phone before you go, will you? It's on top of the bureau.'

Eleanor looks at me, straightens her spine, squares her shoulders. 'If you do anything that gives me the slightest cause for concern, I'll be straight on the phone to the police. Understood?'

I give a small nod.

The second the phone is in Eleanor's hand, I start walking towards Toby's bedroom. 'Come with me, there's something I need to show you.'

24

I go straight to the toy chest. It's a sturdy thing, around two feet high and painted a pretty shade of yellow. On top of it sits an object that seems slightly out of place in a toddler's bedroom: an old-fashioned crystal vase. It's filled with fresh flowers – an amateurish arrangement, but a colourful one, the sort of thing that would be instantly attractive to a young child. I turn around, expecting to see Eleanor right behind me, but she's hovering in the doorway, clearly wary of sharing the same space as me.

'You see these,' I say, pointing to the flowers. 'They're poisonous. Every single last one of them.'

Eleanor stares at me, clearly confused. 'What are you talking about?'

I pull a stem from the vase. 'Oleander. An exquisite plant, known for its star-shaped flowers. It also happens to be highly toxic – so toxic that just eating honey made from its pollen is enough to give an adult a nasty stomach ache.' I pause for dramatic effect, before adding, 'A single leaf is enough to kill a child.'

I snap the oleander's neck and try to ram it back in the vase, but it won't fit and slips out of my hand on to the pale beige carpet.

I choose another specimen – not a flower this time, but a stalk laden with vibrant red berries. 'Let me introduce you to black bryony. It's a pretty name and my goodness, those berries look good enough to eat, don't they?'

Eleanor swallows and puts a hand to her throat.

'I wouldn't advise it, though. They contain a chemical called saponin with a distinctive foaming characteristic. It irritates the membranes of the digestive tract; definitely not something you want to be putting anywhere near your mouth.'

Eleanor tries to say something, but all that comes out is a croak. Smiling grimly, I swap it for a taller variety with distinctive tubular flowers. 'I expect you recognise this one, don't you?'

She takes a couple of steps into the room. 'It's a foxglove, isn't it?'

'Correct – or *digitalis purpurea* to give it its full scientific name. Despite being a staple of many a country garden, every part of the foxglove is poisonous to humans. It contains a chemical compound that interferes with the heart's natural rhythms – it's actually the active ingredient in a type of medication used to treat congestive heart failure. I wouldn't recommend it for a healthy person, though.'

After returning the foxglove to the vase, I gesture with a magician's flourish to the final stem – a dazzling species with dark blue flowers that are almost leathery in texture. 'As for this little beauty . . . personally, I wouldn't even touch it unless I was wearing gloves.'

'Why not?' I can see how shocked Eleanor is and I take no pleasure in the collapse of her facial muscles, the deathly pall that inches across her face.

'This is aconitum, also known as monkshood. Its poison can be absorbed through the skin, usually via an open wound. Swallow a big enough dose and you'll end up with paralysis of the respiratory system.' I fold my arms across my chest. 'Dead, in other words.'

Eleanor gives a guttural moan and slumps against the mural. I can only imagine how she's feeling, knowing that any moment her precious offspring might've grabbed one of those poisonous blooms or berries and stuffed it into his eager mouth.

'I think it's safe to assume Toby hasn't come into contact with any of these plants, as he looked perfectly healthy when I saw him just now. But make no mistake, whoever put this vase here intended to cause him serious harm.'

The pain in Eleanor's eyes is raw. 'But what kind of person would do such a thing?'

'The same person who pushed Izzy out of a window and stabbed James. Someone out there is gunning for your family, Eleanor – and given that they clearly have access to your home, it has to be someone close to you. So I need you to think very carefully . . . when did this vase appear in Toby's room?'

She crosses her arms over her chest. 'It must've been some time yesterday. It was Izzy's funeral; we held the wake here at the house. I came into Toby's room to get some of his clothes, things he's grown out of, to give to one of the guests who's just had a baby. The vase wasn't here then, I'm sure of it.'

'What time was that?'

'One . . . one-thirty. This is the first time I've been in here since then. Katya put Toby to bed last night, while I was at the hospital with James, and got him up this morning.'

'How many guests did you have at the wake?' I know I'm bombarding her with questions, but we have to get to the bottom of this before someone else gets hurt.

She looks at me, her eyes brimming with panic.

'Fifty or so.'

'Any one of whom could presumably have slipped up to Toby's room without being seen.'

Eleanor nods her head in agreement. The next moment her face contracts as if she's bitten into something rotten. 'Hang on a minute, how do I know *you* didn't put the flowers there?'

'If it was me, why would I come to your house to warn you?'

'Perhaps that's why you did it in the first place – just so you could rush round here, acting like the heroine,' she says, her voice rising in pitch. 'How did you get into the house? Did you steal a set of keys at Izzy's party? Katya was only saying the other day she couldn't find the spare ones that are usually hanging up by the back door.'

I reach a hand out towards her. 'No, Eleanor, you've got it all wrong; I don't have any keys.'

'Don't touch me,' she says, recoiling in disgust. 'It must've been you. How else would you know the flowers were here?'

'Oh yeah, I never said, did I?' I jerk my thumb towards the bedside table. 'Your baby monitor; my phone's paired with it. I checked the footage first thing this morning; that's when I saw the flowers.'

'You must think I'm stupid,' she scoffs. 'You'd have to be connected to our WiFi to pair your phone with the camera.'

'I know and I *was*.'

'When?'

'Yesterday morning, when I was delivering the flowers for the wake.'

She screws her face up in fresh confusion. 'James's PA asked *you* to do the flowers?'

I nod. 'I guess nobody told her I was *persona non grata*.'

Eleanor's face is a rigid, righteous mask. 'What about the password for the camera app?'

'I bypassed the password and answered your memorable question instead.'

'What memorable question?' she says disbelievingly.

'Orthodontist,' I say to trigger her memory. 'Your dad's job came up in one of my conversations with Izzy.'

She still doesn't look entirely convinced, so I take out my mobile phone and open up the app. 'See,' I say, showing her the live feed.

'Is this supposed to reassure me?' she spits. 'Forgive me if I don't fall at your feet in gratitude, but your actions are a gross invasion of privacy – if not downright illegal – and anyway, none of this proves your innocence.'

I rake frantically through my memories, searching for the silver bullet that's going to save me. Compelling evidence that I couldn't possibly have pushed Izzy from the bell tower, or attacked James last night. Unfortunately, my brain is firing blanks.

'Can we discuss this later? I just saved your son's life, didn't I?'

'Yes, but—'

I hold out a hand to stay her. 'Look, Eleanor, I understand your reluctance to trust me, I really do – but time isn't on our side.' I hear the ugly desperation in my voice. 'Whoever booby-trapped your son's room could strike again – and who knows which member of your family will be their next target.

'Right now, we need to put our heads together and work out who had the means, motive and opportunity to put these flowers here. It's our best chance of running this monster to ground.'

She opens her mouth to protest, then snaps it shut, offering a shrug of surrender instead. 'Fine,' she says, venom pooling in her eyes. 'But I'll warn you again: one wrong move and I'm calling the police.' She holds her phone aloft to drive home the point.

'Understood.'

'We should start by viewing the camera footage from yesterday,' says Eleanor who, now that we've negotiated a fragile ceasefire, is suddenly all business. 'We always keep the camera pointed at Toby's bed, but there's a chance that whoever left that vase here wandered into its field of vision.'

'I've already checked; there's nothing.' I tap my phone

against my chin. 'Can you think of anyone who might have a grudge against your family?'

'There's no one that springs to mind.'

'What about James? Did *he* have any enemies? A disgruntled business associate, perhaps?'

'He's had his fair share of difficult customers over the years, but James is very good at handling people. He'll bend over backwards to make sure clients are completely happy, even if it involves some element of compromise on his part. It's the same with his employees; I don't think you'll find anyone at Cole & Elliott who has a bad word to say about him.'

'What about his personal life?'

Eleanor frowns and rubs the side of her temple. 'We've known most of our friends since before we were married. To the best of my knowledge, James has never fallen out with any of them.'

I stare down at the floor and scuff the thick pile carpet with the toe of my shoe, trying to work out how best to frame my next question. 'What about his, er . . . intimate relationships? Were there others besides Izzy?' When I look up again, Eleanor's wearing a look that could melt tungsten.

'They *were* having an affair, weren't they?' I say when she doesn't respond.

Her nostrils flare almost imperceptibly.

'I know this is difficult, but if you want my help, I need you to be completely up front with me.'

She draws in a breath. 'Yes, they were, but I only found out about it after Izzy died.'

'How?'

She links her fingers behind her neck, cradling her head in her hands. 'James was completely devastated by Izzy's death. They'd always got on well, so of course he was going to be upset. But his grief seemed so profound; it just didn't quite add up to me, especially as he's usually so stoic. Five or six days later, I found him sobbing in the garden shed. Believe it or not, it's only the second time I've ever seen him cry – the first was when Toby was born. I just had a feeling.' She lets her arms fall down by her sides. 'I asked him out-right if he and Izzy had been sleeping together. He looked up at me, with tears rolling down his cheeks, and said yes. Apparently, it had been going on for three months – which is right about the time my relationship with Izzy started to go off the rails.' She pulls a wry face. 'Funny, that.'

'Did he tell you how it started?'

'He offered to, but I didn't want to know; I thought I'd spare myself the gory details.'

'Do the police know they were having a relationship?'

'No, James begged me not to tell them. He said it would make him the number one suspect in Izzy's death.'

'How did you know he *didn't* do it?'

'Because right before she fell, James was with me – helping me put some empty bottles in the recycling box at the side of the house. He'd just gone to get another crate of empties from the caterers when I heard someone screaming. He was out of my sight for less than a minute;

nowhere near enough time to get to the bell tower and back.'

I nod slowly, absorbing this information. 'Do you think it was serious between the two of them?'

Her gaze remains steady, but her lips give a series of tiny convulsions, betraying her inner turmoil. 'If you mean was he thinking about leaving me for her, then I don't know the answer to that question. What I do know is that it's not the first affair James has had and it probably won't be the last. As for Izzy, I have absolutely no idea what her intentions were. She's always been a complex character; I stopped trying to work out her motivations for doing anything a long time ago. Did she confide in you?'

'About her and James? No.'

'So how did you know they were having an affair?'

'I didn't know for sure, not until you confirmed it just now.'

'But you had a suspicion?'

I rub my index finger back and forth across my lips. Fessing up to the baby monitor is one thing, but admitting I hid in Eleanor's wardrobe is a humiliation too far.

'I saw them together at the party. Let's just say they were looking a bit more cosy than the average in-laws.'

'You're not the only one who noticed; my mother saw them too.' She gives a thin-lipped smile. 'I must say, it's not like James; he's usually very discreet. I think they'd both had a bit too much to drink that night.'

'You sound so matter-of-fact. Don't you mind about his affairs?'

Her hand rises defensively to her neck. 'Of course I mind, but I've come to think of them as a necessary evil. James finds family life boring, restrictive. He needs his play time, otherwise he gets sulky and irritable.'

'You make him sound like a five-year-old.'

She shrugs. 'Aren't all men big kids at heart?'

'But sleeping with his own sister-in-law,' I persist. 'That's a really shitty thing that the two of them did to you.'

'It is, isn't it? Izzy's always been needy, selfish, attention-seeking, even when she was a little girl, but I never thought she'd be capable of something like this. If she was still alive, I don't know that I'd be able to forgive her.'

'Have you forgiven James?'

'What choice do I have? He's the father of my son.' She swipes a tear away from the corner of her eye. 'Anyway, we mustn't get sidetracked. You asked me about James's other women. Do you think one of them could be behind all these attacks on my family?'

'It's possible.'

'I suppose it does make sense. If this woman, whoever she is, was a guest at the party and spotted James and Izzy together, she could've pushed my sister out of the window in a jealous rage.'

'And when that didn't send James running back into her arms, she decided to punish him as well.'

Eleanor's gaze strays to the flowers. 'But what about Toby? He's a complete innocent in all of this.'

'Maybe she did it to hurt *you*. You are James's wife after all.'

Our eyes lock together. 'You know, for a while, I actually thought *you* were sleeping with James. When Izzy died, my head was all over the place – and then I found a receipt in his jacket pocket for a lunch he'd had at the café next door to your shop. Even after Maria convinced me you weren't his type, I still thought there was something off about you.'

'Oh? Why's that?'

'I don't know; it's just an odd vibe you give off. Maria felt it too.'

I feel a pinprick of hurt. 'Did she?'

'She told me you were fixated on Izzy . . . I think "obsessed" was the word she used. The two of us even speculated that you might have had romantic designs on her.'

I press my lips together and look down at the floor.

'Sorry,' Eleanor says. 'But you did say I should be up front.'

It's a fair point.

'I saw what you wrote on Izzy's Facebook – implying I had something to do with her death. You sounded pretty convinced.'

'I was at the time. I'd just found out your best friend drowned in mysterious circumstances when you were both teenagers. Clearly, there were similarities between that case and what happened to Izzy, and I thought it was strange that you were living under a different name now. It just made me wonder if . . .' She pauses and chews the inside of her cheek.

I say what she seems reluctant to. 'If I'd pushed my childhood friend off a bridge and then dispatched Izzy the same way?'

She nods. 'It was silly of me to vent on social media and I'm sorry you saw it. If it's any consolation, I've had Izzy's account deleted, so no one else will see it.'

'Is that when you decided to share your suspicions about me with the police?'

'Not then, I didn't want to say anything until I was sure; I didn't even mention the newspaper article to James. But then he got attacked and I knew I had to act. I showed the article to the detectives and said they needed to take a long, hard look at you.'

That figures, I think to myself. What with Eleanor naming me as a suspect, *and* the type of weapon used in James's assault, it must've looked like a slam dunk to DI Kilner. She must've been kicking herself when she had to let me go.

While Eleanor's been speaking, something's been niggling me, like an unreachable itch between my shoulder blades.

'So how did you stumble across the connection between me and Sophie Douglas? Most people don't even remember the Frances Bellamy case; it happened such a long time ago.'

'I got a tip-off.'

I feel a crawling sensation at the base of my spine. 'A *what*?'

'Someone sent a DM to my Instagram, a few days after Izzy died.'

'A friend of yours?'

She shakes her head. 'Someone I'd never heard of; they had a weird username made up of numbers and punctuation marks. They didn't give their name; I don't even know if they were male or female.'

'What did the message say?'

'That I should be very careful about who I welcomed into my family. There was a link to a website – an old newspaper article, written on the tenth anniversary of Frances's death. The person said I should pay close attention to one of the photos in it, the one that showed a girl in school uniform. "She may look harmless enough," they said, "but remember, every rose has its thorn."'

I give a snide little laugh. As cryptic clues go, it's a pretty good one.

'When I saw the photo of Sophie Douglas, I knew right away it was you.'

'Did you reply to this mysterious person?'

'I tried to, a couple of days later, but by then their Instagram account had been deleted.'

Unease dangles inside me, a heavy weight suspended from a fraying thread. There's something very sinister at play here; something I can't get my head around. Whoever sent that DM to Eleanor wanted her, and the police, to think I killed Izzy. Just like they want them to think I'm responsible for the attack on James – and the attempt to

poison little Toby. Not many people can boast my ency-
clopaedic knowledge of plants, but all the information
needed to make up that lethal bouquet is readily available
on the internet, and a pair of professional-grade snips can
be bought easily enough on eBay.

I experience the collapsing sensation that comes with
a realisation so terrifying that my brain has no immediate
means to decipher it.

It's not the Elliotts they're trying to eradicate. It's *me*.

Eleanor drapes a hand across her forehead like a Victorian heroine with a fit of the vapours. 'I don't know about
you, Amy, but my head is spinning. I appreciate what you
did in coming here today, but we're never going to crack
this on our own. Why don't you and I go to the police
station right now and tell them everything we know?
Hopefully, they'll be able to work out who's behind all this
before anyone else gets hurt.'

'Good idea, but you'd better call Katya and tell her
where we're going. If she comes back here and finds us
both gone, she'll probably think I've kidnapped you.'

Eleanor cocks an ear towards the door. 'Actually, I
think she might be back already. I thought I heard someone moving around downstairs just now.'

'Really? But they've only been gone for ten minutes.
That's barely enough time to walk to the park and back,
never mind squeeze in a hot chocolate.'

Then I hear something too.

The tiniest squeak of a floorboard.

But it isn't coming from downstairs; it's right outside the bedroom door

'Katya?' I say. 'Is that you?'

When there's no reply, I feel a spasm of alarm. Eleanor feels it too; I can tell by the look in her eyes.

I start towards the door, but I've only taken a single step when suddenly it swings open. As I see who's standing there, my shoulders instantly relax.

'Claire!' I say, breaking into a smile. 'What are you doing here?'

Eleanor frowns. 'Did Katya let you in?'

My assistant doesn't answer either question; she just stares at us, her eyes blank and indifferent like an animal's. Then I see that she's wearing my favourite pruning gloves; I'd recognise them anywhere. They're made from a pretty bee-print fabric and have sentimental value as they were a birthday present from my ex.

What happens next is so sudden and so shocking I don't have a chance to process it in real time. Claire, who still hasn't spoken a word, lunges at Eleanor, pinning her against the mural. There's a flash of silver and I see to my horror that she's holding a knife. Before I can stop her, she drives the knife into Eleanor's flank. With a rasping cry, Eleanor slides down the wall, clutching her side with her hand. Then Claire pulls the knife out and raises it in the air again.

I feel as if I'm in one of those twisted dreams that only happens after a night of heavy drinking. You wake up in the wee small hours, completely disoriented, dry-mouthed, heart hammering in your throat. Then, the terrific sense of relief when you realise it's not real. There isn't an ogre chasing you through the forest. You weren't walking naked down a busy Soho street. One of your employees isn't butchering a woman, right in front of your eyes. Except this isn't a dream. This is actually happening.

'What are you doing, Claire?' I cry. 'Get away from her!'

The knife comes down in Eleanor's right bicep as she lifts her arm to ward off the blow.

I hurl myself at Claire, grabbing her around the waist in a clumsy rugby tackle. She utters a low growl and starts thrashing in my arms. She's a skinny thing, but her strength is incredible. The next moment I feel a sharp pain in my chest. The shock of it makes me loosen my grip and Claire wriggles free from my embrace.

For a moment, we just stand there, both breathing heavily. There's a malicious gleam in Claire's eyes and her face glows with a dark victory. I touch a hand to my breastbone and when I bring it away and look down I see that my fingers are bloody.

My eyes flicker to Eleanor. She's lying on the floor, eyes half open, cream pyjamas now stained with crimson. I could make a dash for it, but Eleanor is blocking the door, leaving only a narrow gap. Still, it should be enough for me to squeeze through. I could run to a neighbour's house . . . get help for both of us.

I don't even get halfway across the room before Claire

is on me. She grabs me by the hair and drags me backwards, pushing me against the chest of drawers. The impact sends photo frames and a set of wooden building blocks crashing to the floor. As Claire lifts the knife to stab me again, I kick her in the shins as hard as I can. She falls over, landing heavily on her backside, but somehow manages to keep hold of the knife. As she picks herself up I back away towards the window.

The fire in my chest is getting worse. My brain is finding it difficult to engage too. I'm like a nineties modem, whirring desperately, screaming with the pain of trying to connect. I don't understand why Claire is doing this. What have I ever done to her?

I hold on to the windowsill for support. My arms feel heavy and cool; my fingertips tingle. Air leaves my lungs in shallow puffs. I try to speak, thinking that maybe I can try and reason with her, but all that comes out is a high-pitched hiss, like the sound of a balloon deflating. As my legs start to buckle, I grab on to the curtain for support. I'm still holding it as I slump to the floor. There's a popping sound as one by one the curtain hooks snap, showering me in pieces of broken plastic.

As I lie sprawled on my side, utterly helpless, Claire comes over to me. I can see her measuring me with her eyes, as if she's trying to work out what level of threat I present. It's getting harder and harder to breathe, but I manage to push out a single word. 'Why?'

She gives me a smile like a clenched fist. 'It's payback. For Rosie. You do remember Rosie, don't you?'

A sharp jolt from somewhere deep inside me. How could I forget? The memory is like a noose around my neck. Sometimes it pulls so tight it nearly chokes me. There are some memories we can never outrun. This is one of them. I always knew it would catch up with me one day. I just didn't imagine it would be like this.

You see, Frances wasn't the first of my friends to die.

Before Frances, there was Rosie.

'H-h-how do y-you . . .' Each word feels like I'm expectorating a large and jagged chunk of metal.

'How do I know her?' Claire drops to her knees beside me, lips peeled back, revealing her incisors. 'Haven't you managed to work it out yet? Rosie was my sister.'

The fear starts somewhere in my gut. It rushes past my lungs, across my heart, into my throat, shreds itself against my teeth. Now I see it. Now it's starting to take shape. The bigger picture is emerging. Just like Rafe said it would.

'S-s-sorry,' I wheeze as my lungs struggle to inflate.

'You killed my sister, and that's all you've got to say for yourself?'

She shakes her head wearily, like a judge scoring a lacklustre performance: one out of five for effort.

'Fuck you, Sophie,' she says as she plunges the knife into my body for a second time.

I must've blacked out momentarily, because when I come round, Claire is picking a child-sized pillow up off the bed. I look across at Eleanor, lying behind the door. I know she's still alive because I can see the rise and fall of her chest.

I watch in horror as Claire straddles her body and places the pillow over her face. I know she's going to suffocate Eleanor if I don't do something to stop her, but my limbs are leaden and my throat is horribly constricted. I have a strange anchor-less feeling, as if I'm not in The Sanctuary at all, but adrift on a vast sea, being carried further and further from the shore.

As dark shadows begin to gather at the edges of my vision, my head rolls to the side. I feel a slight tickle on the side of my face and realise it's the stem of oleander I dropped on the carpet earlier. Crushed by the weight of my head, its apricot perfume fills my nostrils. The fragrance is so powerful, so unbearably sweet, it acts as a kind of smelling salt, nudging me back to full consciousness.

Gritting my teeth against the pain, I haul myself up on to all fours. Claire is fully focused on Eleanor, who's now making a horrible gurgling noise. There's no sign of the knife; I assume it's still in Claire's possession.

As my eyes cast frantically around the room for another weapon, they alight on the toy chest. It's only a few feet away, but it feels like ten miles.

Using every ounce of strength I have left, I push myself up off the floor and into a half-standing, half-crouching position. My chest is heaving, one breath not following the other as it should; instead elusive, impossible to grasp.

I pick up the heavy crystal vase, still filled with flowers, in both hands and stagger towards the door. At the last second, Claire looks up, but her reactions aren't quick enough.

I bring the vase down as hard as I can on top of her head. It shatters as it makes contact with her skull, a nauseating crunch.

She topples sideways, landing with her arms and legs spread wide, like a starfish.

I back away from her, half-expecting her eyes to snap open. When they don't, I fall to my knees. I feel stomach-churningly dizzy, as if I'm plummeting headfirst into space. Adrenalin squeezes my chest, my head filled with explosions of light and colour.

I close my eyes to watch the agonising fireworks and slide backwards out of the world.

Now

25

'If you could just tell us in your own words what happened at The Sanctuary.'

I place two fingers on the tender spot between my eyebrows. 'It's all a bit of a blur, to be honest,' I say, the words feeling sticky in my mouth. 'I think I'm still in shock.'

Detective Inspector Kate Kilner's face fills with sympathy as she leans forward, resting an elbow on the starched white sheet of my hospital bed. 'You've just had a very traumatic experience, it's perfectly natural to feel a little confused.'

I lie back on the pillows and take a few long, slow breaths. It's barely twenty-four hours since I regained consciousness and my brain feels sore. There's a long silence. It stretches out, thinning until it becomes awkward.

'What if we rewind . . . go right back to the beginning?' says DI Kilner's colleague, whose name has momentarily escaped me. He's a big man; his corpulent bulk fills the room in a way that feels slightly intrusive. 'How did you first come to meet the Elliott family?'

If only they knew the truth: that this all began way before I ever laid eyes on the Elliotts. Before I even knew they existed.

'Through work,' I tell him. 'Darling Buds has been doing the flowers for James Elliott's office premises for several years. He's one of our best customers.'

'And his wife, Eleanor?'

'Also a client. We supplied the floral arrangements for a couple of social events at her home.'

DI Kilner steps in. 'So were you at the Elliotts' home in a professional capacity on the morning of the twenty-second of September?'

A wave of exhaustion washes over me. The kind of tiredness that creeps up behind you and climbs on your back, its clammy tentacles slithering round your throat. I don't think I can do this now. I need more time to get the facts straight in my head; iron out any creases.

'I'm sorry, I know you're only doing your job, but I don't think I'm in any fit state to answer questions right now. Perhaps you could come back tomorrow.'

DS Pearce, whose name has just popped into my head, smiles stiffly. 'Your doctor's given us clearance to speak to you. It really would be better to get this out of the way now, while events are still fresh in your mind. One person is dead and another is in a critical condition. You're the only one who can tell us what happened.'

'Actually, that's not strictly true,' Kilner corrects him. 'We do have another witness.'

A flicker of surprise in the centre of my spine – like a

match being struck. What does she mean? It was just the three of us in that room.

She pulls out her mobile phone. 'Here, let me show you.' She presses a button to adjust the volume, then places the phone on the bed where I can see it.

As I look down at the screen, Kilner's eyes are on me, alert to the smallest tell. I manage to maintain a neutral expression, but it takes every ounce of energy I can muster.

When the video has finished playing, I shut my eyes. I can feel the throb of a headache starting in my temples. My thoughts are like rats in a burning building, running along one wall after another, desperately looking for the escape route. I'm inclined to take DS Pearce's advice. Tell them everything.

In light of the surprising new information DI Kilner has just presented me with, what other choice do I have?

26

*Transcript of interview between DI Kate Kilner and
Claire Fogarty, University Hospital, Lewisham*

CF: Before we talk about what happened yesterday,
I need to tell you about Rosie.

KK: Rosie?

CF: My little sister. She was murdered three days after
her fourteenth birthday by Amy Mackenzie – or
Sophie Douglas as she was then.

KK: *Murdered*, you say?

CF: Yes. I'll explain what happened, but can I give you
some background first?

KK: Please do.

CF: Rosie suffered from asthma. As she got older it
seemed to get worse. When she was nine she had
a serious attack that landed her in hospital. After
that, she never left the house without her inhaler.
A few months before she died, she joined a local
youth club. She made lots of new friends there, but
there were two girls she was especially close to –
Sophie Douglas and Frances Bellamy. I didn't know
them – they went to the Catholic grammar, not the
comprehensive like us – but Rosie used to talk about
them a lot. One night at youth club, she had a falling

out with these two; we never did find out what
it was about. For some utterly incomprehensible
reason, this pair of morons decided to teach my
sister a lesson by stealing her inhaler. Another kid
at the youth club saw them take it from Rosie's bag
when she wasn't looking – except, at the time, he
didn't know whose bag it was. Two hours later, my
sister was waiting for her bus home when she had
a massive asthma attack that was almost certainly
triggered by a man who was smoking in the bus
shelter. Usually, Rosie would've steered clear of
cigarette smoke, but as it was raining quite heavily
that evening she obviously decided to risk it, secure
in the knowledge that her inhaler was safely in her
bag. Except this time, it wasn't. The ambulance
took ages to arrive – some kind of mix-up over
the location of the bus shelter. By the time the
paramedics got to her, she was already dead.

KK: And you hold Sophie and Frances responsible for
her death.

CF: Of course they were responsible. Unfortunately,
the police didn't see it that way. Instead of treating
them like criminals, the senior investigating officer
described what they did as – quote, unquote – a
foolish prank that had unforeseen consequences.
What a fucking joke. We're talking about two clever
girls here, *grammar school* girls. Of course they
could've foreseen what might have happened – so
why weren't they held accountable? The little bitches

showed no remorse; they didn't even have the decency to apologise to my family.

KK: How did that make you feel?

CF: I've never felt pain like it, not even when I had my two miscarriages. Rosie's funeral was the worst day of my life. Seeing my parents standing at her graveside, utterly broken, is an image that will haunt me for ever. That was the day I made up my mind to get justice for my sister, no matter how long it took.

KK: By 'justice', do you mean you wanted to see Sophie and Frances punished?

CF: Yes.

KK: And just so we're clear, are we talking about the same Frances Bellamy who drowned in the River Wye in 2004 after she fell from a bridge in the town of Bakewell?

CF: She didn't fall. I pushed her.

KK: You're telling me that you *deliberately* pushed Frances off that bridge into the river?

CF: That's what I just said, didn't I?

KK: How long after your sister's death did this incident take place?

CF: One year, seven months and eight days. I knew she couldn't swim because Rosie told me. Apparently Frances had mentioned she was going on a family holiday to one of those posh Club Med resorts. She said she'd have to wear armbands in the swimming pool and she was worried the other kids would take the piss. The irony is that Rosie had actually offered to teach Frances how to swim before she went away. That was typical of my sister – always looking out for other people.

KK: Since you knew Frances couldn't swim, you must also have known there was a possibility she would drown.

CF: Are you not listening to me, DI Kilner? I *wanted* her to drown.

KK: Did you feel any regret when you heard that Frances's body had been recovered from the river?

CF: Not in the slightest. I was pleased that the first part of my plan had worked so well.

KK: What was the second part?

CF: The part where Sophie Douglas was charged with Frances's murder.

KK: You mean you tried to make it look as though Sophie had pushed Frances off the bridge? For the benefit of the tape, Claire Fogarty is nodding.

CF: Sophie wasn't punished for killing my sister, so I figured the next best thing was to make her pay for killing someone else. The fact it was her best friend would be the cherry on top.

KK: And how exactly did you plan to achieve that?

CF: I'd recently left college and I was working as a cleaner for an agency that had contracts with lots of the schools in Derbyshire – including, as good luck would have it, the local Catholic grammar. That particular school wasn't on my roster, but I managed to find a colleague who was willing to

swap out a couple of shifts. It wasn't too difficult
to find a locker in one of the corridors with Frances
Bellamy's name on it. Early one morning, before
the kids arrived, I slid a note through the gap in
the door – written to make it look as if it was from
Sophie. I printed it out from my dad's computer, so
there wouldn't be an issue with the handwriting not
matching up.

KK: What did the note say?

CF: I asked Frances to meet me after school so she could
help me choose a birthday present for a friend.
I said I wanted to nip home first to get changed, so
we should meet at the bridge. It was a place I knew
well – a nice quiet spot where there weren't usually
too many people about.

KK: Weren't you worried Frances would mention the
note to Sophie when she saw her at school later that
day?

CF: Of course I was. That's why I warned her not to say
anything when she saw me, because the friend I was
buying the present for might overhear us talking
about it. It was a pretty pathetic cover story, but it
obviously worked because Frances showed up, bang
on time.

KK: What happened then?

CF: I was already there, hiding in the bushes at the
side of the lane. I watched as she went up on to
the bridge, sat on the parapet wall and got out her
mobile phone. I checked to make sure there was no

one else around and then I started walking towards the bridge. Frances glanced up as I approached, but then her attention went back to her phone. I acted like I was going to walk straight past her, but at the last minute I turned and shoved her in the chest as hard as I could – and over the wall she went.

KK: You make it sound as if it was easy.

CF: It was – and as the police never questioned me, or any member of my family, I don't think they even considered the possibility there might be a connection between Rosie's death and what happened to Frances.

KK: You must've been disappointed when they also failed to link Sophie Douglas to Frances's death.

CF: That's an understatement. It appears the police never found the note I left in Frances's locker. It would've backed up what she told her mum when she left the house that day – that she was going to meet Sophie. But since the note was never mentioned in the press coverage, or during the inquest, I'm guessing Frances chucked it away at school after she read it.

KK: And after Sophie was exonerated . . . were you still intent on exacting some sort of revenge on her for your sister's death?

CF: Not revenge. Like I said before . . . *justice*. There's a big difference. And yes, I still had Sophie in my sights, but other stuff got in the way.

KK: What kind of stuff?

CF: Oh, you know . . . life. I met a guy, became Mrs

Fogarty, lost a couple of babies, got divorced.
While all of that was going on, I put Sophie to the
back of my mind, but the memory of what she'd
done to Rosie was always there, like a big chunk
of gristly meat I couldn't swallow. Then I got made
redundant from my job as a supermarket manager
and suddenly I had more space in my brain. It's time,
I thought to myself. Time to finish what I started.

KK: You wanted to kill Sophie?

CF: Not kill her. Destroy her.

KK: What do you mean by that?

CF: Killing her wasn't enough for me. I'd learned that
lesson with Frances. The coroner reckoned she
drowned within five minutes of entering the water. It
was all over too quickly – for her and for me. With
Sophie, I wanted to savour the experience, to have a
front-row seat as her life fell apart. I wanted her to
suffer, to feel the unbearable pain that I'd felt when
Rosie died. That's why I took the job at Darling
Buds. So I could learn about her. Identify her weak
spots. Work out how to inflict maximum damage.

KK: Given how you felt about Sophie – or Amy as she'd
become – it must've required quite an effort on
your part to work alongside her; play the dutiful
employee.

CF: It did – and believe me, there were times I thought it
would be easier just to slash her arteries with a pair
of branch cutters, or garrotte her with some floristry
twine. But I kept reminding myself that I wasn't in

this for instant gratification. That was the mistake
I'd made with Frances. This time, I was playing the
long game. In the beginning I focused on ways I
could sabotage Amy's business, as it was pretty clear
Darling Buds was the most important thing in her
life – the *only* thing in her life. She ran a pretty tight
ship, though, and my options were limited. Anyway,
ruining her business wasn't sufficient; I wanted to
ruin her entire life. Finally, when I'd been working
for her for about six months, I saw an opportunity.
There was going to be some collateral damage, but
that couldn't be helped.

KK: When you say 'collateral damage', what are you
referring to?

CF: The Elliotts. Amy was completely infatuated with
them.

KK: Why do you say that?

CF: Well, for starters it was bloody obvious she had the
hots for James Elliott. I don't blame her actually;
he's a good-looking man. Not that she would ever
have made a move on him – she's far too strait-laced
for that. Then she met his wife, Eleanor, and her
obsession with the family ratcheted up another gear.
When Amy got back to the shop after meeting her
for the first time, she was so bloody pleased with
herself. I had to listen while she went on and on
about Eleanor's magnificent home and her amazing
sense of style. Amy knew she'd hooked a big fish.
She was hoping the Elliotts would open doors for

her – not just professionally, but socially too. She was so desperate to ingratiate herself with them, she Facebook-stalked Eleanor's sister, Izzy.

KK: How do you know that?

CF: I caught her red-handed at work. She told me she was looking at a friend's Facebook profile, but at that stage she'd never even met Izzy. I looked up Izzy's profile myself later and that's when I saw details of an upcoming hiking club event that she'd expressed an interest in. Amy must've seen it, too, because she signed up for the hike. I'm pretty sure she went along just to meet Izzy – certainly she'd never shown any interest in hiking before then. I couldn't believe it when the two of them actually hit it off.

KK: Why were you so surprised?

CF: Because, on the face of it, they didn't seem to have anything in common. I don't know . . . maybe Izzy felt sorry for her. Anyway, whatever the reason, they started meeting up quite regularly. Amy was totally smitten with Izzy. The way she used to talk about her . . . it was almost like she was in love with her. Just for the record, I'm pretty sure Amy's straight. She was always banging on about her ex-boyfriend – Rob something or other.

KK: Now that we're on the subject of Isabel Harkness, what can you tell me about the events leading up to her fall from a second-storey window on the twenty-ninth of August this year?

CF: I'm not sure I want to talk about that.

KK: Why not? You've been very forthcoming so far.

CF: That's the problem; I think I might have said too much.

KK: You know, Claire, a judge is much more likely to exercise lenience if they know you cooperated fully with our inquiry at the earliest possible opportunity.

CF: Yeah, but there are no guarantees, are there?

KK: Don't forget, we have the evidence you saw on my phone. We know most of what happened already. Come on, Claire, help us fill in the gaps – you'll be doing yourself a favour, trust me.

CF: Oh, all right then, I killed her. Is that what you wanted to hear?

KK: Why? What had Izzy ever done to you?

CF: Nothing, but she was Amy's friend and it was too good an opportunity to pass up. Two best friends. Two mysterious falls from a tall structure. Too many similarities to be a coincidence, huh?

KK: So your sole purpose in killing Izzy was to frame Amy for her murder?

CF: Well done, DI Kilner. Keep this up and I reckon you'll be in line for a promotion.

KK: I don't remember seeing your name on the guest list the Elliotts gave us. How did you gain access to the party?

CF: I knew Eleanor had hired professional waiting staff from an agency because Amy had asked me to text her with a couple of recommendations. I know what

agency work's like; there are new faces popping
up all the time. I just turned up to the house at the
appropriate time in a black skirt and a white blouse,
looking like all the other waitresses, picked up a tray
and started working.

KK: Had you already worked out what you were going
to do?

CF: More or less. Amy mentioned that The Sanctuary
had been featured in the *Evening Standard* property
pages and I managed to find the article online. I
studied the photos and the floorplan, so I knew the
exact layout of the house. When I saw the bell tower
I knew straight away it was perfect for what I had
in mind. I just had to find a way of getting Izzy up
there.

KK: So how did you do that?

CF: I followed her when she went into the house for a
pee. The downstairs loo was occupied, so she had to
use one of the upstairs bathrooms. I went upstairs
too and stood outside the secret door that leads to
the bell tower. There were quite a few kids at the
party and when Izzy came out of the bathroom I
told her I'd just seen a little boy run upstairs, who
looked as if he was up to no good. I said I'd chased
after him and had seen him slipping through the
door. 'Is that some sort of cupboard?' I asked her,
playing dumb. 'Because if it is, I think that kid might
need rescuing.' She laughed then and explained
about the bell tower. 'I'd better go and find him,'

she said. 'My sister will have a fit if she finds out
there's a child running loose in her bedroom.'

KK: And you offered to help.

CF: Yeah, she seemed glad of the company, to be honest.
I'd already worked out that it would have to be
the guest bedroom – the master didn't have the
right kind of windows. When we got there, there
was no sign of the kid, obviously, so I told Izzy to
check under the bed, while I had a quick look in the
wardrobe. While she was on her hands and knees,
I went over to the window and pulled my shirt
sleeve down over my hand, so I wouldn't leave any
fingerprints. Then I opened both windows as far
as they would go. 'There's an amazing view of the
garden from here,' I said when Izzy stood up.
'It looks so pretty with all the fairy lights.'
Naturally, she couldn't resist coming over to see
for herself. I stepped aside and watched as she
leaned out of the window, taking it all in. She was
so drunk, so unsuspecting. By the time she realised
anything was wrong she was falling through the air.

KK: What did you do then?

CF: I went back downstairs and left the house through
the front door. I didn't need to hang around to see
the fallout, if you'll pardon the pun; nobody survives
a fall on to paving stones from that height. I walked
to the next street, where I'd left my car, and drove
home.

KK: When did you find out Izzy had died?

CF: The next day; Amy told me at work. A friend of Izzy's had texted her with the sad news.

KK: I expect Amy was very upset, wasn't she?

CF: She was a wreck. I put on a good show of sympathy, said I was there for her if she wanted to talk about it.

KK: And did she?

CF: No – which was a bit annoying. A couple of days later, I sent an anonymous message to Eleanor via Instagram. I directed her to a newspaper article about the Frances Bellamy case and dropped some heavy-handed hints about Amy Mackenzie and Sophie Douglas being one and the same person. I thought that once Eleanor worked out that Amy was the common denominator in the two deaths, she'd take her suspicions to the police.

KK: But she didn't, did she? And so you decided to hurry her along by assaulting another member of her family.

CF: Well, here's the thing, DI Kilner – I didn't set out to attack James. It just sort of happened.

KK: I find that very hard to believe.

CF: I'm telling you the truth. I was bored that evening, so I thought I'd take a little drive over to The Sanctuary.... see how James and Eleanor were bearing up after Izzy's funeral. I parked my car opposite their house. It was dark outside, but the lights were on in the living room so I had a pretty good view. Eleanor was sitting on the sofa by herself, not doing anything, just staring into space.

She looked dazed, like she'd just been run over by a
truck; I actually felt quite sorry for her. After about
ten minutes, James appeared from round the side
of the house with a big plastic box. He unlocked
his car and put the box in the boot. When he pulled
out of the drive, I decided to follow him. I wanted
to know what was so important he'd leave his wife
on her own on the day she'd buried her sister. When
he turned into the recycling place, I clocked that his
was the only car there. It suddenly struck me that I
had an opportunity here – the kind of opportunity
I might not get again. I carried on driving and
parked a bit further down the street. Although I
hadn't come prepared, I remembered that I had
a pair of secateurs in the glovebox – not the bog
standard type you get in the middle aisle at Aldi,
but professional-grade ones from the shop. They're
really sharp; sharp enough to slice your finger off.
I got them out and cleaned the handles with a wet
wipe. Then I put on a pair of those plastic gloves
you get free at the petrol station. I was worried
about CCTV cameras, so I wrapped a scarf around
the lower part of my face and flipped the hood up
on my coat. When I got there, James had his back
to me and the sound of the bottles smashing as he
tossed them into the recycling bin was so loud, he
couldn't hear my footsteps. I walked right up to him
and stabbed him in the neck with the secateurs. He
staggered forwards, clutching his neck. I was going

to stab him again, but then I heard a voice that sounded like someone calling to a dog, so I dropped the secateurs and legged it back to my car.

KK: Did you intend to kill James Elliott, or just to injure him?

CF: Either or. As long as it looked like Amy had done it, that was all I cared about. That's why I dropped the secateurs – hoping they'd be traced back to Darling Buds. How's James doing by the way? I know he's still alive because the guy who called the ambulance wasted no time broadcasting his heroics all over social media.

KK: Do you care?

CF: Just wondering whether or not he's going to be fit enough to testify at my trial, that's all.

KK: Oh, he'll be there; don't worry about that. Let's move on to the twenty-second of September, shall we?

CF: Do we have to? I'm really not feeling very well.

KK: Come on, Claire, we're nearly at the end now. Let's wrap this up.

CF: If I talk, will you let my mum and dad come and see me? The hospital staff said you lot had banned me from having any visitors.

KK: I'll see what I can do.

CF: Sorry, not good enough.

KK: I really don't think you're in a position to negotiate.

CF: Fuck's sake. OK . . . so, before I attacked James, I'd put a little insurance policy in place, just in case

Eleanor needed some extra encouragement to go
to the police with the information about Sophie-
slash-Amy. I did a ton of research, compiled a list
of poisonous plants – stuff I could easily order in
from Darling Buds' suppliers, all in Amy's name,
of course. While she was out delivering the flowers
for Izzy's wake, I was at the shop, making up a
pretty bouquet of my own. As soon as Amy got
back, I went off on my lunch break – except I didn't
bother with lunch, I got in my car and drove to
The Sanctuary. The wake had already started and I
tailgated some guests when the au pair opened the
door to let them in. If anyone noticed me they would
naturally assume the bouquet I was carrying was a
sympathy gift for the Elliotts. As soon as I could, I
slipped upstairs to Toby's bedroom. In my bag was
an old vase I'd taken from the shop. I filled it with
the flowers and put it on top of the toy chest, where
the kid could easily reach them – and before you
ask, I didn't intend to kill him, just make him sick.

KK: So why go back to the house the next morning?

CF: I got a text from Amy, not long after I'd arrived at
the shop, telling me she had an urgent appointment
in West Dulwich and would be in later. I thought she
was probably going to The Sanctuary, but I had no
idea why. I tied myself up in knots, imagining all the
possibilities. In the end I couldn't bear it any longer,
so I shut the shop and drove over there. I didn't
have a particular plan in mind, but I wanted to be

prepared for any eventuality, so before I left I took a knife from the shop, one of the ones we used for cutting floral foam.

KK: And utilised it during a violent and entirely unprovoked attack on two defenceless women.

CF: I suppose that's one way of putting it. You know the rest, so I guess we're done here.

KK: Not quite. I want to hear your version of events. I need you to tell me every last detail of what happened at The Sanctuary yesterday morning. But before you do, can I ask you something?

CF: Knock yourself out.

KK: You've barely shown a flicker of emotion during this entire interview – except when you were talking about your sister. Do you have any remorse at all for what you've done?

CF: I only have one regret. That I didn't kill Amy Mackenzie when I had the chance.

Four Months Later

I stand on the beach, gazing out to sea. In the west, the sun is just setting, a fat, fierce ball that spills gold on to the surface of the water, making me squint and raise a hand to shade my eyes. The days are long and loose here, bookended between the fanfare of the dawn chorus and the dance of the bats at dusk.

I had my doubts about coming here. I thought I'd miss my flat, my shop, my customers, but I don't. I don't even miss my flowers, as the native varieties here are far superior. The hotel's well-stocked gardens are filled with fragrant jasmine and frangipani and bougainvillea so bright they hurt my eyes.

I try to empty my head of thought as I continue my mindfulness practice, focusing instead on the natural beauty around me. I inhale a waft of iodine seawater, listen to the gentle murmur of the waves rhythmically lapping the shore.

This is the first proper holiday I've had in years. It was Dad's idea. He said that after everything I'd been through, I needed to get away from London for a while, give myself the time and space I needed to heal. I have to say my parents have been brilliant. We've had our ups and downs over the years, but they've always been there when it counted. It's a special kind of love that holds families together, even ones as dysfunctional as mine.

I'm glad now that I took his advice and escaped to this pretty island in the Indian Ocean. The kinks and bruises of the past few months have faded a little more with each passing day, and the terrifying nightmares I suffered in the aftermath of the attack have all but disappeared. The first knife wound punctured my lung, the second grazed my small intestine. The doctors have assured me there won't be any lasting damage, but if Eleanor's cleaner hadn't shown up when she did, it might have been a very different story.

Sadly, Eleanor wasn't as fortunate as me. When the paramedics arrived, she was still clinging to life but, despite their best efforts, she couldn't be saved. It breaks my heart to think of that little boy growing up without a mother, but I'm grateful that at least one of his parents is still alive.

As for Izzy . . . I was grief-stricken when I lost her and now that I know the full circumstances surrounding her death, the pain feels even sharper. Like all of us, she had her imperfections, but she was my friend and I miss her every day. I know the ache will lessen in time, but right now it's like a deeply lodged piece of shrapnel inside me, shifting and tearing flesh every time I think of her.

I haven't seen or spoken to James since Eleanor died. Attending her funeral was out of the question as I was still recovering in hospital, but I sent some flowers and a sympathy card to the house. Once I'd been discharged to complete my recuperation at home, I called James's office a couple of times. My messages were never returned. The next thing I knew there was an email from his PA in my inbox, terminating Darling Buds' contract for the office flowers with immediate effect. I'm not surprised he's cut me out of his life. After all, everything bad that happened to his family happened because of me.

I'm still struggling to come to terms with the depth and breadth of Claire's deceit. I've always considered myself a pretty good judge of character, but she suckered me in completely. When I think about how I opened myself up to her, exposed my soft underbelly, it makes my flesh crawl. I welcomed her into my life, shared my expertise, showed a keen interest in her personal life. And all the while, beneath that warm and empathetic exterior, she was busy selecting her next weapon, cleaning it off, then getting ready to slip it between my ribs with a cold-blooded precision.

Considering the lengths I went to in order to conceal my identity, I'm amazed Claire managed to find me. It emerged during one of her police interviews that, having failed to find any trace of 'Sophie Douglas' on social media, she decided to look for my parents instead. Remembering my dad's name and knowing that he'd worked as an accountant back in Bakewell, she tracked him down to his current employer in Colchester. His firm has one of those 'Meet the team' pages on its website, with photos of every staff member and a potted biography. Dad's biog describes him as 'a wine connoisseur and keen cyclist'. Rather touchingly, he goes on to reveal that, beside his forty-year career as a chartered accountant, his proudest achievement is his daughter, 'a successful florist, who recently won an award for the tiara-shaped floral sculpture she created for a London park to commemorate the late Queen Elizabeth'. Suffice to say, it didn't take Claire long to find out that the award-winner was one Amy Mackenzie, owner of Darling Buds in Forest Hill.

Armed with my new name and a payout from a recent job redundancy, Claire left her home in Derbyshire, moved to London and set about trying to find out as much about me as she could. According to DI Kilner, she spent hours in her car, staking out Darling Buds, observing my routines, learning my habits, trying to find a way in. She followed me home one day, where she continued her surveillance, even rifling through the bins outside my flat, hoping to find something she could use against me. She must've been jumping for joy when, barely a month into her campaign, I put an ad in Darling Buds' window: *Part-time assistant required. No experience necessary.*

Partly due to the meagre salary I was offering, most of the other applicants were school leavers. No wonder Claire, with all the skills she'd picked up from more than ten years as a supermarket manager, stood out. By that time, she also had a convincing South London accent and a well fleshed-out back story, complete with imaginary boyfriend. And since she was using her married name of Fogarty, there was no reason to suspect she had any connection to my childhood friend.

I have to give it to Claire – she planned her assault with military precision. I was shocked to learn she'd masqueraded as a waitress at Izzy's birthday party. She confessed to DI Kilner that at one point I'd beckoned to her as she cleared tables in the gazebo. Fearing I might recognise her beneath the blond wig and coloured contact lenses, she pretended not to see me.

Her success wasn't just down to planning though; I think even she would admit she had a healthy dose of luck on her side. The job opening at Darling Buds, the absence of any witnesses when she ambushed James, the downstairs window that Katya had left open, enabling her to enter The Sanctuary unseen and eavesdrop on my conversation with Eleanor. Realising her plan to turn Eleanor against me had failed and that the two of us were now working together, it seems Claire felt she had no alternative but to silence us both.

Although there can never be any justification for what she did, I do at least understand what drove her. The prank I pulled on her sister wasn't just reckless; it was downright *wicked*. No wonder Claire hated me with every bitter, wire-wool fibre of her being.

When I found out Rosie had died, I hated myself too. I was physically sick in the toilets at school when I heard the news from a teacher, who knew that Rosie and I were friends. In the days and weeks that followed, I couldn't eat, couldn't sleep, couldn't think about anything except what Frances and I had done. What I remember most vividly is my desperate desire to escape. I just wanted the ache in my head to cease, the wrench in my gut to evaporate, the tightness in my chest to loosen. I wanted to disappear.

I know Frances and I were minors, but even at the time I thought we got off far too lightly. That's not to say we weren't chastised once our part in Rosie's death became public knowledge. The school principal called us to her office and gave us a stern lecture about the importance of making the right decisions in life. A close friend's mother refused to let me come to their house any more, describing me as a 'bad influence', and my own parents cancelled a long-booked family holiday to Menorca as a way of showing how disappointed they were in me. However, the police declared that because no crime had been committed, no action would be taken against Frances and me.

In the absence of any real punishment, I was left instead with the crushing weight of guilt, a weight that I naively hoped might lighten some day, not knowing that it would only go on to hurt in new and varied ways for many years to come.

Perhaps if I'd reached out to Rosie's family at the time – showed them how truly sorry I was, then Claire wouldn't have spent the best part of twenty years plotting her revenge. I did think about writing to her parents, but my solicitor advised me not to, warning that any such correspondence could be viewed as an admission of culpability. I *was* culpable though – even more so than Frances. You see, stealing Rosie's inhaler was my idea.

I liked Rosie but I was also deeply jealous of her. She was so pretty, so lively, so comfortable in her own skin. I, on the other hand, was plain and unremarkable, with a slight lisp that affected my confidence. On the night she died, I was annoyed with Rosie because instead of hanging out with Frances and me, like she usually did, she chose to play pool with a boy who went to my school. It didn't help that I'd had a crush on him since Year 7. I don't know where I got the idea to take her inhaler, but when I ran it past Frances, she was up for it – so up for it she even volunteered to do the deed.

Although I knew Rosie was asthmatic, I didn't realise how severe her condition was, let alone that it could be life-threatening. It goes without saying that if Frances and I had had even the faintest inkling of what was to unfold on her journey home, we would never have done it. We just wanted to frighten her, to see the look of panic on her face when she opened her bag to freshen her lip gloss, which she usually did at least once an hour, and realised her inhaler wasn't there. Except she didn't open her bag – or if she did, she didn't notice the inhaler was missing. If I'd seen her leave that evening, I would've run after her, pretended I'd found the inhaler lying under a table some-where and given it back to her, but I never had the chance.

According to the boy from my school who was the last person to speak to her, Rosie had lost track of the time. Realising her curfew was fast approaching, she left in a hurry, without saying goodbye to any of us. By the time I realised she'd gone, it was already too late.

The police visited me at home two days later, after an eyewitness came forward from the youth club. When they asked me whose idea it had been to take Rosie's inhaler, I lied and said I couldn't remember. As the inhaler was still in Frances's possession when she received her own visit from the police, it was generally accepted that she had been the ringleader, while I was the passive, but still morally reprehensible, onlooker.

I don't know if Frances ever knew what I'd told the police, because we never discussed it. All I can say is that, while we remained friends, things were never quite the same between us. Then Frances died, hurling me headfirst into another boiling cauldron of hurt and confusion. Even though I knew I hadn't been anywhere near the bridge that day, I still felt immense guilt for the suffering my parents went through. The three of us tried to start afresh with the move to Essex, but the memories were always there, like clots, sitting in our veins, just waiting to come unstuck and wreak havoc.

I'm still reeling from the revelation that Claire pushed Frances off the bridge – in the full knowledge she couldn't swim. I can only imagine how Frances's mum and dad felt when they found out. The CPS are still mulling over what, if any, charges to bring against Claire in regard to her death. In the meantime, I hope Frances's parents will draw some comfort from the fact that their daughter's killer is already behind bars and will be for a very long time.

In relation to her more recent crimes, Claire pleaded guilty to everything: two charges of murder and three of attempted murder (nobody was buying her story that she hadn't intended to kill James or Toby). It meant there was no need for a trial, for which I am grateful; I don't think I could have faced her in a courtroom. As well as the taped confession from her hospital bed, there was also the evidence from the baby monitor in Toby's room. DI Kilner showed Claire the footage on her phone and that's when she must've realised the game was up. Although it only captured part of the assault, it's pretty clear from the audio alone that Claire was the aggressor and Eleanor and I the victims.

Predictably, Claire's lawyer tried to claim diminished responsibility, but the psychiatric assessment that formed part of the pre-sentencing report concluded that her mental functions were in no way impaired when the offences in question were committed. At the sentencing, the judge gave her credit for pleading guilty at the earliest possible opportunity, but she still received a life sentence with a recommendation that she serve a minimum of twenty-five years. It's not really enough for all the pain she caused, all the lives she destroyed, but DI Kilner told me that in the circumstances it was the best we could have hoped for.

As for me, I don't think I'll ever be able to forgive myself for what happened to Rosie – or for the unwitting part I played in the deaths of Frances, Izzy and Eleanor. I've had a lot of time for reflection these past few weeks and I figure this can go one of two ways. Either my guilt can be an ocean for me to drown in, or I can use it as fuel to fire me up; to inspire me to lead a useful and productive life, the kind of life where no one else has to pay the price for my stupid mistakes. Needless to say, the latter option is infinitely more appealing, but it's going to take a conscious effort on my part. With that in mind, I've offered my professional services to a national asthma charity – gratis, of course. We haven't ironed out all the details yet, but it looks as if I'm going to be providing a spring-themed floral installation for one of their upcoming fundraisers. I'm hoping it will be the start of a long and mutually rewarding relationship. I know it's only a small gesture, but it's a step in the right direction.

I have six more days in this tropical paradise and then I'll be heading back to London to reopen the shop. I don't think I shall advertise for another assistant; Ewan and I will just have to manage between us. He visited me regularly during my recuperation and we've been texting back and forth these past few days. He said that when I get back he's going to take me out for a 'welcome home' drink. I don't want to read too much into it, but I have to say I'm really looking forward to spending more time with him.

With the sun all but disappeared behind the horizon, I set off back to the hotel. I'm feeling quite excited because I've arranged to dine with another solo traveller, also from England, this evening. We've only had two conversations so far – once when we were queuing for the breakfast buffet and another as we travelled on the courtesy bus that runs twice daily from the hotel to the local town. Not much to go on, I know – but still, I have a very good feeling about her.

Regrettably, she doesn't live in London, but Portsmouth's perfectly doable. I checked the route on Google Maps and was pleasantly surprised to find it's less than two hours in the car, traffic permitting. And if I don't feel like driving, I can always take the train: four an hour, changing at Norwood Junction and East Croydon.

I think my new friend will be good for my personal development, just like Izzy was. She's very animated, very assured. I overheard her talking to the general manager earlier, about an issue with the shower in her en suite. Personally, I find the general manager slightly intimidating, but there wasn't a hint of self-consciousness in my new friend's demeanour. As for her physical appearance . . . she's not what you'd call beautiful, but she has an interesting look, with the poise of a dancer and a face like a cut diamond that catches the light from every angle.

As I stood behind a potted palm, watching her take the manager to task so ably, I had a rush of affection – of *love*, almost – for my fellow countrywoman. It was so strong I had to fight the urge to grab her hand and soar with her out of reach of everyone, to a place where the views are to die for and the air is too thin to breathe.

Acknowledgements

I am, and always will be, immensely grateful to Mari Evans for giving me so many wonderful opportunities. Other members of the hugely talented Headline team who deserve a special mention are Toby Jones, Lucy Dauman, Isabel Martin, Lisa Horton, Grace McCrum, Ruth Case-Green, Joe Thomas and Ana Carter.

You should never have let her in . . .

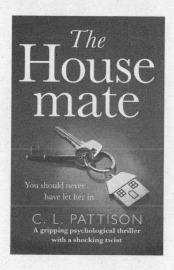

YOU LET A STRANGER INTO YOUR HOME

Best friends Megan and Chloe have finally found the perfect
house. And when they meet Samantha, she seems like
the perfect housemate.

YOU DON'T KNOW WHAT SHE'S HIDING

But Megan thinks there might be more to Samantha than
meets the eye. Why is she so secretive? Where are her friends
and family? And why is she desperate to get close to Chloe?

YOU'RE ABOUT TO FIND OUT

When strange things start happening in the house, Megan
and Chloe grow more and more alarmed. They soon realise
that letting a stranger into their home – and their lives –
might be the worst idea they've ever had . . .